Cries In the Wind

Judy Bruce

BENNINGTON, VERMONT
2016

First published in 2016 by the Merriam Press

First Edition

Copyright © 2016 by Judy Bruce
Cover design by Joseph Gentzler
Book design by Ray Merriam

ISBN 9781576385227
Library of Congress Control Number: 2016946654
Merriam Press #F5-P

This work was designed, produced, and published in
the United States of America by the

Merriam Press
133 Elm Street Suite 3R
Bennington VT 05201

E-mail: ray@merriam-press.com
Web site: merriam-press.com

To Jenny and Tom

Other books by Judy Bruce

Death Steppe
Voices In the Wind
Alone In the Wind

Chapter 1

I killed the chief of police, but I didn't plan to tell anyone. I also shot that scumbag DEA agent. They committed crimes that rocked our small, rural community—they even killed a young autistic man. No, I didn't see it all happen, I just knew. I'm strange in some ways—I feel, I hear, I know things. And going to prison for killing two murderers wasn't going to help anybody, especially me.

Five months later, I was still trying to put it behind me. I humbly believed God gave me permission to move on with life, so that's what I tried to do. Nightmares, both bizarre and realistic, still shook me, but now only once or twice a month. I'd stopped trying to ease the horror with bourbon; after all, I was four months pregnant.

Scanning the rugged terrain to the west of the highway, I drove southward to my law office on an early summer day. This was the harsh, semi-arid high plains with scraggily buffalo grass, crusty ridges, massive bluffs, rocky buttes, and dry gullies interspersed amid the fertile pastures of the cattle ranches. Despite the brutal winters and the devastating droughts, I belonged here. I considered my land beautiful, yet haunting—the furious wind howled, taunting me with mysteries I was forced to solve.

Today, I was simply going in to my office for an unusually early appointment. People didn't usually want to meet this early, but I didn't mind. If it wasn't for the strange uneasiness that nagged at me, I would have thought this would be a Tuesday like any other. After I parked in the lot behind my law firm on Benson Street, I called my husband Brian, urging him to come as soon as he could.

My client, Frank Morgan, arrived promptly at seven. I knew nothing about him, for he booked the appointment with Glenda, my receptionist and former second grade teacher. I unlocked the front door to a stocky man of sixty or so with a gray-brown mix of thinning, curly hair. I pegged him as an office worker, for he lacked the robust, weather-hardened look of the ranchers in the area; also, he wore a fine-quality suit most men in the area either couldn't afford or didn't bother owning. As I led him across the lobby to my office, my brain told me this was merely a businessman from the suburbs, but my guts roiled, arguing to the contrary. I left the office door open during an appointment, a rarity.

After some small talk, he came to the point. His request stunned me.

"Why would anyone want to buy the old Hexam wasteland?" I asked.

"I think it can be improved," he said as he folded his arms across his chest, revealing thick wrist hair and a slim, black-faced silver watch.

"Excuse me, but I don't understand your interest. You just told me you're an insurance executive in Kansas City."

It was ridiculous—that was obvious—I didn't need my rising blood pressure to tell me what my mind understood. The back door opened and closed. As I studied the man's face, Brian walked into the lobby and looked into the office. I waved at him. He nodded and left to go to his office across the lobby. He was an accountant and taxation specialist who had intended to go to his Sidney office this morning—but he knew me well enough to heed my sense of alarm. I would feel foolish when I told him it simply pertained to an absurd request by a stranger.

"I have no intention of selling a single square foot of my family's land," I said.

"I'm just looking for a place to retire in a few years," he said.

He lied, said my bones.

"I think our conversation is at an end," I said, rising from my chair.

"That's it?"

Something I couldn't identify flashed across his face.

"Yes, that's it, Mr. Morgan. I wish you a safe trip home."

Dejection, that's what his face revealed, and it was probably the only bit of truth he divulged. He slowly rose. I walked around my desk and held out my hand to shake his. Yet he just turned and slowly walked toward the door. I followed him to the lobby and watched him go through the front door to his car, a black Chrysler 300. Bear Lake Beulah, my elderly friend, backed her maroon Chrysler out of her driveway across the street, paused in the road, stared at the man for a few moments, looked at me in the doorway, and then drove away.

"What was that about?" Brian asked.

"Damned if I know," I said. "But I don't think I've heard the last of it."

Halfway through our lunch at Custer's, Beulah shuffled toward our table. She was trying to shove a clump of coarse gray hair back into her holder, but failed. She stared intently at me as she stopped next to the booth where we sat.

"Scooch over, hon," she said.

I'd known Beulah since I was a toddler; yet, this was a request I'd never heard. After I moved, she yanked that ornery tuft of hair over her ear then slid in next to me. Brian and I stopped eating and leaned toward her.

"I forgot my pills this mornin'…that's why I was home. That's why I saw him. Been years, but he still looks like his dad and younger brother."

"You saw my appointment…Frank Morgan?"

"That's the name he gave? Heh. Gettin' tricky like a wizard. Gettin' fishy."

Brian broke in. "Beulah, please explain what you're getting at."

"That was Clay Bolger...though it coulda been Andy. They always looked alike."

"As in the Bolger family west of here?" I asked.

"Yep, the same. So I called Ellie Bolger and said how nice it was that her son was visitin'. She huffed and said I was seeing things. But then we chatted for a bit about nothin'. Heh...fishy...like I said."

"How bizarre," I said. "Why would he lie to me?"

"Depends on what he wanted, I 'spect."

Just above a whisper, I said, "It was strange. He wanted to buy the old Hexam land."

Her face slackened for a moment then tightened. "Don't say no more and to nobody. Read about the van. I'll see you at James' party."

With that, she slid out of the booth and hastened back to the kitchen. Brian and I sat in silence, struck by the odd conversation and the rare glimpse of Beulah hurrying to do anything or to go anywhere. We finished our meal without exchanging another word. Brian bought a copy of the Omaha World-Herald from Carol as we paid for our meal. However, we didn't have a chance to discuss the matter again, as I was tangled in a messy child custody case for most of the afternoon. I didn't even have a chance to tell him another stranger from Kansas City named Jack Haley had booked an appointment for six o'clock in the evening the next day.

That evening, I discussed the strange events of the day with Patty White Horse, our Lakota Sioux housekeeper, and my mom, Beth, who was temporarily living with us. Brian dug through our recycling bin for old newspapers. Together, we tried to make some connection between the discovery of a van in Lake McConaughy near Ogallala last Friday and my deceitful morning visitor.

My mom abruptly laughed. I didn't see the humor in any of it until she explained.

"Don't you get it—Frank Morgan and Jack Haley? And this isn't even Kansas."

"No," Patty said, "But it's lookin' more like Oz."

Brian and I grinned at each other as we finally understood.

"On Thursday, you'll get a visit from a lady on a broom with green skin," added Brian.

"Wait...was it the Tin Man or the Lion who was played by someone named Bolger?" I wondered.

"Ray Bolger was the Scarecrow," said my mom, Beth.

"Geez, this is getting' weirder by the minute," Patty said. "And we're not going to figure this out on our own. Too bad Beulah didn't say more."

We definitely needed outside help, so for supper, we invited James Wilson, our next door neighbor, and Uncle Bill, who lived down the block.

When the two men arrived, we questioned them about the van and old Hexam land. Likewise baffled, James shrugged. Yet, it was as if a dark shadow fell upon Uncle Bill. He said he needed to eat before discussing the matter. In a flash, the mystery changed from bizarre to ominous. So the story waited for Uncle Bill to finish eating and for me to return from some hormonal nausea.

Once we had all gathered in the family room, Bill cleared his throat then said, "Been lots of buzz around town since Friday when they pulled that van out of Big Mac." He dropped his chin into his chest. The mantel clock ticked on and on till I wondered if he'd continue.

"But the newspapers don't mention the significance of it," I ventured.

"No, they wouldn't...not till they've run all the tests on it."

"Dammit, Uncle!" I said. "Spit it out or I won't tell you who shot at me this morning."

"What! When?"

"Nobody shot at me, but you better get on with it or I won't tell you what did happen."

"Don't you be scaring me like—"

I hit him square in the shoulder with a sofa pillow.

"All right." He reached down from the recliner and picked up the pillow and held it against his chest.

"It's the van that went missing on the day of the Quinn murders. Mary, the mother, and her daughter, Julie, were killed in their house...then it was set on fire." His face reddened. "I was young, just twelve, but I knew them both."

"I remember hearing stories about those murders as a kid," I said.

"I heard about it when I was living in Denver," James said. "Nobody could believe something like that could happen in western Nebraska. Just a shocker. Walt Bolger is sitting in prison for doing it. Let's see, nearly forty-five years it'd be."

I'm sure I wasn't the only one who thought of Charles Starkweather and his murdering rampage through Nebraska in 1958. It gave me the creeps thinking about it.

"Yep...July of 1968," said Uncle Bill. "The van was found because the lake dropped so low from the drought. I wish I didn't recall it all so well. Like to forget it...but I never can."

"Wait...Bolger you said?" Brian asked. He looked at me.

My uncle nodded. "They caught Walt Bolger fleeing from the scene with kerosene and blood on his clothes. He'd burned down the house."

"I heard about it when I first moved out here. It was still a hot topic in the nineties. What's the big mystery about it?" Patty asked.

"They never found any bodies, just blood on one of the un-burnt walls," Bill said. "Oh, and the charred shoes...saw those myself."

"Well, if they didn't find the bodies, how do they know they're dead?"

CRIES IN THE WIND

"The disappearance of Mary and Julie Quinn and the blood on Walt's pants turned out to be enough to convince the jury of second degree murder and arson."

"But the sons think he's innocent," I said.

"How do you know that?" Bill inquired.

"Because one of the sons booked an appointment with me for this morning. The other son has an appointment tomorrow. They're using aliases, but Beulah spotted one son this morning."

"What'd they want with you?"

"Us. He wanted to buy the old Hexam land. I suppose the younger brother will ask the same thing."

"That was Quinn land first. In fact, that's where the house was."

That sent a shiver up my spine and made my head buzz with alarm.

"Was there a father?" Brian asked.

"Sean. But he wasn't home. Had an alibi, though I don't recall what it was."

Bill dropped his head back into his chest. I had a string of questions to ask, but I sensed he was done talking about it. I could do my own investigation now that I knew the connection to the murders. Bill roused himself from his thoughts, said goodnight to us, and then lumbered out the back door. James shuffled out the door behind him, both men in a haze of sadness.

"I think a can of worms has been opened," Patty remarked.

"Sounds more like Pandora's box," said my mom, who like Patty and Brian, sat upright and alert.

"Sounds like we need a plan," I said. "Mom, you've been antsy...so tell me, how are your research skills?"

"I'm on it, Sherlock," she said.

"If you'll focus on the murders and arson, maybe Brian could play Sam Spade and find out about that van."

"And me?" Patty asked.

"It's amazing what you can find out in a bit of small talk. Bill said the town was buzzing with the news. See what you can find out about the people involved, Miss Marple."

"And what about you?" Brian asked.

"I plan to do nothing—nothing obvious, that is—till after I meet with Jack Haley."

In fact, my mind was galloping with ideas. Getting spies on the move was a necessary tactic. By noon the next day, I received a call from my first spy, Bud, one of Bill's cowhands. Not only was a black Chrysler 300 sitting in the gravel in front of the Bolger house, a silver version was parked next to it. Also, an old white Buick was parked under the carport next to the house, which I assumed was Mrs. Bolger's car. I thanked him for the information then emailed Joy, my assistant, to send fifty bucks to him for his services. She would comply without questioning. Everybody in the office knew the golden rule—privacy was next to sacred in the law firm. Nothing seen, heard, or read was ever to be repeated or questioned.

Similar cars, similar plan—perhaps this was a brother who frequently followed his older brother's lead. My second spy, Beulah, peeked her bright-eyed, aged face into my street side office window ten minutes after Jack Haley arrived. Within a couple minutes, Brian's text message confirmed my Tin Man was actually Andy Bolger.

"Mr. Haley," I said, after some chitchat, "what can I do for you?"

"I would like to buy some land from you…a section just south of the interstate."

"Strange, but another man wanted to buy that land, the old Hexam acres. That's just wasteland. What could you possibly want with it?"

"That's my business."

"I disagree. It's acres of ugly, scraggily wild grass, dirt clods, and bluffs. It's also my backyard. I care very much about what happens to the land bordering my childhood.

You see, I'm wondering if you're a front for somebody who wants to build a warehouse or a superstore in that area."

"What?"

"It would be a prime spot for a mail-order warehouse with both the railroad and the interstate so close. No, I'm not interested in selling."

"But you haven't even heard my offer."

"I don't need to. I may lease that land to a company that operates wind turbines."

"Wait, no, you can't put those monster windmills on the land…it's too unsteady, there's lots of—"

He stopped, fully aware that he had divulged more than he meant to. I waited, hoping he'd feel awkward in the silence and say more. He cleared his throat and shifted in his chair. His resemblance to Clay was distinct—both stood about five feet eight inches tall with a stocky build, and possessed office-worker skin and gray-brown hair in the same balding pattern. The younger man wore a fine, gray suit and his wrists revealed the Bolger hairy arms. The brothers were up to something, though I refused to show my hand. He cleared his throat again, abruptly rose, thanked me for my time, and then hastened out the door. With him went the uneasiness I'd also sensed with Clay. This man didn't seem dangerous; if he was a threat, he was less so than Clay. And what was it about that land that made it "unsteady"?

Why did I feel alarmed by it? I just wanted to be peacefully pregnant. Now this.

Chapter 2

AFTER supper was cleared, my partners in mystery, Brian, Patty, and Beth gathered at the kitchen table. Both Brian and Patty placed their laptops in front of them, though my mom carried a half-inch stack of printer paper. After all, she was a baby boomer, someone who still relied on paper rather than computer screens.

"Okay, first thing—we need to be careful," I said. "It's not just that we're dealing with a murder and arson event, we may also be dealing with desperate and bitter people. Both the Bolgers and Quinns had family and some of the people we know may be relatives. That's something we need to find out."

"Barb Shuster is a Bolger and so is Marva Gush," Patty remarked.

"Really? Well, that just shows how careful we need to be. I don't think we want it known that we're investigating this. So, Patty, just play the busybody. Brian can just act like a guy who grew up in Chicago and doesn't know anything about this. I can act curious because two people have expressed interest in purchasing area my family owns. Mom, I want to keep you in the shadows. You've probably uncovered a ton of info, but if you need to go to a library, go to Kimball or Sidney."

"Well, one thing I found out was that people still have doubts about it all," Patty said.

"How so?"

"Sounds like some folks just don't believe Walt did it. And they wonder about Hank Eldritch—that would be Lew's uncle."

"Oh, that's touchy," said Brian. "Like that guy needed any more trauma in his life."

"Well, we know the mystery men are Clay and Andy Bolger. They're not working very hard at hiding their deceit." I told them about my spies and their reports. "Uncle Bill seems traumatized by the topic, as does Beulah…but she'll talk away, I think…if I can get her going."

"Okay, my turn," Brian said. "Now the van may turn out to be just a coincidence, but we'll see. The one thing the State Patrol has said, and I'm getting this second hand, is that no bodies were found inside. That's all they're saying. But the North Platte paper is speculating that something was found, since they called in forensics." He took a sip of his Bear Lake Beulah root beer, but kept his gaze on me. "I know it's sensitive stuff, but…um…I kind of thought Trooper Merritt was quite kind to you after, you know, in the barn."

Yes, Officer Merritt acted kind to me after I gunned down RT, the crooked DEA agent. Of course, everybody thought RT killed Chief of Police Ray Dobbs and I shot RT in self-defense. Actually, I provoked RT and blasted him the moment he wrapped his hand around his gun. When Dobbs arrived—he murdered Davey with RT—I slid my small, leather-gloved hand over RT's trigger finger and shot down Dobbs. Their poisoning of the young autistic was impossible to prove, yet clever, as was my impulsive, black-hearted act of revenge. So, it seemed that the officer did at least respect me. He even called the house a few times to check on me after the "Shootout," as the locals called it.

"I'll give it a try," I said. "I think talking to Officer Waters would be like talking to a brick wall."

"The only other thing is that the van was stolen from Kimball. But it looks like your mom has a ton of information for us."

"Well, a lot of this is duplication. Most of the newspapers have archived their older articles. The thing is, every

CRIES IN THE WIND

newspaper in the Midwest covered this. It didn't go national like the Shootout," she gave me a wink, "but there's still quite a bit I haven't read.

"So, here goes. Walt Bolger was convicted of two murders in the second degree and arson. He was thirty-seven at the time of the murders. The three sentences were ordered to run consecutively, so he's not due for release till he's ninety-seven. He's been denied parole three times. He has claimed innocence for the murders from the time of his arrest...though he confessed to the arson."

"That doesn't make sense," I said. "But I can understand how that would irritate a jury and a judge. They were convinced he was lying...probably hoping to get a lighter sentence with a manslaughter conviction. But they socked it to him."

"He has never implicated anybody else," said Beth. "But the papers make a big deal out of the fact that he was caught fleeing the scene."

"Still, a good attorney could have gotten him a manslaughter conviction, maybe even convinced Mr. Bolger to make a deal...plead guilty to manslaughter and arson to get a lighter sentence. They didn't have DNA testing back then, so they had no proof that the blood on Bolger's pants belonged to Julie and Mary."

"Hey," Patty said, "I just remembered...there's another son, Bert. He works over at Smokey's."

"What is this Smokey's place?" Beth asked.

"It's a sales yard," said Brian. "He sells everything you can think of with a motor—farm machinery, cars, four-wheelers, lawn mowers, motorcycles...he even sells Hoover vacuum cleaners. And he has a repair shop and runs a monthly auction. It's quite a place. You should see it sometime. Gets customers from several counties and northern Colorado."

"And it employs a good chunk of this town," added Patty.

Damn, my stomach began to percolate. "Excuse me," I said as I hastened to the bathroom. My nausea and vomiting had gotten better the last couple of weeks, but it still hit me at times. My mom said it was just a good, healthy dose of hormones attacking my stomach. I was supposed to be gaining weight, but it was hard when I kept losing my meals. After a few dry heaves, I returned to the table.

"What did I miss?" I asked.

"Nothing," said Patty. "Brian decided we needed bourbon."

"How could we proceed without our commander-in-chief?" said Brian as he set three bourbons on the table. "Just you promise that you'll not do anything dangerous. You have plenty of people who can do things."

"I can't do anything dangerous unless there's a bathroom nearby."

"Okay, then, I've got something big that Bill didn't mention," said Beth. "There was a third woman."

"Oh, Lordy," said Patty. "Isn't two dead women enough?"

"More than. A girl named Linda was visiting Julie."

"But you said Walt Bolger was convicted on two counts of murder, not three," Brian said.

"That's right," Beth replied. "Lots of people place her there, but in the rubble, they didn't find any of her things...no clothes, no suitcase. Bill said something about charred shoes. They must have belonged to Mary and Julie. Yet this Linda disappeared, too."

"Beth, do they think she could have been kidnapped?" Patty asked.

My mom just shrugged. "She was never found. It's like she dropped out of the story."

"What time did the murders occur?" I inquired.

"About one in the afternoon."

"So she could have left before then," I said. "But if she did leave, you would think she'd come back to give evidence. The police would consider her information very important. Then again, she wouldn't come back if she was the murderer. She'd run."

"And it doesn't explain how Walt comes into the picture," Brian said.

"Okay, so, we've got three disappearing women, Walt with blood and kerosene on him, a van pulled out of Lake McConaughy with no bodies in it, and two sons trying to stir up something," I said.

Patty rubbed her temples. "Lordy, this is clear as mud."

"Patty, did anybody mention a feud between the families?" I asked.

"No, but I didn't specifically ask about it. And nobody under sixty could remember much. We need to talk to some oldsters. Hey, what about your dad's old law partner?"

I smiled. "I have an appointment with Art Meyer next Tuesday. He's pushing early eighties, but he's still sharp."

"Megan, this is all very interesting, like a murder mystery in a book. But now that you've said no to those two men, is this really our business?" Brian asked.

"No, says my brain, but my guts say otherwise."

"Here we go again," Patty said with a sigh.

We all knew what she meant—I was a magnet for trouble. Or maybe I was trouble, some disaster in the making, even though I hadn't even hit thirty. My date of birth in February 1984 indicated I was a "Millennial," though I did a poor job of being a part of the ME ME generation. I did own a smart phone, but I ignored apps that didn't involve a dictionary or weather predictions, and the only photos I'd taken lately weren't selfies, they were of suspected criminals, which tied into my investigation of meth in the area last year. Oh, and I killed three men in three years. Yeah, I was trouble. Still, I hadn't instigated this Bolger problem. Maybe it would just blow over, though I hoped it more than expected it.

Friday evening, I wandered through the Seven Dwarves, the five small buttes, out in my "backyard" as I had described it to Andy Bolger. I still roamed this area, the playground of my childhood, where I had grown up with Derek and Vonny Wilson, James and Beverly's kids. I bet I was eight or nine before I really understood how unusual it was for a kid in a Midwestern rural community to grow up with two African American kids as my playmates. James had been my friend and neighbor from my first memory; yet, it was Beverly I embraced as a mother. My dad provided me with Mrs. Crenshaw, "Crenny," as a nanny and housekeeper, and I had loved her; when she passed, my dad gave me Patty, and I loved her. Still, nobody held a place in my heart like Beverly, who died four years ago—nobody till my own mother turned out to be alive. She came into my life just after my father and my twin died—though the truth of their existence had been kept from me for twenty-three years by my father.

The wind bellowed from the southwest, rushing through the tough gray-green buffalo grass and the sparse conifers, and whipping around the rocky mounds to slash at my body. A reddish Swift fox rose out of a den to peer at me, her large ears twitched as she wondered if I was a danger to her cubs. I always came out here alone—I never told Brian I wanted to be alone, but he gave up once he figured out that I didn't respond to his chatter or questions. So he stayed inside or sat on the patio with a beer. Patty was probably watching a movie in the family room. She didn't live with us, but she was almost always here. She complained that her apartment was dull and lonely compared to the "big house."

Just as I sat down on a tuft of buffalo grass, James walked around the far side of Rufus, the small knoll directly behind our houses. Rising from the ground, I waved him over. The clouds overhead were wispy and sunlit, though the ones in the west were dark and menacing. As he approached, he turned to look at the sky.

CRIES IN THE WIND

"Maybe we'll get some rain outta those," he said.

"We need it," I said, wondering if he had been listening for Beverly. "Why do you think I still hear Beverly?"

He smiled and studied me for few moments. "She'd say, if she ever spoke words, that a mother's work is never done."

I nodded. I was going to be one of those, a mother. Would I think that way?

"I saw Lew out here last night. I told him long ago he's always welcome."

James nodded. "And the dogs like him."

"I think he listens for his mother. From what Bill says, they were close…and it was tough on Lew when she died."

"Tough on all of them," he said. "I don't think that family ever recovered. So, yeah, I bet he listens for her."

"I never hear Scott. I think he's at peace," I said of my twin.

"Did you ever hear your dad?"

"I'm not sure. I think I did right after he died, but who knows? And why don't other people hear voices in this wind?" I wondered out loud.

"I don't know why I hear. For years I thought I was nuts, thinking I heard my dad."

"And how come I never heard anything in Omaha? I don't even hear anything inside the house…out of the wind."

"I don't either," he said.

"I felt Scott's heart attack, but I suppose that was a twin…thing."

"That makes as much sense as anything."

A sense of disquietude crept up from the ground, sending prickles up my legs. James said something, but it was lost in the wind. When the shivers started in my spine, I shuddered, and then whirled around to look east.

"Someone else is out here," I said.

"Are you sure...of course you are." He scooped up a couple of fist-sized rocks and trotted east, toward the bluff, Big Leo. "Stay with me, Megan!"

I grabbed a couple of rocks and followed him, my pulse racing faster than my legs needed. We looped south of the bluff, yet saw no one. I scrambled up the side of the bluff toward the Fort, my hut on top of the Big Leo. Once I made certain it was locked, I picked my way across the top of the bluff to scan the area to the north and east. Nothing. James worked his way eastward along the bottom of the bluff. My heart continued to pound—as it should after climbing 200 feet up the steep side of the bluff. However, it was the queasy feeling in my guts that concerned me, and then it was the need to vomit. I heard James yelling, but I stubbornly insisted on barfing in private. I took one last look around then scooted down the side, using outcroppings to slow my descent.

"I didn't see anybody," I said to James when I reached the bottom.

He shook his head. "Do you think it was those Bolgers?"

"That would make sense, but they would need to know this land well to know how to escape. And they looked a bit soft to be moving easily across those rocky ridges where I bet they would hide."

We both turned and looked at the sky, which was becoming unnaturally dark due to the black clouds rolling in. Neither one of us wanted to be out here in the dark. Two summers ago, we both nearly died when Salt Eldritch decided to shoot us down in the dark. He was a lunatic out for revenge—I killed him, too, with the help of a steak knife, a dirt clod, and a deep ditch we called "Miss Gulch." Hastening back to our houses, we parted at the edge of my backyard where the crunchy soil ended and the watered fescue started.

Chapter 3

The next morning, Brian and I rode our horses north to the old Hexam-Quinn land. Brian rode a tall palomino named Rohan, while I rode my black stallion, Gondor. It was four miles from the barn to the old Quinn homestead, over rough ground in the Docket wasteland. Uncle Bill told us where to find the plot for the old house based on its distance from Highway 51 to the west and Hexam Road to the south. But I didn't need his directions.

It hit me so hard I jumped off Gondor before he came to a full stop. Dropping to my knees, I heaved great gasps. I knew where they died—their cries in the wind walloped me. I suppose Brian thought I was throwing up, at least till I started crawling westward. I dug my hands into the dirt until I found the edge of the concrete that indicated the edge of a wall.

"What are you doing?" he asked as he walked over, holding the reins of both horses.

"Here," I said.

Oh, sweet Jesus, their wailing was like a dagger to my guts. Please, Lord, never let me die with this terror.

Brian was talking to me, but I couldn't respond. Although the family didn't survive, a couple of old bur oaks had weathered abandonment. Brian tied the reins to low hanging branches so they could graze. I tried to shift from my squat, but my body had gone to lead. This hadn't happened to me since last winter, though I'd blamed it on the cold. Brian walked around me looking confused.

"Help," I managed.

He squatted down and scooped me up. When he saw how my body was clenched into a ball he carried me over to the shade of the trees and gently set me on the ground. My former Husker linebacker managed to straighten by body by yanking my legs down while flattening my torso. Gondor sensed something was wrong, for he nuzzled my shoulder.

Comforted by two males, I took deep breaths. "That's where they died. I found the frame of the house."

"Should I go look at it or stay with you?"

"You go. I don't hear them here."

With the south wind protecting me from hearing their screams, I gulped air to calm myself. I reached up and stroked Gondor's neck. He stayed with me, not even turning to graze on what would have been the former yard of the Quinn house. The oak comforted me, too. I studied the branch to which Gondor was tied—I bet a tire swing once hung here. I craned my neck to watch Brian. He dragged his boot along the border of the basement, stomped down a few times, crept across the ground, then finally reached down to dig to what must be the floor. I couldn't bear to cower like a damsel in distress, so I mustered a deep breath, rolled over, rose to my knees, crawled a few yards, and then gathered my legs under me. I tottered over to the ghost house and started exploring the floor with him. Someone had torn down the burnt walls, but left the floor, which seemed solid. The cries swirled around and through me, but I persisted.

We never found an opening for steps, so we looked along the sides of the house and found where a shelter had been dug out. The wind had covered the shelter door in dirt, though we found a handle that broke off in Brian's grasp. Finally, the agony of the wailing made me walk away from the house and throw up. Both horses must have thought that unusual behavior, for they both stopped grazing to stare at me. Rising from my knees, I walked southeast.

CRIES IN THE WIND

Brian walked up beside me. He squeezed my hand and I smiled at him. I was glad I hadn't divorced him after he broke one of the Ten Commandments with some Italian whore in Colorado last August.

"The barn should have been right around here," I said.

We located the embedded wood frame that must have been the foundation for a massive barn. According to Bill, the Quinns held a large tract of pastureland to the west for decades and the ranch prospered—at least until the murders. Making inquiries as to the precise disposition of the land would be easy, as the Thornton family now owned much of the land to the west. Back under the shade with the horses, I sent an email to my office from my smart phone to research the history of the land sales and purchases for the area west of Highway 51 and all the former Quinn land.

Even as Brian mounted Rohan, I walked back to the house, certain I needed to complete the one task I had neglected. Back in the cries, I steadied myself and listened hard. As the tears rolled down my face, the older woman's shrieks became distinct from the younger woman's. Wait, that wasn't right. I steadied myself to hear them again. No, it was right.

Two voices.

"Something else?" Brian asked as we started southward.

"She had left…Linda. I could only hear two voices."

Several obvious questions should come to his mind—how and why do you hear things? Couldn't she have been asleep? Are you really sure? Are you just being hormonal? Yet he merely nodded.

As we approached the bluff called the Joker, I thought I saw a flash of a shadow near the base on the west side. I hastened Gondor to a gallop, but swung westward away from that hulking mass of rock; Brian followed, but didn't question me. On the south side of the bluff, I saw no one, but some dust had been kicked up in the air along the slope.

Had I seen someone? Was he hiding in one of the deep crevices? Was someone watching us?

That evening we held a party to celebrate James' sixty-fifth birthday. It was also a chance to show off the rebuilt brick patio James' landscaping company completed last month.

"I'd like me one of these," Beulah said. "Sit outside all day...never make it in to work."

"Oh, you'd go, even if just for the chatter," said James as he finished his burger.

Beulah chuckled, even as she gave me a long steady gaze. Before she could speak, my young friend intercepted me.

"Did you see?" Kayla asked. "They were putting in the carpet, like, all day."

To the shock of the community, we sold a plot of land on Harney Street to Paul Ritter, Kayla's father, to build a house. They were a family initially torn apart by divorce and then by the death of Sheila, the mother, on a meth meltdown.

"First house to be built around here in some time," Beulah said. "So what grade you gonna be in next year?"

"I'll be starting high school in Sidney."

"My, my, that's somethin'."

When Kayla turned to talk to Vonny, Beulah nodded for me to follow her.

"Did you find out about the Quinn murders and that van?" she asked.

"The basics," I replied.

She wanted to have a private conversation with me, but she tended to talk loudly, so most of the dozen attendees could easily hear her. The conversation stopped around us.

"It just tore us up. Bolgers and Quinns both had lots of relatives and friends. Ever'body knew ever'body back then. But no one could believe it. Useta babysit Julie. Knew Ellie

Bolger well. My God, liketa shocked us to death. Never forget it. Never."

"I was hoping this wouldn't come up," Bill remarked.

"What are you talking about?" Kayla asked.

No one said a word.

Kayla looked around then asked Vonny, "Do you know?"

She nodded then looked down.

Finally, I said, "The Quinn murders…a mother and a daughter."

Kayla's eyes got big. "When? Where?"

"It was 1968," Bill said.

"Oh," she said, disappointed.

"I was just a kid…twelve…when it happened," Bill continued. "It was like the world was caving in on us. RFK, that would've been June…and Martin Luther King in April." He looked up from his boots. "Not like people around here were in favor of the Civil Rights movement…but it wasn't lost on folks that a man who pushed for peaceful change was so violently killed. Then our murders in July…right after the Quinn's big Fourth of July party they always had."

"But that was, like, a long time ago," Kayla said.

"A couple of things have come up recently," I said. "They found a van that was stolen near here on the day of the murders, July fifth."

"Yeah, I never did get why people cared so much about that van," Paul said. "They caught Walt Bolger fleeing the scene of the fire he admitted he started…and he had blood on his clothes from it."

"But where did the bodies go?" said Tom Sedlacek, an old classmate of mine and an occasional laborer for James. "My grandpa was chief of police back then. He says those bodies were not in the house. The FBI said so. So people always wondered if Walt or someone else took those bodies away."

Lew, who had started pacing along the edge of the house when the topic began, suddenly bolted forward.

"I know some folks think my uncle done it, but they're wrong. Uncle Hank would never hurt anyone. He didn't even hunt. Those folks who think so are just wrong."

Beth walked up to Lew and said, "Come, let me cut you a piece of cake." She tugged on his arm and he followed.

"Now wait, Megan," Tom said. "You said there were a couple of things. What else besides the van?"

"This week I had two offers to buy the land where the murders took place," I said.

That hushed the group.

"But my uncle and I have no intention of selling any land. So that's done. And I've decided not to look into the matter any further. Look how it's affecting everyone. And besides, I just want to think about happy things…especially the baby I'm expecting next December."

Well, that changed the mood. The black cloud that had descended upon us lifted. People congratulated me and patted me on the shoulder. Marva Gush gushed. So many people wanted to shake Brian's hand that he had to stop eating his cake. He'd been so excited with the news. The same day I told him, he started moving things out of the upstairs guest bedroom in preparation for a nursery.

"Aren't you supposed to have a big bump?" Kayla asked.

I gave her a hug. "In time…I'm not that far along."

Shortly after dark, the wind slackened and the mosquitoes came out, so people went home. However, Lew, Beulah, and the Wilsons lingered, so we invited them inside and handed out glasses of bourbon.

"Megan, hon, you know there was another woman stayin' with the Quinns," Beulah said.

"Yeah, Linda. Brian and I rode out to the house today. Only two women died."

"How can you possibly know that?" Bill inquired.

"I just do."

Bill stared at me for a few moments then sighed. "I'm not sure it's over. Yesterday, Jack and Drew chased a couple of men off that old Quinn and Hexam land. Jack said they were east of where you were."

"Well, I need it to be over," I said. "I bet those two men were Clay and Andy Bolger. They can't stay forever...they have jobs in Kansas City. And—"

I paused. Did I really want to admit this?

"And what?" said Bill. He placed his meaty hands on the sides of my shoulders. "You need to tell us."

"Well, I think someone may be stalking me."

"What?" Brian asked, his brows scrunched. "Dammit, Megan! Why didn't you tell me?"

Now Derek and Vonny were in my face, too. Beulah tried to peek over Vonny's shoulder at me. Yet, it was my mom's eyes that bore a hole in the side of my head.

"But what do I know? Just because I heard two wailing women doesn't mean someone is spying on me. I've never actually seen a person, just dust and shadows."

"But what do you feel?"

Shit. Patty was always the one to ask that question. Now I was stuck. I tried to look away, only to see Beulah's flip-flops on the floor. She was standing on the sofa to get a look at me.

"I think backing off will be the end of it," I said to divert the question, though I wasn't convinced my answer was true.

That night, I awoke four times in a sweat to the screams of the mother and daughter.

No, it wasn't over.

Chapter 4

The relief from getting out of the Quinn conundrum ended abruptly when I awoke Monday morning— my mind raced as distress smashed against the sides of my skull, my heart thudded against my ribs till they nearly bust open. I flipped over, Brian was fine. Running down the hall, the orange sun of dawn lit my steps. I flung open the guest room door, she stirred; Mom was fine. I called Bill, he was groggy but fine; James, Derek, and Vonny were fine; Patty was fine. I dialed Bo's number then hung up because it was well before the start of shift. He rang me back then answered that he was fine and hadn't heard of any trouble. He promised to check with Chief of Police Joe Janowicz, the former FBI undercover agent who'd stayed on after the meth ring was broken up in December. I called Beulah; she was fine, but alarmed by my call. She promised to hustle over to Custer's to check for news. Then I called Paul, who kept me on the phone while he peeked in on a sleeping Kayla.

What the hell? My guts were on a rampage, but everybody was fine. I started to pace the hallway, but I'd made only one pass before the doorbell rang. Brian stopped me before I could get to the stairs.

"I'll go, you change," he said.

We both looked down at the skimpy nightie I was wearing—one meant for his eyes only. I retreated to my room. By the time I made it downstairs, Brian, Bill, and James were milling about the kitchen. Patty rushed in the front door. A couple minutes later, Beth appeared.

"Paul's standing on his front porch," Brian said.

"I'll go tell him we'll call as soon as…well…whatever," said James as he left.

All eyes were on me.

"Did you dream something?" my mom asked.

"I don't remember any dream…just waking up in a panic," I said. "Maybe I'm wrong…about something happening."

"Have you ever been wrong when you felt this way?" Bill asked.

"No."

He turned away and started making phone calls.

"Do you feel any better…now that you've been awake a few minutes?" asked Beth.

"No."

All the eyes on me should have pierced my skull, but the black cloud that hovered in the room dulled my senses. I walked stiffly over to a chair and sat down, while everyone else stayed stuck to their spot in the room.

After a few minutes, Patty cleared her throat. She, my mom, and Brian started on breakfast. James returned, accompanied by Chief Joe J, as he was dubbed—we already had a Joe, not that anyone could confuse the burly rancher Big Joe McCready with the tall, half-Lakota police chief. James might have tried to explain me to Joe J, but I was beyond comprehension. Joe J just stood and stared at me. I guess he thought if he waited long enough, I'd reveal the answer to the puzzle, which was so complicated even I didn't understand the mystery attached to it. I just knew the result would be terrible.

The trauma of my portent was briefly upstaged by the smell of cooking meat—that sent me to the bathroom with dry heaves. Afterward, I stayed in the hallway, even as Patty pressed guests into chairs for scrambled eggs and ham. To me they smelled more like green eggs and ham, and I didn't want to be near it, Megan I am. So I paced the hall. A half hour later, a call to Bill's cell phone brought me back into the room.

All I heard him say was, "Okay."

"Um…it's not in Dexter, but you might want to come with us, Joe J. Bud called the State Patrol. Megan, I know there's no way of keeping you away—"

"It's Gondor," blurted before my brain fully understood. "But you need the police, so he was murdered."

Shit.

Chewing stopped, breathing even stopped, at least mine did.

Gondor lay with his back pressed up against the side of his stall. The single bullet wound between the eyes had sent a stream of blood down his jaw where it pooled underneath his head. Chief Joe J kept Bill, Brian, and me away from the stall, as Officer Merritt photographed the horse and the surrounding area. Bo was busy inspecting the barn door padlock.

"Dang, there's gotta be seven or eight different cowboy boot prints here," said Officer Merritt. "Megan, do you wear boots, like um, equestrian boots?"

"Yes, Officer. Brian and I were in here yesterday around four in the afternoon. We went for a ride."

"These would be your tracks, they're smaller," he said pointing to marks in the dirt. "But the rest of these…no way to distinguish them. Someone came in here, probably let the palomino out into the pasture then came back and shot your horse."

Bud stepped forward from the corner, "I saw Rohan out in the pasture…so early…too early. And Gondor nowhere I could see. Then Bill calls, so I come here to check the barn. I saw right way the chain cut through and the padlock on the ground. Then…Gondor. Miss Megan, I'm so sorry."

"That shot would've killed him damn quick," said Joe J. "Megan, Brian, at least he didn't suffer."

"But why?" I asked.

Silence. Shaking heads. The shock of the senseless killing.

After a while, nothing was to be done but go home. Mom made me tea as I sat in trance at the kitchen table. In time, the tears came. Brian hugged me—it wasn't the first time I'd dampened his shirt with my tears. Once I regained my composure, I eased myself back into my chair then drank more tea. Patty made me wheat toast then she went out in the hall to call Beulah with the news. James, Paul, and Kayla stopped by the big house.

"Why just kill one horse?" asked Kayla. "Why be nice to the other one?"

I shook my head.

"Rohan's gonna be, like, so upset."

I remained quiet, except to give Bill permission to make arrangements for removal and burial of the horse. Kayla reluctantly left for school, soon Paul and James left for work. Brian had a morning appointment, so he showered and left. I stayed at the kitchen table as I didn't have any appointments till the afternoon; besides, I was the boss and I was starting to feel mean.

It just made no sense. Clearly, Gondor was the sole intended victim. But why? Then I knew—I was the target. That truth made me jerk. Who was angry with me? In a flash, I formed a plan, but I didn't want to alert Mom or Patty. I wandered out into the hall and began to pace. They watched me, but didn't question me—they'd given up on trying to get me to talk. I kept pacing until they went back to the kitchen. Then I darted into the study, threw open a cabinet, and pulled out a box. I tore open the mailing paper sent from the State Patrol. There it was—I touched it then I grasped it in my hand. Last year I killed two murderers with cold resolve and this gun—my soul still suffered. I took two lives with gun-fueled bravado. I'd done it on impulse, yet I entered that barn with foolish daring and invincibility, as if I'd been some high school guy driving a Camaro on a Saturday night. Regardless of my anger and grief, I never would've been that bold without that Glock. I'd hoped to never see that gun in my hand again, but I

CRIES IN THE WIND

needed an extreme level of persuasion. Ever so quietly, I took a cartridge from a side desk drawer, but then shoved it back in the box and closed the drawer.

I paced a couple more times before dashing up the quiet, carpeted front stairwell to my room. I made three calls then grabbed my purse, which I stashed in the study. I resumed pacing. Mom and Patty continued to check on me, but I was waiting. The first call came; a few minutes later the second call came. I put my handgun in my purse and charged through the kitchen to the garage door.

"I'll be back," I said, certain the two women would be too slow to stop me.

I parked the Shark right in front of Custer's and that damn fire hydrant. I called Bo and said he needed to come right away. Jack was leaning against the brick outside Custer's.

"Thanks, Jack. I'll let you know if I need you. Send Bo in."

I thrust open the door with such vigor that everyone in the five occupied tables turned to look at me. I walked up to a booth and glared at the two occupants.

"I'm making a citizen's arrest of you two Bolger clowns," I said.

"What are you talking about?" Clay asked.

"How about fraud, trespassing, and the killing of my horse."

Clay huffed, while Andy stared at me.

"You gotta be kidding," said Clay.

With that, I pulled the gun out of my purse and placed it against Clay's forehead. He gasped. The diner went silent.

"Holy shit! Lady, you got this wrong," said Andy.

"Do I?" I said as I rammed the gun up under Andy's chin. "Now, leave your money on the table for your meal and tip then get up. And just remember, I killed a cop with this gun."

They both stared at me, jaws slack.

"Now!"

Clay jolted then slid to the edge of the booth. Andy followed as I backed away from the table. Andy opened his wallet with shaking hands and dropped a twenty dollar bill onto his plate.

"Megan," said Deputy Bo, who walked up behind them.

"I'm making a citizen's arrest." I said.

"I can see that."

"Will you lock them up?"

"I think that would be best."

As I looked down at the gun, I said, "This gun is scary—I didn't even need to load it for it to be effective."

"Come with me, you two," he said, grinning.

They walked through the front door with Bo close behind them. I sat down in the Docket booth. I shoved the gun into my purse. Beulah and Carol hustled over to my table. Blaine and Dane Shuster stood behind them.

"It's too early for lunch," I said. "How about a stack of buttermilk pancakes and coffee? Thanks. Oh, and invite Jack in. He's the cowhand standing on the sidewalk. Give his bill to me."

Still, they stood there. Beulah broke the silence with her cackle.

"Damn, girl! You got some moxie, you do, by God." She slapped her hand on a table a couple of times. "Lordy be…never dull with you around." She began to cackle again.

The Shuster brothers drifted back to the kitchen. Carol went out the front door and Jack followed her in. He sat down in the booth nearest the door then gave me a nod and a grin.

I was only halfway through my stack of pancakes when Bill burst through the door. Brian arrived a few of moments later.

"What the hell, Megan?" Bill said as he removed his Husker cap.

"I believe the Bolger brothers were out to get me. They just hadn't heard I intended to drop the matter. If they are innocent, Joe J will let them go. It's as simple as that."

I entered Custer's in a rage, but I was feeling content now that the Bolgers would see the inside of the jail.

"What if they didn't do it?" asked Brian, who slid into the booth seat across from me.

"Then they'll get a bit of punishment for deceit and trespassing."

Bill took off his red Husker cap and ran his fingers through his graying hair. "Too bold, too bold" he said. "You're gonna get yourself in trouble again."

"You got it wrong. Trouble came to find me—twice in my office and once in my barn. I didn't ask for any of this. I was ready to back off. Well, forget that. I plan to find out what the hell is going on. Now, if you'll give me some room to get out of this booth, I plan to go home and get ready for work."

"Remind me to never make you mad," said Carol as I paid my bill.

Beulah stood with her hands on her hips, smirking at me.

"We need to talk," I said to Beulah, who then dropped her head.

The news of Gondor's death and my persuasive arrest of the Bolger brothers spread throughout town and beyond by dinnertime. After supper, I rehashed the events to both Derek and Vonny over the phone.

"Emily thinks you're so cool," said Kayla as we sat on the patio after supper.

"And what do you think?" I asked.

"I think you're scary, but in a good way."

James chuckled. "Bo says that Judge Shelton took his sweet time setting bail."

"Yeah and I'm loving the fact that those two scumbags spent the day in jail," I said. "I thought Chief Joe J would turn them loose right away. But he came up with the argument that he couldn't release them on their own recognizance because they had each used an alias...so their identities had to be verified. He managed to make that process last for hours."

"Maybe the Chief was just trying to keep them safe from you," said Brian with a smile.

Patty handed out root beer floats.

"Patty, it's a good thing I don't pay you by the hour," I said. "Don't you ever want to just stay home?"

"Hell, no. I'd miss all the action." She handed Kayla a tall glass of foaming root beer and vanilla ice cream. "Megan wasn't always scary. When she was young, she was just ornery."

"So, what do you plan to do next?" Beth asked.

"You mean what do we plan to do? Well, we take up where we left off. Tomorrow, I'm meeting with Art Meyer, my dad's old law partner."

"What does he have to do with anything?" Brian asked.

"He formerly represented both the Bolger and Quinn families."

"But your dad refused to keep them as clients when Art retired," said Bill.

"Why would that be?" Brian wondered.

"Mmm, long story. Frank told me he knew too much about them. He and I grew up with the Bolger boys. And he disliked Sean Quinn."

"You know you'll be telling me that story," I said.

Bill sighed and hung his head. I needed more information before I could pry anything more out of him.

Later I slipped up to the nursery. It had become a sort of haven for me. I'd sit and imagine how the room would be transformed—we'd have the crib on the east wall to avoid the afternoon heat and sun; along the south wall we'd put the rocker and the changing table; and in my arms would be our chubby-cheeked cutie with a toothless smile, dimples, and big brown eyes like Mom and Dad's. I sat on the carpet and felt the heat of that little body radiate through my arms and chest then into my heart where it made my chest swell.

Chapter 5

The Meyer house was located on the southeast corner of Hickory Avenue and Fifth Street. The red brick and white trimmed two-story house in the ornate Queen Anne style featured a wraparound front porch that extended to the east side of the main floor. The lush half acre lawn sported a green ash, four majestic oak trees, a Colorado "blue" spruce, and a limber pine where Vonny and I gathered pine cones as kids. I made a point of driving by the house several times each fall. Trees, excluding the cottonwoods that grew along the creeks, were sparse and therefore highly valued by homeowners for their shade and beauty.

Arthur and Laura Meyer were native to the panhandle, but had become "snowbirds," retirees who lived south during the harsh winter months, Tucson, Arizona, in their case. My earliest memories included Mr. Meyer, my dad's law partner. Art took on Frank as an associate when my dad and I left Omaha to return to his Docket origins. I always liked Mr. Meyer; he was kind and always spoke gently to me.

Mrs. Meyer was kind to me, too, but I knew her to be a petty, racist bitch. She referred to James as "that black man," though she hired him on multiple occasions. However, she allowed Vonny and Derek to visit and treated them kindly, as if they were not responsible for their blackness. Particularly impressed by Vonny and Derek's good marks, she gave us oatmeal-raisin cookies whenever we brought over our report cards. She defended the Wilsons in public, derided African Americans at home, but always sent over a vat of chicken noodle soup if she heard any of the Wilsons were ill. After Beverly died, she bombarded James with home-cooked meals for two months. So maybe she was a closet racist, one who didn't realize how closely I listened and observed. In fact, she was probably like many people in rural, white America—prejudiced against those unlike them, except for the individuals in minority groups they knew, liked, and respected.

At the door, they greeted me like a long lost daughter, though I'd seen them at the funeral for Chief of Police Dobbs in December. Mr. Meyer was eighty-two, tall and thin; he was one of those people who only carried chub in the first year of life then was meant to be skinny thereafter. His shoulders sloped as if age was pulling them down, and he was bald but for the close-trimmed hair on the lower half of his skull. Laura, age seventy-six, possessed skinny arms and legs with a thickened mid-section and a compacted spine. They were a childless couple, but were popular with neighborhood children, including Joy Breeley's kids, Emily and Chelsea.

Seated in a pastel floral print chair I'd never choose, with a cup of coffee and a lemon bar on the end table beside me, we discussed the weather—it was just the warm-up for my scolding. I took a couple of bites of the lemon bar.

"Now, young lady, you've become very bold," began Mrs. Meyer. "You must be mindful of your condition...but let me wish you congratulations on the happy event. If you had a mother, she would be very worried for you. Now, no more toting guns...that will just cause trouble."

"Of course, you are right, Mrs. Meyer," I said. "By the way, this is delicious."

"Oh, pshaw. Call us Laura and Art. You're old enough and the senior partner in your law firm now."

"I'm sorry about your horse," said Art. "I grew up riding quarter horses in Gering, even though we lived in town. Like you, I had an uncle who had a good-sized ranch."

"Thank you. It has been a blow. Gondor was a good, steady horse."

"And his murder is a mystery," he said. "Why do you suspect the two younger Bolger brothers did it?"

I told them of their deceit and the strange requests by the brothers to purchase the old Quinn land. I glanced out their front window.

"Yes, I've seen that silver SUV pass by here three times now," he said.

"And I'm being stalked...and was even before Gondor was killed. I don't know who it is. The Bolger brothers both drive Chrysler 300s with Missouri plates."

"Did you know that Clay and Andy are my nephews?" asked Laura.

Whoa, shit, as Brian would say.

"Then can you tell me what they are planning? They wanted to buy the land where the murders were committed."

"I don't know. But it is strange. I'm not in close contact with my sister, Ellen. And it's a shame, but I haven't talked to those boys in quite a while. Not boys really, both married with two kids each. No, Clay has three."

"Art, I understand you were the attorney for both the Quinns and the Bolgers."

"Yes, but I backed away once the murders were committed. I never did criminal work and I didn't want to get involved. After the murders, Sean just wanted to get away. I handled the sale of his land to the Thorntons. He wouldn't sell to anyone else."

"Why would that be?" I asked.

"Well, his wife Mary was a Thornton, so he thought the land should go to them since he now had no close benefactor."

"Did he make a will?"

"After the murders, I drafted a will for him that gave everything else to two cousins in Wyoming."

"Has it been probated?"

"Not in this county."

"So as far as you know, Sean Quinn is still alive."

He nodded. "Though I have no idea where. And he could have died elsewhere."

"Do you think Walt Bolger killed Mary and Julie Quinn?" I asked, looking first at Art then at Laura, who both took deep breaths, almost in unison.

Laura spoke first. "Truth is, he didn't seem the sort. I thought Ellen had married as well as she could."

Was she insinuating that Ellen couldn't have done as well as she could in marrying an attorney? Did she think a successful rancher was her sister's best hope?

"They argued like cats and dogs," she continued. "But my sister could be unreasonable."

"The motive was always a problem for me…it just didn't make sense," said Art. "Of course, the circumstantial evidence placed Walt on the spot. But without the two or three deaths clearly proven, a good attorney should have plea bargained for manslaughter."

I nodded. "Has there ever been any…well, suspicion that the killings did not take place?"

"No, and people did wonder. But those three women disappeared completely."

"Was there any indication of a feud between the families?"

Laura shook her head.

"On the contrary, the two families seemed very friendly," said Art.

"And even got along with the Eldritch family, and some folks didn't," said Laura.

"What about the Bolger kids and Julie Quinn?"

"I never knew of any problem," said Laura. "Let's see now, this is going a long way back, but Julie was about nineteen or twenty and then all the Bolger boys were younger. I doubt they socialized together. Julie had a job as a secretary at a boarding school…can't think where…but not far. That's where she met Linda. You've heard of her?"

CRIES IN THE WIND

"Yes," I said. "She disappeared also, but none of her things were found in the partially burnt house."

"You've been doing your homework," said Art.

"And I plan to do more. I can get the accounts of that time, but as to motive…only people know that."

Actually, I was drowning in questions. Why kill those two women? Why did Linda leave? Where did she go? Why did the Bolger boys want to buy that land? Why did someone kill my horse? Why was I being stalked?

"Laura, dear, don't forget you have that lunch appointment. And I need to talk business with Megan."

Laura rose, wished me well, and then left, taking my empty plate.

"I have a proposal for you," he began. "I've kept a part of my old office building to store old files. Now some of them could be lawfully destroyed given the parties concerned are deceased, the documents are decades old, and no outstanding legal issues remain. There are a few files that should be maintained and safely stored. I did pro bono work till five years ago."

Laura stopped by to refill my coffee cup.

"I would like to come to terms with you to take possession of those files for safekeeping. My lease for the property with the Cheyenne County Bank is due for renewal and I'm tired of the hassle of it."

Meaningful silence passed between us. He wanted to get rid of his obligation and give me access to all the old Quinn and Bolger records.

"I think we could come to an agreement on that," I said. "There's no space upstairs, but my firm has a full-sized basement with nothing but computer boxes to take up space. I've upgraded our security in every way the experts have suggested. If I get a room built down there, I could provide a secure area for your records."

"Excellent."

"Oh, Megan, if you are done with Art, may I take a few moments of your time?"

I spent the next ten minutes teaching Laura and Art to use and program contacts into their "dumb" cell phones.

Afterward, I said, "I've been wondering something. May I?" I said as I walked toward the back of their house. I stopped just outside the kitchen.

"Oh, you still have it!" I said, genuinely pleased.

Along the west wall was a large window with dozens of little cubicles. In each space was goblet or vase or figurine in a variety of bright colors. The sunlit day diffused the colors into the room in a stained glass effect. As kids, Vonny and I would roll around on the carpet letting the spectrum of colors illuminate our faces and bodies.

"Vonny and I loved this window. After a visit, we'd go home and get out the crayons and try to recreate the window and all the little cups and things."

She smiled at me in a grandmotherly way, pleased that I remembered.

"I never thought of it till now, but that has to be a pain to keep dusted."

"Oh, I hire help," she said with a chuckle.

Laura left for her lunch and Art came with me back to the firm to inspect the basement. He found the arrangement satisfactory. We then sat down with Gus, my law partner, and agreed on the details for the contract.

Before he left for home, Art said, "Forget what Laura said...keep that gun with you."

Later the crew gathered at the kitchen table.

"Nephews?" my mom remarked.

"And sisters. It's a shame that they don't get along," said Brian. "You could find something out."

"I saw Betty Finch at Shaver's today," said Patty. "She said the McCracken sisters, Laura and Ellie, used to be close."

"I wonder what changed that," I said. "Anyway, once we get those files in our building, I'll take a look at the Quinn and Bolger records."

"And who's driving the silver SUV?" wondered Brian. "It's like he always wants to know where you are."

"But maybe doesn't intend to harm me...he's had a dozen chances to do so," I said.

"Is it eating at you, like something's going to happen?"

"No, I don't feel harm is coming," I said, but truthfully, some danger persistently hounded me; yet it felt too muddled to understand.

My mom had concern plastered all over her face. "Still, maybe you shouldn't go anywhere alone."

"I do have my friend Mr. Glock with me. I'm protecting two now."

After a few heavy moments, Brian broke the silence.

"I've been thinking we should paint the nursery white. That way we could have the other stuff in the room have colors...you know...depending on whether it's a girl or boy."

Smiles broke out around the table.

"That makes sense," I said.

"And it would work for our next baby, too."

I chuckled. "Ah, yeah."

"By the way, when do we get to find out if it's a girl or a boy?"

"Ummm," I said with a shrug. "I'll need to ask."

"Okay, Ma and Pa Kettle, unless you have something else, I'm going home," said Patty.

That night in bed, I lay awake wondering—what do other people do out there? I could get back on Facebook, maybe that might give me a clue. Other people didn't have mothers masquerading as aunts. If they had a horse, nobody killed it. If they had a twin, he lived. They didn't have fathers who died from guilt disguised as a heart attack. And they didn't have a cold-case homicide haunting their lives.

Chapter 6

Whatwas wrong with me? Why couldn't I just be a pregnant attorney? I sighed as I folded my arms across the menu I'd memorized two years ago. Brian was a couple minutes late; his appointment at his Sidney office must be holding him up. I felt anxious, though I didn't know why. Maybe the frequent nightmares of wailing dead women were getting to me. I glanced out the window into the alley and the brick wall across the way. I could have staked out a booth by the front windows, but then people on the sidewalk could see me eating. I didn't want to be on display; I wanted to be at peace. Brian approached from across the street. The sight of him pleased me—I'd settle for that right now; I was going to be a mother—that delighted me. What could go wrong?

A tall, thin man with a fair complexion and scraggily gray hair climbed off his stool at the counter. I didn't recognize him as a regular at Custer's, though he exchanged a few comments with Beulah. He carried a soiled red Husker cap in his hands. The moment he turned my direction my stomach cart wheeled. Prickles danced along my spine, taunting me, warning me.

He stopped at the side of my booth. Beulah hurried out from behind the counter. He smelled of oil, grease, and sweat. His hands looked like they'd been washed without removing the grease that lined his fingernails. His watch was cheap, with a thick black band; I didn't like black watch bands, and I loathed this man before he even spoke. He appeared to be healthy and in his sixties. His green eyes were set close together, as if they crowded his nose to a thin point.

"May I help you?" I asked.

"Are you gonna pull a gun on me, too?" he asked.

"Only if you want me to."

"Oh, a smartass."

"You watch your language in here," chided Beulah, who stood off to one side.

"I don't believe I've made your acquaintance," I said, noting that the area around us had gone silent.

"The name's Bert Bolger and you've been causin' my brothers trouble."

"I believe you have that backward."

"Is there a problem here?"

Bert turned to Brian.

"Because it looks to me like you're harassing my wife."

Brian stepped forward so that he knocked Bert back a step with his chest. The churning in my stomach eased a bit.

"Look, I'm not trying to create problems with your family. My Uncle Bill says he grew up with you and your brothers. He said you guys had lots of fun together. Do you remember hunting prairie dogs with BB guns?"

Bert glared at me for a few moments then nodded.

"Beulah, next time Mr. Bolger comes in, give him a Frank Docket steak on me...just to show there's no hard feeling."

He meant to argue with me, but I squelched the battle. All he could do was don his cap and walk away.

Brian slid into the booth. I was already texting Melanie, who was eating lunch with Joy, two tables away. She walked over to Eldon Strumple, the retired Methodist minister, who rose from his booth and walked out the front door.

Brian gazed at me. "Danger?" he asked in a quiet voice.

I nodded. We gave Carol our orders. Eldon Strumple came through the door and stopped at the cashier. He wrote a note then delivered it to Melanie. In a flash, my phone was vibrating. The text read: "Gray chevy suv," which I showed to Brian.

"Bastard," he said.

That evening, the crew met again. I described our meeting with Bert Bolger.

"He's definitely the Lion, and I don't mean the *Wizard of Oz* kind," I said. "I think at some point I'm going to need to make a visit out to Ellen Bolger."

"Leave the gun, take the aunt," Brian said.

I chuckled. "Good idea."

"I've talked to Betty Finch again," said Patty. "She knows all about the Bolgers. She says they had a good spread out to the west, but none of the sons could handle it after Walt was jailed. Bert, the oldest, was still in high school. So they sold the land and herd to their friends, Tim and Marge Breeley. They gave up on ranching completely. They stayed in the house, and Ellie and the boys worked a big garden. They still own several acres, but it's just rocks and gullies and scrub brush...land they couldn't sell. Bert quit high school to go work at Smokey's...supported the family for years. When the two younger ones got old enough, they moved to Kansas to be near their father."

"Kansas?" asked my mom.

"Well, Walt's in prison at Leavenworth. There was some transfer of inmates from Tecumseh. Anyway, they went to college then got jobs in that area."

"So the family split up," I said. "I wonder what Bert and Mrs. Bolger thought of that? Resentful that they left or proud that both of them made it through college?"

"Hard to know," said Beth. "Patty...anything else?"

"Not today."

"Okay, well, I discovered something," said my mom. "It looks like most people had gathered together on the Quinn ranch for a Fourth of July party they held every year.

The next day, after lunch, the murders occur. And later that day, Hank Eldritch is arrested for the rape of Linda Sharpe. The rape supposedly took place at the party the night before."

"Whoa, shit," Brian muttered.

My mom nodded. "Yeah, no kidding. But Hank is released that same day…on July fifth."

"Well, someone must have stepped forward with an alibi for him," I said.

My mom nodded and said, "He fled not long after that."

"Wait, so who is Hank to Lew?" Brian asked, running his hands through his hair.

"His uncle," Beth said. "Yes, it's getting confusing. So I made a couple of lists. Now the adults at the time of the murders include Beulah, Megan's grandparents Al and Anna, Sean and Mary Quinn, Walt and Ellen Bolger, Hank and Bob Eldritch, Arthur and Laura Meyer, Smokey Lurch, and other folks I haven't come across. All of these people would be in their seventies and eighties now."

"The ones that are living," added Brian.

My mom nodded then continued. "Now there's a younger group and they were in their teens, like Frank, Bill, Julie Quinn, Linda Sharpe, all three Bolger boys…though Andy was only eleven, Lew, and Cecil. Who is Cecil?"

"That's Salt Eldritch," I said. "Put him in the deceased column. And we'd have the Thornton family, Mary's parents and siblings if she has any. They bought all the Quinn land Sean Quinn sold after the murders."

"And the Finch family," said Patty. "Lloyd Finch and Al Docket ran the county bank together, 'course those two are both dead, but Betty, the widow, still has her wits. The Finch son, Stanley, would have been too young. There were two sisters, but they didn't stay in the area, Betty says."

"Geez," said Brian. "This is making my head spin."

"I could make a chart," said my mom.

"That's exactly what we need, but we need more complete info. Mom, the newspaper reports wouldn't have everybody's ages. Do you know how to search the public records?"

"You mean at the county courthouse?"

"Right. I can have Melanie show you, if you're willing."

"Sure."

"Once you get all those dates of births, make your chart. In time, we'll need to figure out who was at the party and who was still around on the next day."

Patty shook her head. "We keep digging and it just gets more confusing. What's the deal with Linda and Hank Eldritch?"

"And why does it seem like they're important? And what's the deal with Bert Bolger? Why does he smack of danger?" I wondered out loud.

"Maybe he killed Gondor," Brian commented.

"Oh, and Officer Merritt agreed to come over after his shift tomorrow," I said. "We'll see what I can pry out of him. And maybe we should move all our research to the study. That way Bill or even Officer Merritt can't see what we're up to."

"Yeah, like those murder investigation rooms the police on TV always have," Patty said.

"Let's call it the War Room," Brian said as he took a bottle of root beer out of the fridge.

"Since it's your idea, you can be Doctor Strangelove," said my mom.

Officer Warren Merritt sat across from me at our patio table with the bur oak shading us from the early evening sun. He was one of those men who really needed to shave twice a day. He could grow a great NHL playoff beard before the first round was half over. His thick neck was topped by a large head with a dark crew cut. I wondered as we chatted about small town affairs if I could get such a straight-laced cop to talk.

"Ever since they found that van, things have gone wrong," I said.

"How do you connect Gondor's death with that?" he asked. "And no, I don't have any more to tell you on Gondor, though I wish I did."

I told him of the attempt by the Bolger brothers to buy the old Quinn homestead and the stalker in the gray SUV.

"It doesn't seem like any of the Bolgers are stealthy or cunning," he said. "But Mrs. Bolger says all three sons were home in bed when Gondor must have been killed."

"Clay and Andy don't seem like the kind of guys that go around killing people's horses just because they didn't get their way. No, I think they look like two brothers who work in insurance and live in the suburbs. Now, Bert, he's different, he's threatening. And someone did kill my horse." I poured the rest of the bottle of Michelob into Merritt's glass. "So, what is the deal with this van?"

"Testing hasn't been completed yet."

I ignored his stonewalling. "It seems like if they found the three bodies in the van, that news would have broken."

He scratched the whiskers on his chin. "We're trying to keep all information out of the news till we know everything."

"Officer, I'm an attorney—the exact opposite of a journalist—I guard secrets, I don't spread them. But I'm in this mess, even though I didn't want to be. And I bet the vehicle ID number on the van matches the one stolen on July fourth of that year."

He shifted in his chair, never losing eye contact with me.

"So...no bodies. But they found something or there wouldn't be the need for testing and secrecy."

"We recovered binding cords for two people."

"Not three."

"Right."

"What else?" I asked.

"Why do you need—"

"I'm being stalked...killing Gondor was meant to get at me. I need information. I'd like to save my skin and that of my baby's."

He ran his hand over his whiskered chin. "They found a plastic bag with a man's shirt and pants in it, somewhat preserved."

"But they weren't Walt Bolger's because they wouldn't fit him." It was a guess, but I knew he'd react.

"How could you know that?"

"I didn't...till now."

His face flushed with anger.

"So do you think the bodies could be on my land? Is that what the Bolger brothers thought? I'm willing to cooperate in any way I can. How horrible that must have been for the family—murdered but never found." Maybe if I kept talking I could quell his irritation. "Dig up any part of my land you need to."

"They dug up several places right afterward, but never found anything."

"A smart accomplice would keep moving the bodies," I said. "Maybe he put them in places already searched. There's a lot of open land around here, but newly-dug ground would have been spotted."

"You'd make a good criminal," he said with a smirk.

"And whoever took the bodies had to get rid of them quickly...he'd know there would be police searches."

"Right. Someone hid those bodies, probably in that van, but got rid of them before he or she sunk the van in the lake. The windows and the rear door were all open so it would sink fast. And yes, searches were made around Lake McConaughy. The FBI joined in pretty quickly."

"The topic disturbs anyone I talk to. It's like an open wound."

"It's a case that haunts us still. Decade to decade, this is the one big case the Patrol has never completed. Finding this van is the first break since the initial investigation."

He leaned back in his chair and shook his head. The tone had changed. I never thought of how this would affect the investigators.

"You should see our Sidney office. We got old troopers coming in from nursing homes, just hoping for some news."

"So this has always been considered an unresolved case?"

"Oh, yeah. It has never been officially closed."

We sat in silence for a few minutes. I'm sure he was thinking the same question—where are those bodies? After forty-five years, mother and daughter would just be bones and teeth; though modern forensics could probably identify them.

The back screen door creaked open and shut. Brian put another Michelob on the table for Merritt and poured more iced tea for me.

"Any reason why Chief Joe J keeps driving by?" asked Brian. "Four times now. He's giving me the creeps. His shift would have ended hours ago."

"What do you think, Officer Merritt?" I asked.

"I'd say that's pretty strange. If he needed me for something, he'd call." He stood then handed the beer back to Brian. "You drink it. I better get going. I promised my son I'd help him build a volcano…he's in a summer science club."

"How old is he?" Brian asked.

"Going into fifth grade. He wanted to build a rocket, but my wife vetoed the idea. I'm glad she's the bad guy on that one."

The three of us walked around to the front of the house.

"What are you using for lava?" I asked.

"Still workin' on that. Now, Megan, you take care of yourself."

"What are you going to do about my stalker?"

"I'll have a chat with Bert Bolger."

As Brian and I watched the patrol car head toward the highway, we both noticed James standing on his front porch.

"I wonder…maybe we should invite James into our little club. He could chat up some oldsters in town and on his jobs," I said.

"And he's bored most evenings," Brian added. "I'll go get him."

Chapter 7

A few minutes later, we'd all assembled in the War Room. I gave James a quick rundown on our investigation, while Patty set up two big poster boards on the cabinets. I then recounted the information on the van.

"Everybody's talking about this," James said. "I could see what people know…older folks…the ones who remember."

"Just remember, don't talk about what we know," I said. "We need to find out more about what these people were like. Motive is the big mystery—besides the missing bodies."

"But finding them may not reveal much," Beth said.

James puckered his lips in thought then asked, "What do Beulah and Bill say? They were around, they would know things."

"They will get quizzed…just not yet…not till we know all we can," I replied.

Patty nodded. "If you ask me, they look traumatized whenever the topic comes up. Notice how Bill's been avoiding us? He's usually here most nights."

"I don't plan to lie to him, but I see no reason to bother him right now," I said as I picked up a marker off the desk.

"Wait, Megan," Brian said. "We've all seen your handwriting…it looks like shorthand. We'll write, you talk."

That was true—I possessed rotten fine motor skills. I was a lousy typist; I'd discovered years ago there was no word my fingers couldn't misspell.

An hour later, we completed a chart on the Quinns and the Bolgers. A third board listed Linda Sharpe, with nothing under it except "friend of Julie Quinn."

"Who is Linda Sharpe?" I wondered out loud. "And where is she? Laura Meyer said Julie was a secretary at a boarding school and that's where she met Linda. What boarding school? It couldn't be too far away."

"I'll see what I can find out," Beth said.

"Wait, there is something I need to ask Bill. Andy Bolger said the ground was 'unsteady' in the old Quinn land. What does that mean?"

I called my uncle on the desk phone. I told him why I was curious and he surprised me, not only by his willingness to talk about it, but also by his answer.

"It turns out, Bill says, that Old Man Quinn was a bootlegger. His bootleg whiskey kept the family afloat during the Depression and, not surprisingly, he made good money during Prohibition. Sean filled in the brewery rooms, but kept the series of tunnels connected to them. It became a favorite playground of the kids in the area. Bill says since Sean didn't have any sons, he enjoyed having the town and ranch boys play on his land. Frank and Bill spent a lot of time there, as did all three Bolger boys and the Thornton boys, Buck and Adam." My mom was furiously taking notes as I continued. "So Mary, the mother, had two brothers, at least. We'll want to get the scoop on that family—who's living, who's running the ranch, etc."

"I can get the names and dates of birth," said my mom.

"My friend Melvin Poots will know everything about the family," said James. "Coffee and doughnuts loosen his tongue lickety-split."

"How did you know to ask about that land?" asked Patty.

"I told Andy that I was thinking of leasing land to one of those companies that operates wind turbines…just to see what he would say. He let it slip that the land was 'unsteady'."

James grinned at me then his countenance changed. "Anybody know why Chief Joe J has been snooping around?"

I shrugged. "Not like we ought to throw the first stones. But I'll find out. Meanwhile, we need to get a lock on this door."

"I can do that," said James. "I'll buy it for you, too. Ritter's hardware will have some. Everybody watches what you do, Megan."

"Do they think I'll shoot someone?" I said with a smirk.

"Nah, it's just that unusual things seem to happen when you're around."

Brian chuckled. I couldn't refute that.

"Anyway, Mom, I mean Beth, and I are visiting Ellen Bolger on Saturday."

"Really?" asked Patty. "How'd you manage that? I would think she'd be mad at you."

"We did it the old-fashioned way," said Beth. "I told Megan to send a note on some fancy stationery suggesting a meeting. She responded likewise…invited us to tea."

"Hey, Patty, would you make a loaf of your Paw Paw Bread?"

"Maybe two," said my mom. "I'm visiting Laura Meyer on Monday."

"Lordy, both sisters in the same week. I'll make them, sure thing. But why does Laura Meyer want to hang with you? No offense, Beth."

I smiled. "Three reasons—Laura's bored, Mom looks interesting, and she knows Mom won't be a hick because she's from Omaha."

"Megan, have you ever seen the Bolger house?" asked James.

"No, why?"

"Well, let me warn you—it looks like the House of Usher. I put in a retaining wall for her flower garden a few years back."

From a distance, the Bolger house reminded me of the Bates house, so we'd find out for sure if the mother really lived or if there was only her sinister son, Bert. When I turned off the street, drove down the lengthy gravel driveway, and then cleared an overgrown hedge, the house on a hill looked like it would make a great Halloween haunted house. I didn't know architecture, but it looked like a mix of styles, with arched ground floor windows, two stories, a steep roof squared at the top with a railing, and dark brown paint that had probably been peeling for several years, but no flying buttresses. The house looked eerie, then once I drove onto the dirt parking in front of it, my guts began to churn so wildly that I rolled down the window, expecting to puke. Was I imagining the presence of evil because the owner was in prison for murder?

I could feel my mom staring at me. "Creepy, I know. We should be okay unless we encounter something phantasmagoric," I said as I regained my composure.

My mom laughed. "I don't think there was a sister."

I smiled at her—she knew her Edgar Allan Poe. "We'll stay out of the basement."

We climbed the rickety steps then crossed the creaking porch. Finding no doorbell, I knocked. The windows were open, so we'd enjoy no air conditioning. We heard shuffling then the door creaked open.

"Welcome! Welcome!" said the form on the other side of the filthy screen door.

Ellen Bolger looked like her sister with the thin appendages and compressed spine, though she was a bit chunkier, and wore a print polyester dress Laura would never be seen in. Soon, Beth—I needed to remember to call her that—and I were seated on an old squeaky couch, drinking lemonade so tart it made my entire face pucker.

"Thank you for inviting us," I said. "There have been some misunderstandings between your sons and me."

"Oh, pshaw, I love company. And don't worry…my sons will get over it. My youngest two got kinda uppity once they moved away. Good to knock them down a notch. Have you met Bert, my oldest? He ain't like them."

"I saw him at Custer's."

"And I bet you appreciate his company," said Beth.

"Yep, he stayed and helped his mother. Now, don't get me wrong—Clay and Andrew send me money 'n all. I'm grateful for sure."

"But it's nice to have a son with you in this grand house," said my mother, the diplomat.

"'Grand,' eh? Thank ya. It's too much to keep up, that's for sure. Got a young girl that comes and helps me."

I nodded. Despite the wear and age of the furniture, the tables had been dusted and the room was generally tidy. She favored lace doilies and curtains; though I wished she had forced her sons to buy her central air, for the sweat was trickling down my neck and ribs.

"I understand Bert is quite the mechanic," I said.

She smiled and nodded, "Yep, yep. He is. Been with Smokey for over forty years."

Yeah, this chit-chat was fine, but the creeps kept racing up and down my spine. Was it the house? Was it her? It was time to find out if this old-timey sweetness was genuine.

"Mrs. Bolger—"

"Oh, do call me Ellie."

"Ellie, why did your sons want to buy that old Quinn land north of my house?"

For an instant, she paused, her glass in mid-air. Her look was intense as she studied my face in those few seconds. She set the glass down without taking a sip.

"You're a bold young woman."

"I've been told that. But I don't like being lied to and please ask Bert to stop stalking me and wash his muddy SUV."

She took a drink, keeping her eyes on me, sizing me up, planning her answer.

"You just don't understand what we've been through...over so many years now."

"No, I haven't taken a walk in your shoes, as the saying goes. But I've known some loss...of a different kind."

She nodded. "I went to your pa's funeral. Sure did. But our Walt is eighty-two. We're afraid he's gonna die in prison. My boys want to find evidence. Finding that van got Clay all stirred up and that gets Andrew all stirred up."

"So they wanted to dig up that area for clues...maybe bodies."

She nodded, though some problem in her neck made her head go askew when she moved it up and down or when she turned her head to the side.

"That would be a very bad idea."

Her knuckles turned white as she gripped the arms of her worn fabric chair.

"Why shouldn't they want to help their father?"

"Oh, I understand that. It's just that if they found something it could be ruled that they tampered with evidence. That would make it inadmissible in court. They should have been straightforward with me."

"Oh. They didn't know that."

"I'm willing to help in any way I can, but the State Patrol needs to find the evidence."

"Then tell the police to dig up the Eldritch land. I never trusted that family, none of 'em, 'cept Lois. I always thought Hank Eldritch did it."

That answered a question I was hesitant to ask.

"So you think Hank murdered the women?"

"Of course, Walt didn't do it. I know him. He'd never murder anyone. Oh, he could have a temper on him...could get kinda violent...knock things around, but I never seen him hit anyone...not even when he was drunk."

"Why would Hank Eldritch murder those women?"

"Resentful, I expect. Quinns got more land, more money, more cattle…more everything. Those Eldritches was odd folk. There was talk of a rape. Maybe Hank done 'em in to shut 'em up. He and his brother Bob were both crazy sons of guns."

I tried to look thoughtful as I nodded.

"Nobody knew where your pa was that day. Never did hear…refused to say, if I recall correctly. But it wasn't him. He was a nice young man."

An urge to choke her came over me, yet I just nodded again and leaned back on the couch. For the first time, I spotted a bit of brightly colored carpet to the left of the staircase.

"Do you have colored vases and glasses in your window? I remembered Mrs. Meyer's window from when I was little."

"Heh. Sure do. My sister would like people to think she invented that…but it was our grandmother that first done it."

"I just might have to steal that," I said then turned to Beth. "Wouldn't something like that look great in the nursery?"

"Oh, yes," said Beth, who'd been quiet during my questioning. "Maybe pastels to start then primary colors later on."

"Yep, I heard you was expectin'. Congrats to you."

Ellie's body seemed to sink back into the chair, revealing how tense she had been until the change in topic.

"Thank you, Mrs., um…Ellie. Say, when do babies see colors?"

She smiled and shrugged, which made her head tip to the side. I turned to Beth for an answer.

"Oh, about four months," she said.

"Heh, haven't been 'round a baby in forever. My boys don't bring their families here. They useta."

"Why not?"

It was a simple follow up question to her comment, but it made her body tighten again, as something flashed across her face, but she was too unfamiliar to read. She knew she had said too much. She tried to shrug, but it made her body hunch sideways. Her seventy-seven years betrayed her, preventing her from acting nonchalant. I took a drink to hide how closely I watched her. I could feel my mom shift slightly on the couch. It was time to leave.

We parted as if we were the best of friends. Anxious to get out of that house, I took a deep breath once I locked us inside the Shark. Mom turned the AC up two notches. It had clouded over during the visit, but that just made the air more humid. Neither of us spoke on the short drive home on Harney Street, though people to the west of the highway called it Road 47, its official name. I think we both wanted to "process" the encounter; however, our opportunity was brief as Patty, Brian, and James awaited our return.

"So?" asked Patty as we gathered in the War Room.

"She comes off as a sweet old grandma, but there's something…" said my mom. "It's hard to nail it down. But yes, the House of Usher, as you said, James."

I paused to reflect and they waited for me.

"Okay, here's my take on it. She favors Bert, resents Clay and Andy for leaving her, resents her sister in many ways, resents the families around her who are better off, probably us included, says Walt is not guilty of murder yet makes a point of calling him violent, then tries to soften it, claims Hank Eldritch killed the women to hush up a rape, has suffered a great deal maybe in more ways than we know, and still has her wits. She's a creepy, decrepit old lady who lives in a creepy, decrepit old house—with no air conditioning. And there's an ongoing rift—the younger sons don't visit with their families."

"And she makes terrible lemonade," added Mom. "I noticed you said 'the women' and I kept expecting her to say their names or specify the number of murders, but she never did."

"I don't think she has any sympathy for the death of Mary and Julie. But that doesn't make her guilty of anything. Walt's arrest and imprisonment for those murders devastated that family. And Patty, I know what you're planning to ask. No, it didn't feel like just any other house...there's something else...more than sadness, resentment, and poverty. Is it more than creepy? I just don't know. Oh, and she said nobody knew where my dad was that day and he refused to say."

"Really?" said Patty. "That's kinda disturbing."

The group was quiet for a few minutes. Brian wrote "resentful" and "creepy" under the Ellen Bolger column on the Bolger board.

"So, let me get this straight," said Brian. "The oldsters, the ones in their seventies or eighties would be Walt, Ellie, Sean, and Mary, but forty-five years ago they were in their twenties and thirties. Oh, and add Beulah, Hank, and Smokey. In their fifties and sixties now and teens back then would be Frank, Bill, Lew, Salt, Bert, Clay, Andy, and then Linda and Julie."

"In the murder mysteries on TV, it seems like it's all about money, but I don't see that here," said James.

"I agree," I said. "The will Art Meyer drafted for Sean after the murders names two out of state cousins as beneficiaries. And he sold all the Quinn land to the Thornton family."

"So we still have no clue as to motive," said Brian. "I doubt we ever will."

James shook his head. "Neighbors just don't go around murdering their neighbors for no good reason."

"All the news accounts—old and new—question the lack of any kind of explanation," said Beth.

"There's a motive...we just don't know what it is...yet," I said.

Maybe it was presumptuous to believe we'd figure it out.

Chapter 8

Not five minutes after my mom left, I flushed hot as my hands became clammy. What now? Creatures in spiky boots stomped around in my acidic stomach. Mom! She left for the Sidney library in the Shark because it was raining and her Nissan needed new tires. Then the phone rang. Triple shit. Patty answered it then rushed into the family room, rousing me, Brian, and James. We jumped to our feet then rushed to Brian's Jeep Cherokee. He drove west then turned north onto the highway as my heart hammered the inside of my ribs.

"Whoa, shit!" exclaimed Brian as he slowed. "That's where last year's crash was."

Brian pulled onto the shoulder of Highway 51. Bo's cruiser and two State Patrol cars were already on the road, blocking traffic. The Sidney ambulance crested the hill then sped toward us. Dry heaves shook my body once I jumped out of the SUV onto the muddy gravel.

Tire tracks on the shoulder and down the embankment indicated this was the same place the Troff Construction truck had gone off the road and hit the concrete support under the bridge over Raccoon Creek. The passenger, Jake Breeley, died on the spot.

A State Trooper tried to keep me back, but a simple fake to the left enabled me to dash around him to the right. The cop yelled at Brian and James. I gasped once I came to the top of the slope. The Shark lay on its passenger side at the edge of the shallow creek. The left rear bumper and tail light were smashed in. Bo and Officer Waters were on each side of the vehicle. My queasiness ebbed a bit—

She wasn't dead.

"She's still in there, Megan," said Bo.

I'm glad he had spoken first, for it reminded me to call her Beth.

"Bo, give me a boost."

"Huh? Oh."

I put my muddy tennie in his hands then lunged over the roof onto the rear passenger door. I scrambled to the driver door. I grabbed the handle and yanked. A blast of air bag fumes hit me, but the rain quickly doused them.

"Beth!"

I maneuvered my body so that it blocked the rain from falling on her.

"I'm okay, hon. But I'm stuck. If I release the seat belt, I'll fall."

"Are you hurt?"

"Oh, here and there. I'm mostly mad."

"Mad? Why?"

"Because I tried to stay on the road…I did for a while…but he rammed me off…like he knew just where to do it."

"Mom," I whispered as I hovered over her. "Did you hit your head?"

She smiled. "It was a big black pickup. It came up so fast…but it rammed me and pushed me off the road. And no, my head is fine, but I think this wrist is broken."

She held her left wrist in her lap with her other hand.

"Okay, just don't move. They'll get you out." I eased the door closed.

Despite the rain, a small crowd was gathering at the top of the hill. A fire truck was now parked on the highway. I waved up to Brian and James, who'd gotten stopped by the cop I dodged. They waved back. I explained the situation to Bo and Officer Waters. Then I opened the rear passenger door and eased into the seat, hanging onto the headrest to keep from dropping. Intending to supervise her removal, I wiggled and scooted until I was seated next to her in the front passenger seat.

"Hi," I said.

She laughed. "You're like a little monkey."

"Thanks."

I saw her shudder.

"Mom, just hang on. You're gonna be fine. It's okay if you want to cuss or cry."

She smiled.

Soon, the firemen placed ladders on both sides of the SUV. Thick arms pulled her up and out of the seat. I kept telling them to be careful, and they were. I rode with her in the ambulance to the Sidney ER then stayed with her until she told them I was pregnant. They banished me to the waiting room when they wheeled her off to radiology.

A larger crowd filled the waiting room, several of them still dripping wet. Chief Joe J and Officer Merritt were now present. When I told them that a black pickup pushed her off the road, a wave of shock crashed through the damp and dry alike. Outrage and questions soon followed.

"She told me she hadn't seen the pickup before," I said. "She doesn't know the make, but says it's not like Bill's front end, so not a Ford."

The second I finished talking to the police, I was dragged to a corner of the waiting room by scrawny old lady with a strong grip.

"Lordy, Megan," Beulah said. "This all gives me the shakes...makes me mad, too. Now she was drivin' your car, right?"

"Yes, I know. Whoever ran her off the road probably thought it was me."

She looked over my shoulder. I turned to find my uncle standing behind me.

"I knew you'd be thinkin' that. Had to make sure. I got another question, hon. Why is Chief Joe J askin' me questions about the Quinn murders?" she asked.

"Yeah, he was asking me, too," Bill said. "I said it was a bad memory and I didn't want to talk about it."

"That's exactly the thing to say—to him, anyway," I said. "There's no way he could be involved in any investigation. This is a State Patrol matter."

"But FBI was involved in the 1968 murders and the paper says FBI is involved with the van," said Bill.

"Well, right now his role is with Dexter police," I said, though I wondered if he didn't still have a role with the FBI. Joe J was undercover FBI last winter then said he wanted to stay on as Chief of Police of Dexter. The town council appointed him interim chief, and then the citizens elected him chief in May, as Bo didn't want the job.

"Yep. Yep. I told him I was busy when he asked me. But if he wants to talk to me, he'll haveta sapeena me."

I couldn't help but smile at her. "That's right. If there's a trial, you could be subpoenaed to testify."

An elderly woman with silver-lavender curls came by handing out cups of coffee. Brian took a cup then joined us. His short, blond hair was mostly dry, but his shirt and jeans were sopping wet.

"I just can't believe this," said Brian. "But she did a hellava job steering clear of that concrete. So there's no doubt this was intentional?"

"It's clear to me," I said. "You saw the damage to the rear bumper and taillight. But the S-O-B that did this didn't know front and side air bags would keep her or me alive."

Brian's jaw went slack. "What?"

A nurse came and told us we could go see her in room 143. I grabbed his hand and pulled him along.

"Megan, this has to end."

He was in my face, yet last night's screams still echoed in my head. If I backed off, I'd never be rid of them. But how could I protect my family?

After Beth was released that evening, we came home. By then, the western half of Cheyenne County had heard the news, and all of them tried to visit, or at least it seemed that way. Patty stood at the front door, accepting baked goods and turning most people away, claiming that Beth was sleeping. When Officer Merritt arrived, he was escorted to the family room where Beth lay on the sofa, her left arm in a cast.

"We found the pickup pretty quickly," he said. "It was parked on an old gravel road north of here, just off the highway. He must have ditched it and ran. He probably had a vehicle hidden somewhere nearby."

"Wait, he didn't park it by a couple of old bur oaks, did he?" I asked.

"Let me check." Merritt backed out into the hall and made a call on his cell.

I looked at Brian, he nodded, he knew. Merritt returned a couple of minutes later.

"Yes, Waters says it was parked in a gravel area just off the road, and yes, near two big oak trees."

"The snake left the truck at the Quinn house," I said.

That hushed the room.

"It matches the description of a truck stolen from Smokey's last night," said the trooper.

That night I lay awake in bed. Danger, Mom, the baby, the wailing women, stalkers, Gondor, a creepy old lady and her creepy son, Brian pushing back—instead of rousing me, it weakened me. Despair washed over me and I gasped for air as tears streamed down my face. God help me.

A phone call at eight in the morning awakened me. Brian was already up. He came rushing into the room.

"Megan, get up! You gotta come see this," he said.

"Tell me what it is," I said, annoyed. How could there be something else this fast?

I brushed my teeth and threw on some clothes then checked on my mom, who was still sleeping. Bill was waiting for us in the driveway. He refused to answer any questions; he just drove to Gondor's old barn. Oh, no! Was it Rohan now? Strange, but I didn't feel disturbed, though my grogginess left me in a flash. We strode up to the barn, and then I saw him. He left me speechless and gasping for air. Breathe, Megan, breathe.

The tallest, most beautiful stallion I'd ever seen stood in front of me. He was black from hoof to mane, without even a splotch of white on his forehead.

"I came by here to tend to Rohan and here he was," said Jack, who was holding the reins.

"Uncle Bill?"

"Nope, not me," Bill said. "I was thinking of buying you a horse, but Beth said maybe I should wait awhile...you being in your condition. I even called a couple of the Kimball ranches this morning, but they knew nothing about it."

I took a couple of steps toward the horse. He looked at me, without registering any alarm.

"He's a good three years or so," Bill said.

"He looks different than most quarter horses," I said.

I was no horse expert, but quarter horses possessed broad, deep chests. They were the sturdy, powerful horses that provided companionship and labor to the American Indian and European settlers. This magnificent horse looked powerful and sturdy, yet his shoulders were a bit longer and sloped more.

"It looks a bit like he has some Thoroughbred in him, but he's too calm to be one," said Jack. "That's a John Wayne sized horse...gotta be seventeen hands."

Rohan snorted. Brian cut a wide berth around the new horse to his palomino, a quarter horse with a gold coat and white mane and tail. Rohan appreciated Brian's attention and didn't seem agitated by the presence of the new horse. I stepped up to the stallion and stroked his neck. His nostrils worked quickly as his eyes sized me up.

"Hello, gorgeous," I said. "Do you know how handsome you are?"

I ran my hands down both sides of his neck, letting him drop his head onto my shoulder. It tickled when he sniffed my hair. I walked alongside of him, stroking his chest and then his back down to his flank. When I walked back to his head, he nuzzled my shoulder then dropped his head and sniffed hard at my belly.

Brian walked up behind me. "Stop seducing the blasted horse. You're making me jealous."

I chuckled. "Give me a leg up."

"You sure?" Brian turned to look at Bill and Jack.

When they didn't protest, he bent over and I put my tennie into his hands. I launched myself up and onto the back of the horse. He bobbed his head up and down. Jack handed me the reins. I walked him down the length of the barn and back. Though it was thrilling to feel the muscles and power of the horse, I didn't intend to ride him bareback again. Brian helped me slide off the horse.

As we backed away from the horse, I said, "This makes no sense. Someone kills my horse. Someone gives me a new one. Why?"

And why did I only sense the advent of bad things?

Bill and Jack looked flummoxed. When we arrived back at the house, Patty and James shook their heads over the news.

In fact, I tried to think of one event in the last two weeks that made sense, but that made my head ache.

No sense, anywhere.

Chapter 9

That afternoon, my mom and my horse became the big attractions. In keeping with our Tolkien-themed horse names, I dubbed my black steed Strider. The horse was so tall, I had to let my stirrups down two notches so that I could climb onto the saddle. Oh, could that horse fly! He possessed the quick acceleration of a quarter horse and the flat out speed of a racing horse. I thought Rohan was fast, but Strider could leave him to eat flying cow turds at fifty yards. Patty told me the crash was the news in the pews. It wasn't till after the service did she and James tell people of the replacement horse. People must have been bored on that mid-June Sunday afternoon, for they gathered to watch the shrimpy girl on the tall black horse blast across the south pasture trail at full speed. Many of the on-lookers were still in their Sunday best.

But life changed. For the first few days, Brian carried my mom up and down the stairs, for she had jammed both ankles in the wreck. Whenever I rode, Bud, Jack, or Drew would be walking along the fence with a Winchester balanced on their shoulders. Zane Whitfield, my old boyfriend and former army captain with Post-traumatic Stress Disorder, volunteered to drive me to work whenever Brian needed to go to Sidney in the morning. Every day, one of Bill's cowhands patrolled the area around the big house, always with a visible handgun or rifle.

While the Shark was being repaired at an Ogallala body shop, I concocted a plan to meet with Smokey Lurch. Brian drove me out to the sale yard, his Glock tucked in his rear waistband—we had his and her versions of the same gun. Smokey invited us into his office, a white A-frame that had probably been someone's dinky house sixty years ago. The sale yard was a half mile east of town on Highway 28, Elm Street in Dexter. Compared to the quiet reserve of the law firm, the place bustled—trucks, Bobcats, tractors, riding mowers, even combines in motion, along with an army of sales people and customers, talking, bargaining, climbing under and onto the equipment. Besides ranching and Bear Lake Beulah's Root Beer brewery, this was Dexter's biggest employer, with its "Smokin' Hot Deals."

Smokey Lurch was seventy-four and a former classmate of Beulah's. He had the gruff, raspy voice of a former smoker. He popped a piece of nicotine gum into his mouth as soon as he sat behind his desk. His gray comb-over covered weathered skin, his arms and hands were leathery and permanently suntanned. He visited our firm on occasion, as Gus was his attorney for commercial transactions.

We chatted about recent events for a few minutes then I handed him a printout of the new vehicle I wanted to buy. He whistled.

"Can you get it for me?" I asked.

"Sure. Never sold one of these before. I sell lots of pickups, but no luxury SUVs. This color? Dark red I'd call it."

"That's my choice, yes."

"Now this is the MSRP, the price suggested by Acura. You plannin' to dicker me down?"

"No, sir…as long as the mileage is minimal when I pick it up."

"Don't want one of my boys drivin' it across the country. Heh? No problem. Need a loaner till then?"

"Nobody will let me drive alone," I said.

"Heh! Don't blame 'em. Say, you two are friends of Beulah's."

"She's a character," said Brian.

"You were classmates…along with Hank Eldritch. Tell me about him," I said.

"Hank? Let's see…unpredictable…that's what he was. Could be a good friend, especially in a pinch. Liked pranks when he was young. Grew outta that when he started workin' so much. Loyal even to that screwy family of his."

"Was he malicious?" I asked.

"Nah. Bad to get on the wrong side of him. Strong and quick…sorry I never knew what happened to him."

"Could he murder two women?"

"Nah, never thought he did that. Always polite to folks, even if it came off rough. Kinda shy, in his way…kinda like Lew."

"Lew is our friend," said my Chicago man proudly.

"Could Hank kill a horse?" I asked.

"Don't seem like him. He wasn't no saint…got in trouble sometimes…he's mean when he's drunk. He'd need to be awful desperate to kill somethin'."

We switched to completing the details of the SUV transaction.

When that finished, Brian asked, "Stacy still handling your books?"

"Yep, yep. My boys are good workers…they'll carry on my business for me, but Stacy is the only one to get college-educated. Proud of her, sure am. Say, she'd be about your aunt's age. I bet she'd like to meet her, be around someone who doesn't smell like grease."

I laughed. "Well, Beth is quite bored at the moment, lying on the sofa all day, waiting to heal. Have her give my, ah, aunt a call." I wrote my home phone number on the back of one of my business cards and handed it to him. I nearly said "Mom," I needed to be more careful.

We didn't hold another War Room meeting till Thursday night. Brian and I discussed our visit with Smokey. Stacy, his daughter, had already paid a call over her lunch hour. Laura Meyer visited Beth twice.

"Say, Paw Paw Patty, I heard you dumped Johnny Two Rivers for Chief Joe J," I said.

"Who told you that?" she asked.

"Who knows everything in this town?"

"That Beulah is a blabbermouth," Patty said.

"Well, duh," said Brian with a laugh. "But she's mostly right."

Patty didn't seem willing to expound, so Mom started discussing the details of her research on the boarding school and Linda.

"Well, there was one of those assimilation schools called Clark House north of Potter. Now, I can't get names of students or employees, but we know that's where Julie Quinn worked. Linda Sharpe was either another employee or a student. I haven't found a date of birth or location of birth for Linda."

"Hold on," Patty said. "If Linda was a student, then she might have been Sioux. She could've been born on a reservation or somewhere other than Nebraska."

"That's what I was thinking," said Mom.

"Okay, wait," said Brian. "I'm not familiar with assimilation schools."

"That's when the U.S. government went into the reservations and took Indian kids and forced them to live in boarding schools," said Patty. "They were trying to make these kids, Sioux, Northern Cheyenne, and Pawnee around here, to conform to the Christian European world...make them speak only English and so on."

"Sounds cruel," said Brian.

Patty obviously thought so, for she started walking around the room, her face flushed.

"The schools started in the eighteen hundreds and were big in the nineteen sixties and seventies," added Beth. "They mostly shut down in the nineties. The Clark House shut down in seventy-five."

I listened and formed a plan for my own research, which I didn't plan to share with Patty around. Now that she was dating Joe J, the dynamic of our group changed; I wondered if our secrecy was compromised.

The next morning, Police Chief Joe J came to my office. He walked up to Glenda, our receptionist then tapped on my open office door. I covered up the bankruptcy materials strewn about my desk.

"Any news on finding Gondor's killer?" I asked.

"No."

His voice was harsh—he came to argue or scold me. I leaned back in my chair.

"Then why are you here? You don't have an appointment."

"You need to back off, Megan. You're meddling in things you shouldn't."

"Such as?"

His face flushed red. He was debating what to say. The fool had come to argue, but hadn't made a plan. Even worse, he'd shown the matter was personal and emotional. How was he connected? He turned and walked out, slamming shut the front door.

I closed my door then pushed the Hadley bankruptcy file to the side. I started to dial my cell phone then stopped. Using the number in my cell phone contacts list, I called Jackson Draper, my elderly friend on the Pine Ridge rez in South Dakota.

After a few minutes of small talk, I came to the point. "Do you know of a Linda Sharpe? She'd be in her sixties by now."

"I know you would only ask such a thing if it was important," he said.

"It is. I mean her no harm. I will protect this information."

"You're calling on your office phone."

"It is more secure," I said.

"I see." After a pause, he said, "The Sharpe family still lives here. Linda grew up here."

"Did she live in a boarding house in the panhandle?"

"Yes."

"But she left Clark House in 1968," I surmised.

"She graduated from the high school that year."

"You have a tremendous memory…though as an elder, many people and many things would be your concern."

"Yes. And I recall her…situation well."

"Is there anything else you would like to share?"

"In time…perhaps. Complete your investigation."

"You understand this involves the Quinn murders in 1968."

"Yes. I recall those murders too well."

"I know that Linda did not die here."

"How do you know?"

"When I went to the ground where the house was located, I heard only two women wailing."

"You are the Woman Who Feels."

"I wish I hadn't heard it—it was terrible. And now I hear them at night."

"Yes, yes."

"Jackson, have others made recent inquiries?"

"No."

"I think they will. You don't need to talk to anyone. Someone named Joe who identifies himself with the FBI may contact you."

"I understand. He will need a subpoena for information."

"Right, good. Be wary of Joe Janowicz. He's the Dexter police chief right now. Our friend Patty is dating him. She may lose…perspective."

"Janowicz. I see."

I told him about Beth's crash and injuries, as well as Gondor and Strider. "I may call you again…though maybe just for counsel."

"Feel free."

My next call went to Robert Foxworthy of the Denver FBI office. I started to tell him about the events of the past few weeks, but he stopped me.

"We'd be foolish not to keep tabs on you."

"Hmm. So tell me, why is Joe still here?"

"I'm not at liberty to divulge—"

"Yeah, yeah. My guess is that he's still FBI…perhaps mopping up some of this area's run in with meth."

Silence.

"If that's the case, why is he stalking me? And why did he just tell me to back off a cold case that involves more than just murder? And why is he so emotional about it? Is Mr. Half-Lakota interested in the Lakota woman who disappeared at the time of the two Quinn murders? And no, Linda wasn't murdered here in 1968."

"How do you know that?"

"I just do. I also know that people must think I know things or I wouldn't have two different stalkers, one of which probably tried to run me off the road, maybe kill me. And don't tell me to back off, because I'm in this mess, even if I don't want to be. So rein in your boy…he's lost it."

"I think you're out of line."

"No, you don't. You think I'm right on the mark and that worries you."

"Are you through?"

"Oh, I'm just getting started. Good day."

I'd just pissed off a FBI regional big shot; he'd get over it. I wouldn't put him in my enemies list, at least not yet.

My next call went home.

"Beth, is Patty around?"

"I think she's upstairs. Should I get her?"

"No, but don't reveal our conversation or just lie about it. Now, this is important. Stop all research on Linda Sharpe. Don't say anything about it. Joe J's been alerted to our research. I trust Patty with my life, but she may have let something slip. More than likely Mr. FBI has hacked into my home computer. I'm going to call Derek—he'll find out for sure."

"Uh-huh. Coming down stairs."

"Okay, start telling me how you're feeling."

"My ankles feel stiff...I may try walking on them."
Pause. "Yes, I'll make sure Patty helps me." Pause. "I took
one this morning." Pause. "Okay, she's in the kitchen."

"Well, done, Watson. So if you do any research, and it
might be good if you did do a bit, do it only on the Quinns.
I don't want to tip him off. And I was planning to ask you
how you were feeling."

"I know. Coming. I'll ask." She took the phone away
from her face and asked Patty what we're having for supper. "Salmon."

"Okay, I'll see you later. Bye, Beth."

"Bye, hon."

I called Derek, again on the firm's line. I told him the
situation with the possible hacking. He promised to check
both work and home computers, including Brian's laptop as
we shared a wireless connection. He said he'd planned to
drive to Dexter this weekend anyway to check on my mom
and to see the new horse.

Just before five, Derek called with the answer—we
had been hacked, both laptops. Shit. Derek didn't think personal information such as credit card information and bank
transactions had been stolen. Still, I needed to cancel credit
cards and get new bank accounts. That bastard! Cleary we
needed a more secure system at home. Derek promised to
bring out two new laptops and to set up a new wireless
connection that weekend.

I made one more call before trying to get my mind
back on my work. Bill had just gotten home. I told him he
should come to supper and that I promised not to discuss
the Quinn murders. He admitted that he wanted to see Beth.
Our meetings had been keeping him away, which was a
shame because he wanted to be near Beth; after all, he'd
loved her for nearly twenty-nine years. Though I told him I
had one matter I needed to discuss with him.

He sighed. "And what is that, dare I ask?"

"It involves Joe J. Has he been poking around again?"

"Yeah, he came to the house last night. Tried to ask me about the Quinns and who they knew...lots of vague questions."

"What'd you say?"

"Well, he seemed a bit too eager. He didn't act like a cop investigating something. I told him it wasn't something I wanted to discuss...like I did before. He got kinda mad. I had to ask him to leave."

"He threatened me today. And yes, this is a personal matter for him. So I'd stay clear of him. If he comes back or comes on our property, ask him for his search warrant. And maybe you ought to tell your hands."

"Is it that big a deal?"

"Oh, yeah. Now this is in confidence, but he's hacked into our home computers."

"How could you know that?"

"I couldn't, but Derek could."

"Damn."

"No kidding."

Saturday afternoon, Derek set up our new computers. After we transferred all the data from the old laptops to the new ones, I called Melanie. By prior arrangement, she came out to the house and picked up a box, which she then delivered to Officer Merritt's house. She told him to call me. She didn't know what was in the sealed box and she didn't ask. When he called, I asked him to keep the laptops in his possession until, and if, I decided to press charges against Joe J.

I felt certain I knew Joe's next course of action. So on Sunday night, while Brian kept Patty distracted in the kitchen, I met with Bill and Beth in the family room.

"I think we may be forced to tell the truth."

Chapter 10

Even though both Beulah and Bill still refused to discuss the events of 1968, I felt certain Lew would talk to me—and I knew exactly where to find him. After I scaled Big Leo, I walked around to the east side of the bluff, next to the rocky outcroppings and conifers. I passed by the Fort and found a football-sized rock to sit on. As I scanned the rocky ridges to the north and east, I kept glancing back at the sun setting into swaths of pink and orange. The south wind blew the powdery topsoil from the newly-dug hole of a prairie dog.

In time, Lew sauntered westward from the direction of his former home, now demolished, where he probably parked his pickup. The last of the Bob Eldritch family, he sold the remainder of his land to us over a year ago. Although I didn't like spying on him, especially when he stopped and turned toward the south wind to listen, I hoped his mother comforted him. Though a loner, he loved being a part of the Harney Street gang. When he looked back west, I stood and waved my arms. I scampered down the east side; he rushed forward to the bottom of the bluff in a chivalrous impulse to catch me if I fell. When I reached the bottom, he stepped back and feigned an interest in the dirt.

"I didn't mean to disturb you, Miss Megan," he said with his head still down.

"Where've you been? You only call me 'Miss' when you haven't seen me in a while. Hey, why don't you come over tomorrow night? We can play poker."

"Heh. I'd like that…Megan."

"You know we'll have plenty of Jim Beam Black on hand."

"I like that bourbon even better," said my favorite hick.

"Good. Say, have you been getting work this summer?"

"Yeah, mosta the time."

"Are you busy now?"

"Finishin' up some dry wallin' over on Washington Street."

"If you're free after that, I'd like to hire you to build a wall in the law firm basement. I plan to put it to use."

"Yeah, I could do that...be grateful for the work."

"I need it done, and you're the best man for it."

As always, he squirmed at compliments. He looked over my shoulder. "Purty."

The pastel sky was now flaming red and brilliant yellow.

"Why is that Chief Joe J pesterin' me with questions about...people?" he asked.

"Who is he asking about?"

"Walt Bolger and his sons and Bill and lots about my Uncle Hank."

"Just tell him I'm your attorney and you don't need to answer his questions unless I allow it. There's no current case he's investigating. I think it's personal stuff and he's been asking other people questions, too."

He looked back at the dirt then up at me. "Are you my attorney?"

"I am if you want me to be."

He nodded. His body began to twitch in the brief silence. "Been keeping an eye out. Those two Bolger boys are back in town."

"They must get a lot of vacation. What do you think of them?"

"I like 'em. Went to school with Andy...Clay was two grades up."

"What about Bert?"

"Hm. Six grades older, not like his brothers. Kinda mean. Tried to bully kids. Frank always protected us, Bill, too, when he got older and bigger. Your pa was always about doin' what was right."

"What about Walt?"

"Oh, Mr. Bolger was a nice man. Makes me sad that he's sittin' in prison."

"All of this is sad. Did you know Sean Quinn?"

"Yeah, Mr. Quinn was nice, too. So was Mrs. Quinn. Never around Julie, she was older...didn't want to be around us stinky boys. Bert tried to talk to her sometimes."

"Were you 'stinky'?"

Lew chortled. "Yeah."

"Did you play in those tunnels up on the Quinn land?"

"Heck, yeah. Lots of fun in those. Julie would never go near them...too dirty. She wasn't hardy like you. Kinda...um—"

"Prissy?"

He snorted his answer then got to laughing. "Oh, that's bad of me. God rest their souls."

Lew went from laughter to sadness faster than anyone I knew.

"Yes, God rest their souls." After a pause, I said, "Lew, I can hear them."

"Oh, Lordy, Lordy."

"It's more terrible than I can find words for. I-I heard them at their old house. They haunt me at night sometimes."

"I ain't been up there since right after it happened. Helped to put the fire out...well, I tried. I was just eleven."

He became so flushed with emotion, I needed to bail him out. So, I picked up a rock.

"See that scrub tree?" I pointed to a scraggily conifer thirty feet away.

I threw my rock and missed it by a couple of feet. Soon, we were both chucking rocks at the little tree. We stopped after we both hit it a few times. The azure sky began to darken and subdue the horizon.

"So, were you at the tunnels before the fire started?"

"Yeah.

"Was my dad with you?"

"Um, no, come ta think of it. Don't recall where he was."

"I like that you come out here…keep watch on things," I said.

"Mr. Finch thinks you should sell this land to some warehouse or big store," he said.

"Yeah, right. I plan to sell this land to Walmart the year the Cubs play the Twins in the World Series."

Lew paused then laughed till he snorted.

"Mr. Finch is a banker. People like him look at this land but they don't really see it."

He nodded. "Hank would like you. He likes people who don't take shit from anyone…he never did. Oh! Sorry about that word."

"Ha! It's one of my favorites. But it's a shame your uncle isn't around here anymore."

Lew jerked his head, first toward me then away from me. "Folks think he done somethin' bad…they're against him."

"I don't know about that. I saw Smokey the other day and he said he was sorry he never knew what happened to Hank."

When I walked toward the narrow streaks of gold and purple, Lew followed.

"Tell me about Hank."

"He'd never hurt no woman. If he was drunk, he'd fight a man…done it plenty of times. Not anymore though. He's seventy-four, just had a birthday. Always drove too fast, like my dad. Useta be friends with the Bolgers and Sean Quinn. Mary Quinn was cranky…had the diabetes. She was big, uh, not tall."

"You mean she looked like a bowling ball."

Lew convulsed with laughter, like he didn't get enough of it so it burst out of him at the slightest chance.

"My uncle didn't really like ranchin' much. He liked ridin' Ole Beauty far out to fix a fence. Taught me repairin' and buildin' stuff."

"And you've taken those classes so now you know wood working...the fancy stuff. Hey, can you make a bassinet? One of those wood ones that rock?"

"Yeah, 'spect I can. Like ta to it for you."

"Great. Hey, have you seen my horse?"

"Yeah, Bill showed it to me."

"Ah, what a looker and he's faster than the wind. I ride him as often as I can. He's some sort of mix."

"Don't look like pure quarter horse. Maybe something else."

"His neck and shoulders are a bit different, and he's so fast, like he's got Thoroughbred in him," I said.

"Or maybe like those old German army horses."

"What are they called?"

He got a bit jerky then shrugged. It was a strange reaction, even for Lew.

He paused then said, "I got somethin else to tell ya. I know you like that young Kayla. I seen her smokin' out here two times with another girl."

"Ah, hell," I said. That upset me. I would need to do something about that. "Thanks for telling me. That's a bad thing to ever start and she's only fourteen."

"Yep," he said, nodding.

He looked down, I looked up. The ink blue sky of the east cast darkness upon us.

"We better get going while we can still see. Remember, poker tomorrow. Come for supper, too. See you at six."

He smiled and twitched with pleasure.

Back at the house, I related the interview with Lew to the crew. Patty wrote on the Hank board, "nice to women." When she finished, I wrote "Frank" on an empty spot on a new poster board, then added "No alibi July 5" before I sat down.

"Oh, c'mon...nobody suspects your dad of anything," said Brian.

"I want to make sure of that. Okay, anything else?" I asked.

James cleared his throat. "I've been talking to Melvin Poots. He likes to talk about old times...he likes talking so much it takes time to get him to say something important. His sermons were like that, too." He smiled and continued. "We know pretty much all he has to say about the murders. But he's known the McCracken sisters since they were kids. He says Ellie and Laura were as close as two sisters ever could be. Then something happened."

"What?" asked Patty.

"He said he never knew. But it was way back when they were teens. And they've acted mad at each other ever since then."

Mom got up and walked over to the boards. "So Ellie got married at seventeen, but Laura didn't marry till she was twenty-two. But they fought when they were in their teens. So maybe they fought over a man."

"And let's see, there were other things, but I don't see how they tie in," said James. "Melvin said Sean was a bit of a 'lothario'—his word. He also fought in the Korean War, as did Walt, but at different times. And Sean was gone for a few years after the war."

"Hmm," said Patty. "We've heard that Mary was obese and Lew says she had diabetes, but who knows when Sean was prowling around and when Mary got sick."

"Anything else?" I asked.

"This is just getting more confusing," Brian said.

"Well, I'm going over to see Kayla for a few minutes. Lew has seen her smoking."

"Why is that your business?" asked Brian.

I didn't bother with a response, except for the look I gave him. I loved that kid. We'd gone through a great deal with her since her mother's death. Why would I abandon her now?

A few minutes later, I sat on the Ritter front porch on an Adirondack chair that left my feet hanging two inches off the ground.

Kayla jumped out of her chair. "Who told you?"

"It doesn't matter. It could have been a number of people."

"Was it James? He's over on his porch now."

"No, it wasn't him. But you're missing the point. Smoking is stupid and disgusting. I'm very disappointed in you."

She sat back down. The anger left her face and she dropped her head.

"Who is the girl you smoke with?"

"Her name's Brittany."

"Well, you tell Brittany that she is forever forbidden from stepping on Docket land again. And you can't come back to the house until you stop smoking."

"Are you going to tell my dad?"

"I don't know. That depends on you. You know how upset he'll be."

"I'll stop."

I wasn't sure whether to believe her, but she looked distressed rather than rebellious, so I was hopeful.

"How come you don't hang out with Emily anymore?"

"They moved into our old house. I don't want to go back there."

"I get ya. But it looks so different now, especially since they painted the outside."

"I think it was stupid to paint it beige."

"Then come by the office. She and Chelsea walk over at about two."

That night, I kissed my stud and he slid his warm body on top of mine. He'd been quiet during the evening, but I guess he wasn't mad at me. Then he took my hand from the back of his neck and pinned it down, off to the side. He'd never done that before. Then he took my other hand and pinned it down onto the pillow. It made me mad, as his weight pressed down hard on my wrists.

"Stop, I don't like this," I said.

He didn't move.

"You got two seconds before I ram my knee—"

He flinched then let go of my wrists, dropping to his right elbow. I slid out from under him. Shit. What was with him?

"What was that about?" I said as I put on my night-gown.

"What? Nothing."

"Don't play moron with me. Why were you pinning me down? Huh?"

"I-I can't protect you, can't control you. Yeah, there's plenty of danger ahead and you know it."

"So your answer is to act like a prick? Don't you understand how upsetting that is to be pinned down?"

He just stood there. I took his pillow and opened the door to the hall. I tossed it across the hall into my dad's old bedroom.

"Take a hint," I said. "And no…you're never gonna control me."

I shut the door behind him.

No apology—he's always been bad at those. I didn't remember him being this much of a jerk when I married him.

Chapter 11

The next morning, I passed by Brian in the hall. He was coming out of his bathroom; I booted him from mine last winter.

"Good morning, goodbye," I said.

"Hey, wait," he said. "I'm not ready."

"I called someone dependable."

I walked on. I'm sure he dashed to the window to see who was driving me to work. He wouldn't like that it was Zane, my virile boyfriend from my college years. Maybe these bouts of immaturity on Brian's part were a permanent part of our relationship. If so, he needed to be ready to get out of my way—I had a life to live and important things to do. I loved him, but he needed to find his own way to grow up. How would he handle fatherhood?

Later that morning, Zane drove me to my meeting with Art Meyer at his old law firm on Elm Street. Zane wouldn't agree to go wait for me at Custer's until I showed him the Glock I now carried in my purse. Art's old law offices were adjacent to the Cheyenne County Bank. The building featured two stories with a heavy rounded arch over the bank entrance, flanked by two large arched windows. Constructed of brick and limestone, and topped by a modestly pitched brown tile roof, the bank building was erected at the "turn of the century," a term the older folks still used for the early 1900s. Located on a corner lot, the law office was around to the side, also with an arch over the doorway to the law firm. I remembered visiting my dad at work when I was a kid. Eunice, the receptionist and secretary, kept a bowl of cinnamon candy on her desk. Now it was merely a massive maple desk covered in dust and leaned upon by Art Meyer, who was staring intently at his cell phone.

He greeted me then asked, "What does this mean?"

"You have a text message. Push that button. Trying using your thumbs. Good. Right. Oh, Laura figured out how to send texts."

"Why didn't she just call me?"

"She probably didn't want to bother you. She figured you could read the message at your convenience."

"Well, anyway, let me show you the file cabinets."

He unlocked a door that was the firm's former conference center. Like the lobby, it was stripped of carpet. A couple dozen tall, gray file cabinets crammed the room, with just a narrow aisle down the middle of the hardwood floor.

"This is more than I expected, I must confess."

"Now remember, this represents decades of work. And Mike Leland passed files to me when he retired. I didn't have a computer to store anything. I retired in 1995 and never bothered to learn about them, even though your dad encouraged it. I do have a list of files I'll give you."

He took a binder off a file cabinet, which was nearly level with my head. I thumbed through the pages, pausing ever so slightly on the pages for Bolger and Quinn. These files, added to the files of my law firm, made me the supreme secret-keeper of several counties.

"I'll let you know the date for the movers."

"That's fine," I said, confident that the bulk of the files would eventually be scanned and stored electronically; but Art wouldn't care about that. Mostly, I couldn't wait to look through the Quinn and Bolger files.

"I'm getting a room built in the basement with a dead bolt lock. Even if it's not finished when the file cabinets arrive, we can lock the door to the basement."

"Fine, fine. Say, Ernie Sedlacek is stopping by. He's bored, wanted to chat with us. I think the discovery of that van has him all stirred up. He was the Dexter Chief of Police back in sixty-eight."

"Great, I haven't seen him in a while."

Art nodded. We both knew he'd been at Ray Dobb's funeral. I peeked at my phone, which vibrated in my purse. It was Bill.

"This is rude, but mind if I take this call? My uncle doesn't call just to chat."

As I listened intently and asked a couple of questions, Art Meyer went to the door. Soon, I joined him and Ernie.

"Hello, Mr. Sedlacek," I said, shaking his hand.

Once a big, burly cop, at eighty or so, he now limped and his shoulders hunched. His hair, a thick shock of silver, had withstood aging better than the rest of him. Every Christmas, he grew out his silver beard and donned a Santa costume.

"Ahh. Call me Ernie. You've earned it."

"Okay, Ernie…Art, this is hot off the wire. Bill just called to tell me someone busted out the windows in Chief Joe J's police cruiser."

"Someone shot them out?" asked Ernie.

"No, he, she, or they just used rocks. It's unfortunate that it happened out near one of our barns…the old Eldritch barn. Joe never saw who did it. Art, just you remember that I've been with you. The Chief's been on my case lately."

"What's he doin' way out there?" asked Ernie. "This is his shift in town…Bo doesn't even start till noon."

"Why is Joe J bothering you?" asked Art, as he locked the records room. "Oh, here are the measurements for this room so you know how big to make the room in your basement."

I took the paper from Art. "Well, I've been making a few inquiries on the old Quinn case…he doesn't seem to like that. I got involved when the younger Bolger brothers tried to buy the land where the murders were committed…they used phony names, which warranted an investigation."

"Then your horse got killed," said Ernie.

"Does everyone know about that?"

"Of course they do," said Art. "The popular opinion is that if it involves Megan Docket, it's going to be interesting."

"Well, right now, the focus will be on Chief Joe," I said.

"He's got some explainin' to do," said Ernie.

"I'm really sorry it's so dusty in here," said Art. "We can't even sit down."

"What do you intend to do with this desk?" I asked.

"Didn't really have any plans," Art said.

I walked around behind it, pulled out the drawers, and inspected the top of the desk. "I'll buy it from you."

"Good, good. Laura was afraid I'd be bringing it home. It's early, but we could go for lunch at Custer's."

I checked my watch. "Fine with me. I have a nasty divorce case to deal with at one…but we'll have time to chat."

After we walked half a block toward Custer's in the bright June sun, my breathing became shallow and the blood began to pound in my ears. Art and Ernie walked calmly beside me. How could they not sense danger bearing down upon us? Twenty feet away from the diner's door my heart began to pound so hard I stopped. As the two men paused and turned to look at me, I whirled around. The only man I saw was Trent Maxwell and he was looking at the window of Clark's. Suddenly, he veered toward the store to inspect the display.

Behind him was Bert Bolger—the thin man slowed, having lost his cover.

A hand wrapped around my right forearm, which I had slid into my purse. The old cop held on tight as Bert approached us. He ignored Art's greeting then continued down the sidewalk past us.

"Megan, are you feeling all right?" asked Art.

"He's been stalking me," I said, then wondered at the wisdom of my confession.

Ernie let go of my arm as I removed my hand from my gun.

"Bert Bolger, you mean?"

I nodded.

"You're in deeper than I thought," said Ernie.

He led me to Custer's with his hand wrapped around my upper arm. Zane sat at the counter. As the three of us sat down in the Docket booth, I lifted my hand to Zane then pointed to the menu. He understood to stay where he was and order lunch. Truly a military man, he knew how to obey an order, even though he couldn't grasp the situation.

"Okay, we don't have much time before the booths and tables around us fill up," I said. "So, why was Sean never a suspect?"

"That's easy," said Ernie, who sat across the table from me and Art. "He had an ironclad alibi from a respected person."

"Me," said Art. "At the time of the fire, he was in my office. I don't recall the reason, but he had an appointment at one o'clock."

"And at noon, he was seen by many witnesses here, at whatever diner this was back then," said Ernie.

"So, he has an alibi for the arson," I said. "What if the murders were committed earlier?"

Both men stared at me then Ernie scrunched his brow and nodded, so I continued.

"Somebody murdered those two women and hauled them away in the van they found in the lake. Either Walt murdered them then went back to the house to burn it down or someone else hauled away the bodies. But the clothes they found in the van weren't Walt's."

When Carol came to the booth to take our orders, the two men were still staring at me.

"Water, for now," I said.

When neither man said anything, she left.

"So, who was the second person?" Ernie asked me.

"No idea. Who hated those two women?"

"How do you know only two women were killed?"

"I just do."

"Carol's a Thornton," said Ernie.

"Really?" I said.

"Distant, but yes. She didn't even recognize her own cousin when she was around here. Remember that State Patrol Officer Rachel McNeill? She's a Thornton, Buck's daughter."

My mind raced back to the Thornton board in the War Room. "Julie's niece."

"Dang, that's right," said Art. "Where did she end up? Never see her anymore."

"She's got a desk job in North Platte," said Ernie.

Rachel and I had been friends, but that soured then ended when I shot down her boyfriend, RT, the crooked DEA agent. It was just as well that she wasn't around to muddy things here. Then I remembered that Bill recently hired a new cowhand. Who was he?

"Plenty of hatred between the Thorntons and the Bolgers still," said Ernie. "It's just been tough talk and glares…not exactly the Hatfields and the McCoys. Ray Dobbs was always worried somethin' would happen, but in the forty-five years since then, nothin' did."

"Seems like there was something else…" mused Art.

"Oh, that's right. A few days before the murders, the police station got broken into. Someone stole a rifle and a handgun. Never did find them or the person who did it. We've never been able to staff a twenty-four hour shift. The chief or one of the deputies always took the night calls at home."

Smokey, his daughter, and his two sons sat down in the booth next to us. Paul and Harold Gush sat down in the table across the aisle, ending our conversation. We greeted our friends then Carol came to take our order. I waved over Zane who announced that he had been hired at Cabela's sporting goods store in Sidney, starting next month. I wondered why he was waiting till July to start, but decided against asking him in public. Big Joe McCready, a rancher and friend of Bill's, stopped by our table to greet us and chat. He knew about Chief Joe J's cruiser and said the chief was "in a rage."

"He'll be by to accuse me," I said. "I should have done this before." While the three men listened, I called Melanie to ask her to lock the front door and post a sign informing people to ring the doorbell for entrance. When I ended the phone call I said, "Joe J will need a warrant to enter the firm."

"Say, you have a full sized basement at your firm, right?" asked Ernie. "You're gonna put those records down there and still have room. You could make your basement a tornado shelter."

"We did go down there in April when the siren sounded, so we're okay," I said.

"Yes, you're fine, but I meant for your neighbors."

"Doesn't everybody have basements?"

"Sure, but they may not want to go in them. The Cutlers behind you have a vole problem and next to them are the Williamsons, they get water whenever it rains. Must not have the money to fix it."

"My dad must have been concerned about being safe," I said. "When he remodeled the house to make it into a law firm, he hired a contractor to place steel beams across the ceiling with metal posts to support them."

"You got a biffy down there?" Ernie asked.

I though Beulah was the only one who used that old-timcy term. "I could easily put one in since the plumbing is set up," I said. The suggestion did get me thinking about it.

I found out after my one o'clock appointment that Chief Joe J did come to the office. When Gus, my law partner, went out on the front porch to ask for a search warrant, Joe stomped away, "madder than a hornet." Another enemy, great, just what I needed.

That evening after supper, I walked down the hallway toward the family room, but I paused. I wanted to ask Bill about the new cowhand, Tony. But Beth and Bill were talking about a trip, yet it was their voices that stopped me. Speaking in low, quiet voices as if they were sitting close together, they sounded like lovers. I retreated to the study door. I was pleased for them; perhaps it was just in the evenings that Bill had been staying away. In a flash, I warmed with anger at Brian for being a jerk and refusing to apologize. Well, the hell with him. Just as I put my hand on the doorknob for the study, the floor creaked. Our house was built in 1905, so it did that often.

"You're still mad at me," said Brian.

"Well, duh. You're lousy at apologies."

"I'm sorry."

"It doesn't count if I need to tell you to do it," I said as I opened the door then shut it in his face.

Living in a house with others hanging about or living with you makes arguments quieter. I disliked arguing, despite my occupation. Tonight, only Beth and Bill were here with us as Patty had gone out with Joe J. I sat down at the desk chair and stared at the nearly blank board for Linda Sharpe. Next to her board was Joe's. He'd become an adversary, though a victim now, too. Who busted out his windows? A few of the cowhands acted loyal to me, but I doubt any of them would risk trouble with the law and a loss of a job over me. No, it was probably some bored teenagers, or maybe even Lew, venting his anger over the questions about his uncle.

The phone rang. It was Patty.

"Joe says Officer Merritt's been questioning him about his whereabouts at the times of Gondor's death and Beth's crash."

"I hadn't thought of Joe J as someone who would do either of those acts," I said honestly. "Is Joe sure Officer Merritt wasn't just trying to provoke him to say something else? I've done that in the courtroom, it sometimes works when the person is emotional."

Her voice became muffled as she talked to Joe.

"Patty, Joe did not kill my horse. I don't know who did, but it's someone unwilling to confront me face-to-face. No, it's my coward stalker, maybe the same person who bashed in Joe's windows."

"Okay, I'll tell him what you said. Bye."

That was strange. I walked around to the other boards, pausing at the name of my father. How well did I really know him? Then I halted at the Quinn board. Mom found newspaper photographs of Mary and Julie Quinn and paper clipped them next to their names. The black and white photos were grainy, but eerie enough to make me swallow hard and recall their cries. I passed on to the Thornton board. The Thornton parents, Michael and Colleen, were both deceased. Their three offspring include Michael Jr., or "Buck" as he was commonly called, Mary, and Adam. Buck and Adam still ran the family ranch. If Mary, the middle child, had survived, then she would have turned sixty-four last week. I went back to her photo. She'd been crying into the wind all these years—how incredibly sad.

Chapter 12

Saturday morning, I went for a run then put on my jeans and equestrian boots, and headed for the barn. As I saddled my black beauty, Rohan snorted his protest. I would usually ride with Brian on Saturday morning, but he was busy sulking in the dressing room. I directed Strider to the south pasture where he knew we'd be racing into the south wind. In his excitement, he rose up off his front legs a foot or so before he sprinted across the field. After a good long dash, I slowed him to a stop. I stroked his neck twice, and then pulled back on the reins with one hand as I held onto the saddle horn with the other. He did it! He rose up onto his back legs and kicked his front legs high into the air.

"Whoo! Yeah!" I yelled.

It was just like the stunt horses in the movies. Lew was right—this horse possessed something else in him. My heart pounded with excitement. My husband should have been the one thrilling me, but I'd need to settle for this. Strider snorted and pranced with his own excitement. We went for another dash then circled back around a herd of lazy heifers. I stroked Strider's neck, pulled on the reins, and he rose up again, this time letting out a joyful neigh.

I laughed then directed us northwest. I couldn't wait to show off my horse to someone, but I needed to spend time with him in the rough land—any horse of mine needed to be able to handle the danger of the rugged terrain of my backyard. We picked our way through a series of prairie dog holes then came to a smoother area. I looked up to see the silhouette of a thin man, lit from behind by the east sun, right before he dashed behind Big Leo. I spurred Strider toward the bluff. I saw one more flash of him in the rocky ridges as we rode around the north side of the bluff. Too rugged and dangerous, I knew better than to proceed. Instead, I veered northward, hoping the man would dash from his cover. But he was smart enough to stay hidden.

What did I see in that flash of him? He looked to be a thin man, medium to tall in height, fairly quick, but not agile like a young man. Twice now, he'd hidden from me in those rocky crests. Riding too close to them would give my stalker a chance to ambush me, so I worked back southward, as I formed a plan.

As usual, Saturday night was dinner and dancing at the Cowpoke, the local tavern. After eating, I claimed a headache. So, Brian drove me home with plans to return for Bill and Beth in an hour. Brian and I watched a baseball game on TV, with me feigning illness. When he left for Beth and Bill, I set my plan in motion. I made three quick calls—to Bud, Jack, and James, my posse for the evening. We met in the barn, with Strider already saddled for me. I donned a black hooded sweatshirt, the same one I wore when I fled from Salt Eldritch into the darkness. With my black jeans covering my black boots, I mounted Strider. Tucking my ponytail into the coat, I pulled up my hood and donned my gloves. With my coal black horse, the only thing that wasn't black was my face.

When I set out due north, James and Bud left for their positions. Beverly's soothing voice calmed me. I kept going north till I passed the old Hexam Road. Just past the bluff, the Joker, the wind began to swirl. Beverly abruptly left me; she was replaced by snatches of the wailing women, whom I would hear for a few moments then the wind would scatter their voices away. Strider was willing to take a slow pace in the unfamiliar darkness. As we neared the gravel road that went past the old Eldritch homestead, I turned hard south and quickened the pace. Once we neared the red barn, now famous for the Shootout, I slowed and whispered to Strider.

"Danger, Strider, danger."

I pulled my cell from my back pocket and sent a text. I slid the phone back into my jeans then yanked my Glock from my rear waistband, which was harder now that my waistline was expanding. Strider was incredibly quiet—as we walked in the buffalo grass I could still hear the nearby crickets. I pulled a flashlight from the saddlebag and sent a beam of light onto the east-facing front door. The padlock was secure, so I guided Strider around to the back door, which Lew installed when he and some cowhands repaired the barn. I yanked on the reins and shone the light onto the door.

It was ajar. I drew my Glock with clammy-cold hands as my heart hammered my chest.

A man burst out of the door and into the darkness. I kept my distance, but stayed even with him, keeping him from turning back or heading north. A quick flash of light on him indicated that he wasn't carrying a gun. Gripping the reins with my teeth, I held the gun with my right hand and sent another text. I saw a flash of light to the south— Jack was riding Rohan alongside the mystery man. Another text, another flash of cell phone light to the west. Then the man began to labor and pant, even though we had traveled only forty yards or so from the barn.

The time seemed right, so I caught my prey in the beam of my flashlight. Two beams quickly lit him from the west. A gasp, a groan, and then a thud as he hit the ground, lassoed by Jack. As the man writhed on the ground and spewed vulgarities, I lit up his face, which was unfamiliar to me. I was pleased it wasn't Bert, but not surprised. This man didn't scare me like Bert would have, though I still felt danger.

"Settle down or you'll hurt yourself," I said. "Who are you?"

"You're Megan, I can tell. But I can't see you, 'cause you look like a ghost rider. A pretty scary one." The man struggled to his feet.

"I'm scary? You've been stalking me out here."

"No, just watchin'."

"Hmm. Bud, check him for weapons."

As Bud removed the rope and patted him down, I decided on the second part of my plan.

"Bud and James, take this man—"

"Oh! You're James. Nice to meet ya."

"Ah, yeah," said James.

"Take Mr. Eldritch in your pickup to the big house. Now listen, they are both armed. Just cooperate so nobody gets hurt."

"Oh, you know me."

"You're Hank, Lew's uncle," I said.

"Will you call him for me?"

"Yes, I will. Time to go. Wait for us in the driveway."

As Bud and James escorted Hank to Bud's truck parked on the Eldritch Road, I met up with Jack. On the way back to the barn, Jack rode on ahead of me, so that he'd be the one to search it. Chivalry, I loved it. All he found was a blanket, a flashlight, and a bottle of water. We swung southward back to Uncle Bill's barn, where we prepped the horses for the night.

"Strider, you did great," I stroked the horse's neck as he stretched his head over the rail toward me.

"If you don't mind me sayin', you were damn scary in all black," said Jack. "I never heard your horse…he was so quiet. That ain't usual."

"Lew told me he might have some German army horse in him. I don't know how he'd know—" I paused. "I get it. Ah, never mind. Let's get to them."

As we approached the house, the back light was on and Brian and Beth were standing in the yard. Bill was probably in the driveway with Bud's pickup.

"Megan? Is that you?" asked my mom as we neared the house. She left for the Cowpoke without her sling, but she was wearing it now, so her wrist must be bothering her.

"Who else is that short?" said Brian.

I quickened to a jog and Jack followed my lead. I didn't want to stop to explain.

"Need to go—Jack will explain where we've been. Beth, will you give him and Bud something to eat?"

"Brian, come with me. I need you," I said, as I ran around the side of the house into the darkness.

"I love it when you say that. Wait, where are you?"

I was a few strides ahead of him. "Right here."

"What's going on?"

"Something big."

"Wait, stop!"

I did, but it annoyed me. He reached for me and missed, so I grabbed his arm.

"You are a mystery…and I can't even see you. Look, I'm sorry for the way I've acted."

His lips didn't miss mine.

"We'll finish this later," I said as I ran my hands down his chest.

He caught my hands. "Now, don't tease me or you'll make my balls ache."

I laughed then took off running and he followed. We found Bill standing outside the pickup in our driveway. Bud and James were waiting for me, just like I told them to. Their obedience amazed me. I asked Brian to call Lew. More obedience.

"Hi, Uncle Bill. Okay then, James and Bud, bring Mr. Eldritch inside. Bud, you'll find Jack in the kitchen."

"You know who this is?" said Bill, looking stunned by the whole situation.

"I guessed right," I said.

A few minutes later, Hank sat with us in the family room. Bud and Jack finished the large hunks of chocolate cake my mom gave them then collected their boots. I met them at the back door where I gave them each a hundred bucks and thanked them. They tipped their cowboy hats and went out the back door.

On the patio, Jack turned back to me and said, "Goodnight, Ghost Rider."

I was still laughing when I joined Brian on the sofa. Bill passed out glasses of bourbon, as I sipped a glass of water. Brian left to answer the front door. He escorted Lew into the family room and brought in a dining room chair as Bill handed him a bourbon.

All Lew could say was, "Wha?"

"They captured me, Lew…trapped me," said Hank. He nodded to me, "And she knew who I was. She flushed me, scared me so bad, and I couldn't see her. She was a ghost…she and that black horse."

"So, first question for you, and I'll call you Hank, if that's okay…why did you kill Gondor?"

Patty gasped.

"Lew told me you'd be the one to figure things out. He said you know things…but then you said you were gonna stop lookin' into it. I had to do somethin' to get you back in…make you mad…that's what I thought."

I turned to Lew. "You helped him kill my horse?"

"No, no, I swear I didn't know he was gonna do that," said Lew. "Honest."

"He didn't know. Did git real mad at me. It broke my heart doin'it…such a fine horse." He hung his head for a moment then took a big swig of the whiskey. "Lordy, this is good. Not like the rotgut I usually drink."

"So, your plan worked, but you felt so bad that you bought me a new horse," I said. "The very horse that helped capture you."

Hank nodded then hung his head again. "Oh, and Lew said you been wonderin' about the breed. It's quarter horse and Holstein."

"Holstein?"

"Yep. Those're fine German soldier and carriage horses, got some Thoroughbred in them, so they're fast, but not too tempermental so they're still steady."

"By the way, where did you buy it?" asked Bill. "Do you have papers on him?"

"I ain't gonna say...beggin' your pardon. You're treatin' me so nice for what I done."

"Hank, you didn't steal it, did you?" I asked.

"Heh! I'm smarter than to give you, an attorney, a stolen horse. No, I got papers...already gave 'em to Lew."

"I put them in a safety deposit box at the county bank, Miss Megan," said Lew.

I nodded. "Where have you been staying, Hank? You didn't have much in the barn."

"You went back to check, just like a detective, Miss Megan," said Hank.

"Now you two stop calling me 'Miss Megan' or I'll have you both thrown in the clink."

Brian and my mom snickered.

"Agin, nice of you...Megan...not to call the police on me," said Hank.

"So why are you doing all of this?"

"I needed someone to clear my name," he said. "People think I killed those two women."

"And you were arrested for rape then released," I said. "Did you murder or rape anyone?"

"No, I didn't. Never been a good Christian...but I ask you to give me a Bible."

James, who was sitting nearest the book shelf, raised his eyebrows. I nodded, so he rose, took a Bible off the shelf, walked over to Hank, and then held out the Good Book. Hank reached his hand out to it.

"Oh, King James, good, good. Okay, I swear before God and all of you that I didn't kill anyone...ever...person, that is...and I never raped no woman ever."

"I believe you," I said, and I did. "Did you know Linda Sharpe?"

"Yes. She didn't get murdered."

"I know," I said.

"How?"

"Just do."

He sat and stared at me. He took the Bible from James' hands, rose from his chair then set it on my lap. Shit. I took a deep breath then placed my hand on the textured black cover.

"Because I only hear two women crying when I go near the house. I heard them tonight." I didn't mention my recurring nightmares—that would just upset people.

Bill drew his breath in sharply, though I didn't return the stares I felt.

Hank looked to Lew and nodded. "Lew said you're the right person to help me."

"But you didn't need to kill my horse."

"Yeah, I done it wrong. I screw up some-times...always have. I'm sorry."

"Hank, where have you been living all these years?" asked Bill.

"Not ready to say right now. Been comin' and goin' from here, Lew picks me up late at night from the barn and I sleep at his house then leave before daylight."

"Huh, right across from my law firm. But your clothes look decent, you keep your hair cut and you look groomed, so you must be doing okay."

"And I been telling Lew that he don't get his hair cut often enough."

Lew dropped his head into his chest in the same manner Hank did. But I needed to get back to the facts.

"So, Linda didn't get murdered. Where did she go?"

"Back up to the rez."

"Is she still alive?"

"Yep, but you won't find her."

"Why not?"

"She changed her name."

Actually, that told me a great deal. I looked at the clock and back at Hank. I leaned over to Beth, who was sitting next to me, and asked if the study was locked. She nodded.

"Take the key to your room and hide it. I have the other one."

She nodded again.

"Hank, I think you should still stay out of sight. But you look tired. If I promise to help you, will you promise not to leave?"

"I gotta go for a few days on Monday, but I promise to come back. I got some work…I do carpentry like Lew."

"Uncle Bill, you will put him up while he stays in town? Hank, I bet you don't get enough sleep, hiding as you do."

"Yeah, that's fine. Be nice if I wasn't sneakin' around. Like to see some people."

"Mmm. Not yet, you just stay with Bill tonight. We'll all talk again tomorrow."

"I want to come home with my head up."

The next afternoon, I summoned the group again. Patty actually stayed home on her day off. I needed to figure out what to tell her about Hank. I was convinced he was tied into the Linda mystery, given that he knew so much about her.

Back in the family room, we started with small talk then I began the interrogation.

"So, Hank, you want me to investigate, but Bert Bolger wants the opposite. Actually, I'm not sure why he's bothering me. I think Beth and I made peace with Mrs. Bolger."

"Can't figure it…can't get a hold of it," he said.

"Bert probably wants people to think Hank was the murderer and not his father," said Brian. "And Clay and Andy were going to try and find evidence."

Bill nodded. But I wasn't sure of Bert's motive. I still wondered about the roles of Sean Quinn and Linda Sharpe.

One or both of them saw the women before they were murdered.

"Hank, who do you think killed Mary and Julie?" I asked.

"I know the jury thought Walt done it...but he never seemed like the kinda fella that would do something like that," said Hank.

"Then who?" asked Bill.

Hank shook his head.

"Hank, why did the State Patrol arrest you for rape?" I said.

"I never knew why, they didn't tell me. But then a couple of guys came forward and said I was with them that night. Megan, one of them was your Grandpa Al. I was with a couple of other guys that night, including your Great-uncle Ned. I don't know who said what. But nobody could challenge your grandpa."

"Lew, you and I were both pretty young, but what do you think?" asked Bill.

"Lord Almighty, I been thinkin' about it all these years...but it don't make sense."

"You're absolutely right," I said. "That's the problem—it doesn't make sense."

Lew squirmed at the compliment, while Hank nodded his approval of Lew's statement.

"We don't know something important. There's one key to it all—the reason for the killings. We won't know the murderer until we know the motive."

Chapter 13

Monday morning, at my request, Jack tracked Lew and Hank to Smokey's lot. Hank probably figured no one would notice an extra truck on their lot. Jack gave me the make and model of Hank's pickup, as well as the license plate number, which was from Nebraska, though expired. A few minutes later, Lew arrived at the office to work on building the records room in the basement. Later, Jack called and said he followed Hank to Interstate 80, and then to Highway 385, where Hank headed north. After I thanked him, I suggested he break off the pursuit and return to work.

"Dang," he said. "I feel like a cowboy detective, though I took off my hat so he wouldn't think it was one of us Docket cowboys, and I kept a distance back, like I see 'em do on TV."

"Oh, trust me, there will be more to do."

That afternoon, I called Officer Merritt. He said he could research the old records regarding statements made by witnesses and potential suspects, but he didn't think he would be allowed to tell me much. I then called Ernie, who was leaving town for a few days, but could meet me next week. Both men were as interested in this old case as I was. What could I eke out of Merritt? What did Ernie recall? Did he know my father's alibi for that day? Then I thought of someone, a computer whiz, who would relentlessly research anything I asked. So I called Derek, my childhood chum, who agreed to find anything he could on Linda Sharpe, Joe Janowicz, the Quinns, and the Bolgers.

Down in the basement, Brian was discussing the room plans with Lew. My hubby had volunteered to supervise building the room.

"Lew says he can put up drywall all around the concrete, make it look more finished, once he builds this wall."

"Lew, we'll be housing some old law files, a lot of them, and putting in a dead bolt lock on the door," I said.

"Uh, huh. I can triple the two by fours around the door and put the hinges inside," said Lew. "Don't recommend a floor bolt…bad idea drillin' into the concrete floor…might not be too thick, could have water seepin' in. Could put in a ceiling bolt easy 'nough."

"Good thinking," I said.

Lew had seemed so professional till he got a compliment—then he squirmed. I liked to praise him because he obviously lacked self-esteem, but it made him uncomfortable. So I quickly continued.

"Brian, did you tell him about the biffy?"

Lew smiled at the term. "I can build a room for it, but I don't do plumbing work, never learned," said Lew. "I can do drop ceilings."

"We're going to hire the plumbing work," said Brian. "Megan, we should replace that blasted upstairs toilet. We're plunging that damn thing every other day."

I laughed and agreed.

At Custer's on Thursday, Barb Shuster came by my table. Brian hadn't arrived from his Sidney office, so I invited her to sit down and have an iced tea with me.

"I thought you were a root beer person," said Barb.

"It gives me heartburn these days, so I've backed off. How have you been doing?"

"Oh, lousy. But Blaine and I carry on. Ashley is so upset that she refused to come home this summer…she stayed in Kearney. She has a job on campus."

"That is so wrong of her! Does she blame you and Blaine for Davey's death?"

"Yeah. She says if we hadn't brought him here to work then he would never have been murdered."

"There's no way you could have known that vermin RT would do what he did. Tell her to look up foreseeability in the dictionary. Dang that makes me mad. I thought she had more sense. Vonny was angry with James for a while after that car accident that killed her mom. But she came around…realized the fault was with Bob Eldritch, not her father."

"I hope you're right. I feel like I've lost both of my children."

"That must be tough. I wish I had some magic words to make you feel better."

She smiled sadly at me. How horrible it must feel to lose a child.

"But hey, I've been wanting to ask you—is the rumor true that you and Bill turned down Walmart when they wanted to buy land to build a store?"

I choked on my iced tea. "What? Where did you hear that?"

"Lots of people are saying it, talking about the jobs we could have had and how our kids wouldn't need to leave the area to find jobs."

I waved Beulah over to the table, now aware that people in the adjacent tables were listening, hell, they were leaning toward us to hear better.

"Beulah, have you heard this rumor that Walmart tried to buy some of our land and we turned them down?"

"Yeah, I heard it."

Beulah knew that if anybody tried to buy an inch of my backyard I would tell them to get lost—but that wasn't the point.

"Well, this is a crock of bull and you can quote me on that. Nobody has made any offer to buy a square foot of our land for retail purposes of any sort. Man, it's incredible that anyone would think Bill Docket or I would act against this community. Feel free to set people straight."

Brian slid into the booth next to me. "What's this?"

"Somebody started a lie that we turned down Walmart."

Brian laughed. "You're kidding…aren't you?"

"Why would they build a superstore near Dexter when they're more likely to build one near Sidney? It doesn't make sense. I wonder if it was Clay or Andy Bolger. They're mad at me. They tried to buy the old Quinn land to hunt for the bones of the Quinns, and then somehow prove their father was innocent. I know people are stirred up about the van being found."

"Oh, Lord, not that," said Barb. "Walt Bolger is my great-uncle. He's a nice man."

Beulah began to ease away from the table.

"Well, that's what people say about Mr. Bolger," I said. "But if he didn't do it, who did?"

Barb shook her head. "Beats me. I used to think I could figure it out…but everybody else had alibis, I was always told."

Clearly, we needed to be looking more closely into alibis and other facts of those two days. As it was a popular event, we'd need to scrutinize a number of people.

I needed to stop Beulah before she backed any farther away, so I said, "Now Beulah, you remember to tell people the Walmart rumor is a lie. I'm counting on you."

She nodded and took her position behind the counter.

When we paid our bill at the cash register, I whispered, "I've seen Hank."

Her jaw dropped as did our change.

"Is he still here?"

"No, but he might come back."

She retrieved the change from the floor then handed it to Brian.

I held her with my gaze then said, "I miss you."

She dropped her head into her chest.

Out on the sidewalk, Brian said, "That's going to make her feel bad."

"Well, I do," I said. "I've known her since I was a tot. And I haven't seen her smile or laugh in weeks. By the way, we need to decide what to do about Patty. She's in tight with Joe J, who I think is connected to Linda."

"Connected how?"

"As in mother and son. That would explain why he's so emotional. He knows she was around here at one time. That's why he stayed on as police chief, to get information."

"But he's FBI still, so he should have access to her records," said Brian. "Damn, he hacked into our system easily enough."

"But he knows the records aren't enough. He needs to find out about the people and the events. My guess is that he doesn't know who his father is, and he's trying to find out. Derek is checking records for me—he'll confirm that the birth record doesn't show a father."

"And it might be Hank, who was arrested for rape," he said. "And you're thinking the rape would involve Linda. Whoa, shit, we need to keep Joe J away from Hank."

"I could probably get Joe's records from the town council, but I don't want to tip anyone off. It's better to wait for Derek—"

"To tell us that Joe J was born in April 1969, exactly nine months after Linda was here."

"Exactly," I said.

"So how much do we trust Patty?"

"Enough."

That evening the crew, including Patty, met in the War Room. We told her about Hank. James told her about the capture and the Ghost Rider, which amused her greatly. She didn't mention anything about Joe J or Linda, so we didn't either. Patty walked over to view the photos of Mary and Julie.

"This room gives me the creeps," said Patty. "I think we need some bourbon floats."

"What's that?" asked Beth.

"That's when you need something stronger than root beer."

Later, when we settled in to watch the Red Sox and the Yankees, Patty's cell rang.

She checked the caller ID and said, "Ah, dang, it's Joe. Better take this."

She walked out into the hall and came back after a brief exchange.

"He's drunk and he's on his way here," she said. "Oh, and he asked me to spy on you, Megan. He has no idea we have a crew working on all this stuff. I told him where he could shove his badge."

"Well, I'm not inclined to argue with a drunk tonight," I said. "I suppose I better call Deputy Bo."

"Maybe I'll go out on the porch and wait for him," said James.

A few minutes later, Joe J came stumbling up our porch steps, wearing jeans and a wrinkled t-shirt. Patty and Brian went out to meet with him. James leaned against the front of the house, ready to be of service. Mom and I stood inside against the front door, intent on eavesdropping.

First, Joe accused Patty of betraying him then he ranted about how Bill or one of his cowhands busted out the windows of his cruiser.

"They would never do that," said Patty. "They know better."

"What? What do they know?" demanded Joe.

"That you're no match for Megan."

"What the hell? She's a goddamn bitch…that's all."

My mom and I grinned at each other.

"And she better back off or I'm gonna—"

"Gonna what? Ram her off the road? I bet you tried that once before…hurt her aunt pretty bad."

Another pair of boots clomped up the stairs.

"Deputy Bo," said Patty. "Joe is threatening Megan—again. I'm wondering if he didn't run her car off the road."

"Well, Chief?" asked Bo.

"You're all fulla shit," said Joe. His boots stomped down the steps.

A few minutes later, Patty, Brian, and James came back inside. Joe's pickup roared down the street with Bo following close behind him.

"Damn, Patty...getting feisty," I said.

"Well, I learned from the best," she said then pinched me on the shoulder.

The next morning, Derek called with information. He couldn't tell me anything new on the Quinns or Bolgers, but he gave me the scoop on the former Linda Sharpe.

"You didn't do anything illegal to get this information, right?" I said.

"It's all about being creative and making a few guesses," he said. "I wish I could be around when it all blows up."

Brian didn't think we would figure out the murderer of Mary and Julie Quinn; whenever we learned something new, it increased my confidence in our ability to identify the killer. Yet at times, I wondered how we could discover information the police and FBI missed. My guts told me two things were certain—I would push on and it would blow up.

Chapter 14

Friday afternoon, Bill called to tell me Hank returned to town and would hide out until he and Lew were summoned. I asked Bill to invite them to supper tonight. A big steak was one of the means I hoped would loosen Hank's tongue.

Promptly at seven, I rode Strider over Rufus to the edge of our backyard. A long picnic table with a blue and white checked tablecloth was set up in the shade of the big oak. The crew plus Bill, Lew, and Hank were milling about the yard. I waved my arm to get their attention, then I stroked Strider's neck and yanked back on the reins. My steed rose up, kicking his forelegs in the air. Hank gave a whoop even before Strider's front legs hit the ground. Lew clapped.

"Look!" yelled Brian. "She made the horse do a wheelie."

I dismounted and handed the reins to Jack, who had been standing off to the side. He led Strider away.

As I walked into the yard, Patty, Beth, and Brian came out to meet me.

"Good Lord, Megan! You're pregnant!" said Patty.

"No kidding. Now listen, it's all a part of the plan," I said quietly. "We need to keep Hank drinking beer." Then louder, I said, "That's why I need to do it now. Strider knows I'm pregnant...he'll understand when I need to back off."

"Yes, but will you?" asked Brian. "Though I have to admit, that was really cool."

I took Brian's hand and walked toward Hank, who said, "That's a damn fine horse. Not so scary in the daylight."

"Did you know Strider won't let anyone else ride him?" Brian asked. "My butt found out the hard way. I saw him send Bud flying last weekend."

Even Bill, who had been glaring at me, laughed. "Do you really think he knows you're pregnant?"

"Yeah, he always sniffs my belly…he doesn't do that to anyone else."

"They know," said Lew, who quickly dropped his head and twitched.

Soon, we gorged on juicy sirloin steaks, sweet corn on the cob, baked potatoes slathered in butter, and plump, sweet strawberries. I was too full to eat the apple pie my mom, I mean Beth, baked that afternoon. Brian kept replacing Hank's Michelob bottles as soon as one would empty. As twilight approached, the mosquitoes and gnats drove us indoors.

Brian got the conversation going as he placed an extra chair in the room for Lew. "Hank, did you live with the Eldritch family when you were here?"

"Nah," he said. "I lived in the old house…built to the north…but I see it's gone and so is my brother's house. My brother would have a fit if he knew. All our land is sold…ain't really no Eldritch to this world anymore. It's all gone."

"That's because the family burden was too much for one man…any man," I said. "Everybody besides Lew either died or ran away."

"I had to go…I told you why…everybody was against me."

"That was a convenient lie you told yourself."

That made his face redden with anger.

"Or were you just not ready for all of it?"

"What do you mean? Dammit, Megan, spit it out."

"Linda left the Quinns on the morning of July fifth. Then she went to the reservation where she gave birth nine months later. Her child was adopted by a family in Rapid City. No father is listed on the birth certificate. Do you know him, Hank? Is he still the same man?"

Hank jumped to his feet. Bill and Brian rose also. Hank looked from one man to the other then back at me.

"Are you going to threaten me, attack me, Hank? It's been tried. You need to understand I want to help you."

He sat down. In a low, quiet tone he said, "We both ran away. Linda gave up the baby for adoption then followed him to Rapid City. She decided he was better off with those folks than with her...she was alone and had no money, no help unless she took him back to the rez. That was my fault." He scratched his head then cleared his throat. "I never went too far, Cherry County, mostly. Didn't keep in contact. Bob and Salt both died and I didn't find out till later when I finally tried to find Lew."

"Tell us about Linda."

"Yeah, I ran away from her, too. But then I went to find her. I loved her but I had shamed her...not married and had a baby. Her father rejected her, but others took her in. I found her in South Dakota a few years later, that's when I found out about the baby. Tried to give her money. She rejected it and me...but I kept tryin'. We've been together 'bout eighteen years now."

"But she married a man named Milner, right?"

"Right. He run off long ago."

"Did she have any kids with him?"

"Yep, two—both girls. They're grown up and married."

"Wait...so, her name's Linda Milner?" asked Patty. "Does she live in Rushville, up by White Clay?"

"Don't know if I should say...though you've found out everythin' else."

"Megan, remember when you came to bail me out of jail?" asked Patty. "One of the women in our group threw a rock through a Whiteclay liquor store window. We were protesting the sale of alcohol to members of the rez. Her name was Linda Milner."

"That's right...two summers ago," I said. "Did you know her before then?"

"Oh, just by sight."

"Heh! Linda said some short white woman paid her bail," said Hank. "I was off on a job in the Sand Hills."

"Uncle Hank, you really need to get one of them cell phones. Nobody can find you. Dang, I couldn't even tell you when my mom died."

Hank shrugged. "Don't always like to be found."

"I think we need some bourbon," said Patty.

Her timing was perfect. Now I prepared to move on to another topic, one I didn't understand, but needed to. I sat on the sofa with Brian on one side and my mom on the left, so she could rest her cast on the armrest.

After Bill and Patty passed out glasses of bourbon to everyone but me, I looked to Hank and Bill then asked, "So, tell us about this Fourth of July party the Quinns held. It sounds fun."

"They were," said Hank. "Always had a monster bonfire...invited tons of people, mostly the ranch families, with some townsfolk. They grilled loads of food, and people brought stuff. Then later, we always broke off into groups. The older guys went off to drink whiskey. I drank some then Linda and me walked south, all the ways to that bluff."

"I call it the Joker," I said.

"Heh! Yeah, 'cause that opening looks like a mouth."

"Me, Frank, Clay, and Andy, oh, and the Thornton boys...we were together," said Bill. "We had some wimpy little firecrackers we set off. Then Sean set off some bigger fireworks. After that, we went inside to watch *Star Trek*. Beulah and Julie were sent to watch us, oh, and Mrs. Quinn and Mrs. Bolger. That was the last time I saw Mary or Julie."

"What about Bert? Where was he?" I asked.

"Don't recall," said Bill. "He and Frank were only a couple years apart in age, but Frank didn't like Bert."

"Were there any fights or arguments…anything like that at the party?" I asked.

Bill and Hank looked at each other and shook their heads.

"It was a party a lot like the year before and the year before that," said Hank. "And I've tried to think of somethin', but I never do. People seemed happy."

"Do you remember anybody else who was there?"

Hank looked to Bill then said, "Oh, Ernie Sedlacek, the Chief of Police back then, came by for supper with his wife after his shift. Then they left."

"The Breeleys were probably there and the Zimmers, but those folks are all dead now…that generation anyway," added Bill. "There were other ranchers on the land to the southwest, but they're gone now. It's all that land owned by Krauss."

"Who are the Krausses?" Hank asked.

"Nobody…it's a corporation," said Bill.

"What about the next day?" I asked.

"I don't remember much about the early morning," said Bill. "But I know some of us played out in the tunnels on the Quinn land in the late morning. We were just getting ready to head home for lunch when the fire started."

"Who was with you, Bill?"

"Lew, Salt, Buck and Adam Thornton. I think that's it…oh, Clay and Andy."

"But not my dad."

"Ah, right."

"I was with Linda at about ten," said Hank. "She was upset because we—" He cleared his throat. "I ate lunch at the Docket house. Anna…Mrs. Docket…was mad because the boys were late for lunch. But it turns out that's when the fire started. Someone called the house. We jumped in our trucks and went out there to help with the fire. I know you're gonna ask—no, didn't see nobody. Police and fire trucks were already there."

"Uncle Bill, what did you see?"

"Well, we noticed too late that we were missing lunch. We all had been underground. When we came out, the fire was already going. We ran to it, but there wasn't anything we could do. We got there about when the fire departments did, um, Sidney, and Kimball, and some volunteer firemen."

"Anything else?"

"Yeah." Bill took a deep breath. "We saw flashing lights, like from a police car, east of us, stopped on the gravel road. You can see for miles from there. Later found out it was the State Patrol stopping Walt Bolger."

"They were able to save part of the house," said Hank. "I remember hearin' someone saw the smoke from the interstate...or maybe it was the highway...and called the cops. So they got to it real quick like."

"And you saw no one at the house, right?"

Both Bill and Hank nodded. Lew squirmed then nodded.

"It was like a big, black cloud we couldn't see out of," said Hank. "Just broke us all to pieces. Then I got arrested. But Bill, your pa stood up for me. They had to release me because nobody there was claimin' a rape. Don't know where that came from, but Lordy, it was real mean."

"Sean just fell apart," said Bill. "He sat in his front yard and wouldn't leave. Dad, Uncle Ned, and some other guys went out and brought him back to our house. Had to hog-tie him, because he fought against them...refused to leave his yard. Mom convinced him to eat and shower. By the end of the week, he was gone. Haven't seen him since."

"Good guy," said Hank. "A talker, told good stories."

Bill smiled. "He used to tell us boys dirty jokes and he let us play in those tunnels."

"Mrs. Quinn had a big garden, I 'member," said Lew. "Gave us sweet corn and tomatoes and cukes."

That big, black cloud seemed to settle over the three men. Bill waved off any other questions. But there was an important one to ask Hank.

"Hank, I told you I wanted to help you."

"Yeah, ya did."

"Then you should hire me."

"Do I need to sue somebody?"

"No, but as your attorney, it gives me some rights when I make inquiries or decline to release information."

"Ah, yeah, okay."

At this point we all seemed to feel the weight of the black cloud.

"Hey! Remember Mrs. Wackles had those triplets?" asked Hank.

That perked up Bill and Lew.

"Oh, those babies were so cute," said Bill. "The whole town and all the ranch folks just kept goin' to see them."

"Lifted us up like," said Hank. "All three had a shock of black hair."

"Babies are powerful," said James.

"Say, you all are friends with Beulah," said Hank. "Any chance I could see her? We courted once."

"Really? She's been hiding from me, from these memories," I said.

I couldn't picture Beulah dating anyone. I needed to talk to her, but I couldn't force her. Until then, I planned to proceed in other ways.

Chapter 15

Promptly at 11:30 a.m., Brian and I picked up Ellie Bolger at her house. He gave Ellie his arm then we escorted her into Custer's and to our booth. She and I sat together while Brian sat with Eldon Strumple and Pastor Ryder to chew the fat, as Lew would say. Her floral print polyester dress was probably her finest. She seemed genuinely pleased to be in town and treated to lunch. Like every other Bolger, she made my stomach queasy with apprehension, yet I couldn't help but feel her loneliness. But did she cause some of her isolation by feuding with her sister and driving off her younger sons' families?

We spent most of the lunch just chatting about trivial matters. She wasn't current on town happenings, so I added some town gossip to our meal. Mostly she wanted to hear my version of the encounter with Salt Eldritch in the darkness. She was also keen to hear about the Shootout last winter in the barn. So I obliged her. I didn't pepper her with questions, though I had many; I wanted to simply show some goodwill toward the Bolger family, as I felt in my bones that something ominous loomed ahead.

As Ellie proceeded to a boring exposition of her garden, my mind wandered as I looked her in the eye. I thought back to my encounters with Bert. Was he like her? Ellie ate with her fork in the left hand, Bert wore a watch with a black band on his right hand—they were both lefties—I'd want to remember that. Something in the face was the same, but that was hard to pinpoint. She possessed prominent cheekbones; her body had thickened and compacted over the years, though she had probably once been attractive. She had a thin nose, which all three of her sons inherited. Patty scrounged around the attic last weekend and found some old photographs that were now tacked onto the boards in the war room. We discovered that Walt Bolger had a broad nose, but was reasonably handsome—though not nearly as good-looking as Sean Quinn, who was paler and thinner with a manly jaw line and thick, light-brown hair.

I tuned in enough to know that Ellie was bragging about Bert, which was odd considering that Clay and Andy were the successful executives. Then she suddenly shifted to talking about the Breeley and Zimmer families, who ranched to the south of the Bolgers, and their financial struggles.

"Lots of folks is hurtin'," she said. "At least during the school year them kids get breakfast and lunch. I wonder about the summers. Bert gets a steady paycheck...it ain't a lot, but money comes in every other Friday. Ranchers have nothing guaranteed. Last summer when the drought started, some folks sold off their herds early. Max Zimmer may be selling off the rest of his just to get through the winter. What he does after that, I dunno."

Hunger in my county—the thought distressed and distracted me; at least until I gazed across the street and saw a lean figure standing in the shade of Ritter's Hardware. Ellie had gone back to talking about her garden. As I took a drink of water, I looked back across the street—the man lifted his right arm to check his watch.

Ellie suddenly shifted topics again, for she said, "If you're trying to get our legal business, we don't really have any."

As if I needed work from white trash. "You have a will, I presume?"

"Oh, yes. Art Meyer retired long ago, but he still made one for me a few years back."

"Good," I said.

"Ain't got much to give."

I nodded.

"Yep, my Bert is good to me."

Did she just tell me her beneficiary?

I felt Beulah's stare. I didn't have the time or energy to worry about her right now. Ellie excused herself and went to the restroom. Though Ellie left, an ominous, eerie force pushed down on my shoulders. Bert. Shit. I texted Zane and asked him to track Bert. He replied immediately—perhaps he was waiting for some mission from me, even though he seemed to be enjoying lunch with Melanie in a table near the front door. He rose and paid his bill as Ellie returned to our table. I glanced at my watch.

"Ellie, I was wondering—do you have a few more minutes? There's something I'd like to show you."

She agreed—retired people are bored, curious, and re-plete with time. She agreed immediately without even ask-ing where we were going. The man in the shadow disap-peared when we left Custer's. Brian drove to our house. A newer Lincoln sedan was parked in the lane nearest our front door.

"That's Laura's car," snapped Ellie. "What's she doing here?"

"She and my, um, aunt, were going to Sidney for lunch," I said.

"My sister don't like to drive."

"Maybe they switched cars?" said Brian then he looked in the rear view mirror at me, aware of his blunder, for my mom was still in a cast and unable to drive.

Ellie was still willing to come in, especially after I started talking about the nursery. Patty opened the front door for us.

"I wished I had me a maid," said Ellie as she handed Patty her cream vinyl purse.

I dodged Patty's pinch as we entered the foyer.

"I been here, long ago," she said. "Your grandparents were nice folks."

"I'm sorry, but the nursery is up the stairs," I said.

"Of course, of course. Quieter up there."

As Brian helped Ellie negotiate the steps, I looked back at Patty, who nodded and pointed upstairs. I made a turning motion with my hand. Patty scrunched her brow then turned and locked the front door dead bolt. I nodded then followed Brian and Ellie. After a few steps, I glanced back—Patty was staring out the front door window. Having known Patty since I was twelve, I could see the tenseness in her body.

At the door of the nursery, Ellie stopped and looked in. "Lookin' older every time I see you," she said.

Before I even saw Laura, I heard her retort: "I've been discussing the Quinn fire with Beth. It's a good thing your beloved Bert wasn't around...he might have gotten burned."

Brian would be thinking, Whoa, shit! right about now.

"Old witch," said Ellie as she shuffled into the room.

A series of little shelves and placed vases, glasses, and figurines in pastel colors in each opening filled the window.. It gave the room a soft, colorful glow that had now been infused with acrimony. I resented making this plan to stir things up—I now wanted to hustle the women out of the room before they defiled it even more with their venom. But hell, they were here so I might as well go with it.

"We've just come from Custer's," I said. "Did your Bert like those tunnels on the Quinn land? My uncle said they were fun."

"He'd grown out of such childishness," said Ellie, trying to act nonchalant. "Nope, we were looking at pickups on the Chevy car lot in Sidney the day of the fire."

"Beth, weren't you supposed to be in Sidney for lunch?" I asked.

"Well, we were, but I hit my bad arm. Laura gave me some aspirin, but it still felt bad so she drove me home. But this room makes me feel better."

Brian walked behind me and insisted Beth sit down in the rocker, the only piece of furniture we'd bought for the room. Laura smiled at Brian's kindness, but Ellie continued to glare at her sister. I heard my cell vibrate in my purse.

The text from Patty said, "Gray suv on prowl."

My blood pressure rose and fear lodged in my throat like a tumor.

My return text read: "Call state patrol, tell where we go."

A few minutes later, Brian escorted Ellie down the stairs and out into his Jeep Cherokee. I figured we were safe as long as Ellie was with us. Yet, her Harney Street house came too fast. We walked with her to her front door then wished our farewells.

"Keep your eyes open for Bert in a muddy silver Chevy SUV," I said after I climbed into the Jeep.

"Do you know where he's at?" Brian asked

"I wish," I said as I dialed my phone. "Zane, do you know where he is? We just turned onto Highway 51 south-bound. Never mind, I see him."

Shit.

He waited for his chance and here it was. God above!

"Brian, that's him, coming straight for us!"

Bert's pickup lurched as he stomped on the accelerator. He swerved into our lane. Brian looked frantically for an escape. He braked hard then started to veer to the shoulder.

"No!" I yelled.

I grabbed the steering wheel, pushing it to the left—we jerked back into the lane. We were close enough that I saw Bert's mouth open wide. My heart was a moment from busting through my ribs.

Bert swerved right and went off into the ditch on his side of the road. His truck rolled over, kicking dirt and rocks into the air. We came to a stop then Brian drove us onto the shoulder. Bert tried to kill us in broad daylight. The witnesses were already stopping along the road. What a bloody idiot. Brian and I both sat still gasping for air. He turned to me, angry.

"He was playing chicken with us," I said.

"Megan, dammit! You almost got us killed."

I shook my head then closed my eyes. I still sensed his evil. He lived. Triple shit. Zane's face appeared in my window.

"Damn! That was gutsy," he said.

"I tried to bail, like a normal human," said Brian. "That was her doing."

Zane looked at me and shook his head. "There's some serious shit going down—you need to let me in on it."

"I agree," I said. "Tell the cops what you saw, but don't tell them about me calling you. I'll be talking to Officer Merritt, even if he's not here."

Brian and Zane walked across the two lanes to the wreck. I called my mom to tell her we were fine, and then I joined the group beside the upside down SUV. Bert's body was smashed against the roof, with his head contorted at a sharp angle. No seatbelts. Idiot. He was groaning, but people knew not to move him. I bent down to look in at him. He tried to talk, but he was too compacted to speak clearly; all that came out were spit and primal mutterings, which I'm sure were foul. When he attempted to grab me with his hairless, freckled arm, I didn't squelch my smile. He spewed a new round of vulgar grunts.

Soon, the sound of sirens joined the chatter of the people as they discussed what they saw. The all too familiar Sidney ambulance arrived. Brian and I gave short, simple statements to the county deputy. Others were more adamant that Bert tried to run into us. Unless Bert confessed his intent, which he wouldn't, they could only charge him with reckless driving. His head was bloody, so maybe a concussion would subdue his danger for a day or two.

Among the crowd was my appointment, Charles Hadley, who was fighting bankruptcy, a divorce, and his gambling demon.

"Come on, Chuck," I said. "Let's go. It's hot out here."

Back at the office, the staff buzzed with chatter and questions about the accident. Before I led Chuck into my office, I said to the staff and a few others who wandered in for news: "Bert Bolger will know better than to challenge Brian again."

As soon as I sat down, Chuck began questioning me; thankfully, it didn't involve the accident. Though I was ready to move past the attempt on my life, my brain still buzzed.

"Yes, Paula did come here," I said. "But she didn't come to complain about you...she's supposed to talk to her own attorney about that. She was annoyed with me and the counseling I've been suggesting."

"Oh."

"Look, Chuck, I came from a broken family. If anything will save your marriage, I'm going to suggest it."

"Her attorney is a jerk. He's pushing her to go through with it."

"It means a much bigger fee for the attorney."

"Oh."

"However, Joy will be sending your bill in the near future—it's one of her late-month duties—but we'll skip today. I'm feeling pretty good just to be alive right now."

He nodded then changed the subject. "I didn't grow up here, but our newspaper says that the van they found in Big Mac was connected to the murders...probably hauled the bodies away. And Paula has been chattering about it. She was a second cousin to Julie."

"Did she know Sean?"

"Yeah. She was pretty young and a relative—she says that's the only reason he didn't 'hit' on her."

"He was that bad, huh?"

"She says it was all talk...just him feeding his ego. But she always said those Fourth of July parties were fun."

After Chuck left, Glenda came in and asked if I had time to talk with Doreen Hutch. I agreed. Doreen was the next door neighbor of the Ritter family before they moved and a teacher at the Dexter middle school.

Her topic took me off guard, though I was a bit flattered by her confidence in me.

"I'm worried about the kids this summer. This drought isn't breaking. During the school year, we teachers started handing out boxes of raisins at about eleven. Still, most of my class spent the last half of class watching the clock, waiting for lunch. Some people would look at these kids and say they have ADD because they fidget so much. Megan, they're hungry."

It was a slap in the face for me. I'd been spending so much time thinking about my baby, work, and the Quinn murders that I'd missed something incredibly important in my community. Ellie Bolger had mentioned it, but I disregarded her warning.

Feeling thoroughly ashamed, I said, "Doreen, we must do something, and we need to raise money pronto."

"But many families are struggling," she said.

"Hang on," I said as I dialed the phone number for my friend and former classmate, Jeff Finch, a banker at Dexter's branch of the Cheyenne County Bank. After I told him the problem, he expressed his willingness to help.

"We need to set up collections for funds…maybe call it the Cheyenne County Drought Fund or something like that," I said to him. "Yes, I know people are hard up, but it has to look like a community effort…take collections all over town. Then the people who have money need to come up with the real backing." Pause. "Yes, like me."

I winked at Doreen. She smiled.

"Right, we need a committee. I'll get you in contact with Doreen Hutch and we can go from there." Pause. "Hey, thanks." Pause. "Yes, Bert Bolger did try to run us off the road. I don't think he'll try that again. See ya."

Doreen and I brainstormed on a few ideas, including gift vouchers for Shaver's grocery, distribution of food boxes to families in need, and setting up a free summer lunch program.

"The kids would come once they saw that other kids were coming," she said.

"What will you do when the hungry senior citizen or the unemployed cowboy shows up? It'll be hard to turn those people away. Just something to think about. Here's Jeff's number. He'll help because he's a good guy and it shows good will on behalf of the bank."

"The very bank that's getting ready to evict the Zimmers,"

"What? Really? I knew Max has been ill, but I didn't know it was so bad. I'll look into it. In the meantime, get some friends together to form a committee. You'll want the bank to supervise the collection of the money. Folks are proud and stubborn…you'll need to find a way to convince people to take charity."

That evening, Zane became part of the crew. By the time Brian and I arrived home, Beth and James had already given him a run down on the investigation. When we entered the War Room, he was walking back and forth between the boards.

He looked from Brian to me then said, "Ever heard of the phrase 'information overload'?"

Brian nodded. "It's a kick in the gut."

For a man who had served three tours in Iraq and Afghanistan, he flinched whenever he looked at the photos of Mary and Julie Quinn. Finally, he sat down and said, "Sweet Jesus."

James left and came back with a snifter of brandy. "You look like you need this." He handed the glass to Zane. "It'll heat you up, but maybe you won't care."

Zane took a big swig and nodded, then said in a raspy voice that made us smile, "Yeah, good stuff." He took another drink. "So, what can I do?"

"Well, if you're going to play bodyguard, then you need to know what we're dealing with," I said. "And with

Chief Joe J and Bert Bolger on the rampage, any of us could be targets."

Zane looked at James and said, "I think you need to be pouring more of that."

"I keep a stash here," said James. "We never run out of reasons to need a restorative."

We convinced Zane and James to stay for supper. Beth and Patty announced that they had invited Paul and Kayla, so we locked the study and waited for them in the family room. I waited until we were done eating then I mentioned my conversations with Doreen Hutch and Jeff Finch.

"I'd like to help with that," said my mom.

Then Kayla said, "Mrs. Hutch is right. I see those kids who stand outside in the halls during lunch. They don't even have food to bring from home. I'll help. But what you need are some little kids to deliver the food. Nobody's gonna scold a kindergartener for being nice."

Ah, the brilliance of youth.

That evening Brian stood at the sink drinking his second bourbon. Glaring at me he said, "We need to end this. You almost got us killed today."

"There's a man sitting in prison who probably didn't kill anybody."

"That's his problem, not ours. You have to get your hands on everything."

"Those Quinn women are my problem—they haunt my sleep with their faces and cries."

"Well, stop thinking about them."

I stared at him—he turned away. If he thought it was that simple or that easy then I'd married an idiot.

Chapter 16

The next afternoon, Art Meyer and Ernie Sedlacek came to the office. We discussed Bert's crash then Brian suggested the two men get a Danish from Glenda and a cup of coffee. Brian held me back as they left.

"Why do you keep telling people that I'm the one who challenged Bert?" Brian asked.

"Because you know he's after me. You've wanted to bash in his brains for a long time...you just didn't think it would be with a car. And you were disappointed he wasn't hurt more than he was. You're no saint." I didn't add that he lacked the nerve to challenge Bert as I did. Still, I wanted him to appear heroic to others.

He ran his hands through his short blond hair as he grinned at me. "I'm getting a Danish."

Just as the four of us started for the basement, Officer Merritt arrived. Gus came out of his office.

"We need to start locking this door again," said Gus. "Dang, look at the riff-raff that can get in here."

The two men laughed. A brief conversation between them indicated an ongoing friendship. Officer Merritt took the coffee and pastry Glenda gave him. Melanie, who was standing behind us, cleared her throat.

"Lew made this," she said, holding up a four by six inch oak placard for the front door with "Please Ring For Service" etched into the wood.

"I suppose we should start," I said.

The basement plans were complete. The carpet had been installed, along with an oak baseboard, as well as counters and cabinets. Art inspected the dead bolt on the empty records room. Then he walked over to the big desk that formerly occupied his office.

"Laura cleaned that up, didn't she?" I said.

He smiled and nodded then took a big sniff, "Lemon Pledge, my house smells like it."

Ernie looked around and said, "You need a generator. When that tornado leveled your uncle's house, plenty of people lost power. That's tough on babies and oldsters like me."

Brian said, "That makes sense. We have one at home."

I nodded as Brian set out folding chairs to sit in. We placed the chairs in front of the desk. Brian sat down in the desk chair and took out a pen and notepad.

"Okay," Brian said. "Alibis."

Ernie cleared his throat then began: "The one thing I've always remembered was that nobody really had a strong alibi for the morning. They all claimed to be out working in the field or in a barn. It was a day of good weather, so it's believable. They would have been scattered over several miles of hills, pastures, and cornfields. Likewise, the cowhands were spread over acres of land and didn't prove to be helpful witnesses, since they were doing their own work. Yet there was enough confirmation that Walt, Sean, Mike, as in Thornton, Hank, Bob, and your Great-uncle Ned were working out on the land. Al Docket was in his bank office."

"That would correspond to the records I found," said Merritt. "We can put the time of the fire at one o'clock and as early as five till one, as it was called in so quickly. Sean Quinn was with attorney Arthur Meyer at that time."

Art nodded.

"We can place Walt Bolger at the scene, obviously. Bob Eldritch claimed to have been finishing lunch at his house. Mrs. Lois Eldritch confirmed that. Bert Bolger was on a car lot in Sidney with Mrs. Ellen Bolger at that time or shortly thereafter. Mrs. Bolger states she served lunch to Bert and Walt at twelve-fifteen then Walt left. Albert

Docket was at the Docket home with Ned Docket and Hank Eldritch eating lunch. Mrs. Anna Docket confirmed that. Michael Thornton was at Smokey's sale lot, as confirmed by staff there. We believe some of the boys were playing on the Quinn grounds, but none of them reported seeing anything."

"Right," I said. "They were playing underground in the old distillery tunnels. Bill states he was with Lew and Salt Eldritch, Clay and Andy Bolger, and the two Thornton boys, Buck and Adam. They saw the fire and ran to it, arriving as the fire trucks did."

"Frank wasn't with the other boys," said Ernie. "It was never determined where he went. He had a secret and he kept it. But no one had a reason to connect him to the murders or Walt. Your dad was never cleared, but never officially suspected."

"Right...okay," I said, stalling to calm myself. "But we don't know when the two women were murdered as the bodies were never examined. They could have been killed earlier and the fire started later to cover up the killings." I paused then said, "Bert is evil...I'm sure of it. But I don't know if he was a part of the murder."

"So, someone drives a blue Chevy van to the Quinn house, murderers the two women, then hauls away the bodies," said Brian.

"It would be so easy to hide the van somewhere in this area, and then move it later to dispose of the bodies...then in time, sink the van into Lake McConaughy," I said.

We were all quiet for a few moments, and then I asked Merritt: "Did Bert Bolger buy a car in Sidney?"

"Yes," he said as he shuffled through his notes. "He bought a 1955 Ford pickup truck at Horst Ford."

"Mrs. Bolger said they went to a Chevy dealership," I said.

"But she's old and it was forty-five years ago," said Art. "Most people, such as the cowhands, if you could even track them down, wouldn't remember that day very well. I don't even remember why Sean needed to meet with me that day."

I nodded yet I thought of two people who did know that day very well.

"I think we still have a problem with motive," I said. "Sane people just don't go out and hack their neighbors to death. And nobody has ever indicated Walt Bolger was a psychopath."

"Nobody reaped a monetary benefit, that I can see," said Brian.

"I've heard Sean was a womanizer or at least a flirt," I said. "Was he messing around with someone's wife during this time?"

Ernie and Art exchanged a quick glance. What did that mean? Officer Merritt rifled through his notes then shrugged.

"But wouldn't a jealous husband go after Sean?" I asked.

"I've always wondered why the authorities never looked more closely at Bob Eldritch," said Art. "Of all the men we've talked about, he's the mean-tempered S-O-B of the bunch. He could've been nursing some grudge against Sean then found out Walt was angry, and they cooked up a plan. But when they went to the house, Sean wasn't there."

"This was a State Patrol investigation," said Ernie, "but they asked me to help out because I knew the families. And I remembered thinking at the time that it seemed impulsive, especially since it was done in broad daylight."

"But the van was stolen the night before," said Merritt.

"We didn't know about the van at the time...not till a day or two later and we didn't know if it was connected."

"We've concluded that the van was connected to the murders. We found cut cords and a bag of bloody clothes."

"Wait, if they were dead, why did they need to be tied?" asked Brian.

"Oh, God, what if they were still alive when they were hauled away?" I asked.

I was glad I was over my nausea because the image that hit us all would have made me puke up meals from last week. Art's face turned green, so I didn't feel like such a wimp.

"Hauling bodies, even dead ones, is awkward," Officer Merritt explained, "especially if one man was doing the moving."

"And I bet the murderer, or the van driver at least, moved those bodies more than once to elude searches," I said. "How long did the searches continue?"

Merritt looked through his notes as Art scratched his chin.

"Not long enough, you're thinking since we never found them," said Ernie. "We had an army of men and we searched every barn and every house, and every loose bit of dirt we found. The FBI brought in a dozen men. My God, it haunted us crazy. We prohibited any digging or even moving of large machinery in the area. But eventually, cattle had to be sent to market and the ranches that raised corn had to harvest. As soon as the stolen van came to light, we put out a national search for it. And yes, we did try to search Big Mac...the FBI even brought in Navy divers. But nothin'."

I didn't say anything, but with all those men and all the vehicles, the police would have driven over any tracks the van left before they knew its importance. Every summer was dry, so the ground would've been hard and a vehicle could drive across a field of buffalo grass without difficulty.

"The van driver committed murder in broad daylight, but he would move the bodies and sink the van at night," I said. "If he was smart, he'd sink that van that same night, before more police could move in. He'd hose off the bodies or maybe even dunk them in water...even the lake, so he could move them in another vehicle without leaving traces of blood."

"Geez, Megan," said Brian.

"She's right," said Ernie. "The murderer would've bled them out like butchered cattle. Then he just had to worry about the smell."

"So he got them underground right away, maybe even wrapped them in a rug or a roll of carpet," I said. "Then he moved them to keep ahead of the searches which now wouldn't find any blood. He couldn't just bury them because you said they checked loosened ground. I bet while you were searching, you were wondering if that van and those bodies were on their way to Mexico."

"Yeah, that's exactly what we wondered," said Ernie. "In 1968, we didn't have the surveillance we do now. Even with the FBI helping, he could drive to another state, swap license plates, get a paint job or paint it himself then disappear."

"But he didn't disappear," I said. "He's among us. He's been gloating all these years, till now. The van has been found—he never took those bodies to Mexico. They're here, too. Clay and Andy wanted to conduct their own search. And a search is what the killer fears. Or maybe the attempt to buy that old Quinn land was a charade, and Clay and Andy were involved in the murder and cover up, so Bert is protecting one or both of them, instead of the father. Hmm. Doesn't seem right. Clay and Andy don't come off like devious killers."

My phone vibrated in my blazer pocket. I read the text from Bud.

"Well, Clay's car has been spotted in the area," I said. "It must be hard to have a parent in prison, but what does he really expect to accomplish?"

"Walt Bolger has a parole hearing in August," said Merritt. "So that and the discovery of the van stirred up that family. Bert spent the night in the hospital with a concussion, but he's home now."

"Great," I said as my stomach flipped over.

I needed to work late, but Brian was antsy to get home. So I packed up a couple of files in my attaché case, and let him drive me home. I worked in my bedroom till supper—the study was now the War Room—I'd never be able to concentrate in there. After supper, I finished a Special Needs Trust then set off for Bill's house. It was time for him to talk.

I meant to catch him by surprise and I did. Of course, he felt obligated to invite me in. After some chit chat, I stunned him with a question:

"Did my grandmother have an affair with Sean Quinn?"

He plopped down in his big, gray recliner, his mouth open.

"Awhile back, you told me Dad found out about Grandma's cheating and that he never forgave her."

"Yes, but how did you know it was Sean?"

"It just adds up," I said. Actually, it didn't—why do people cheat? "Did Grandpa know?"

"He figured it out—Frank made it easy."

"How?"

"Frank came home from school early feeling sick from something. He never did that. He said he heard my mom and Sean talking, and he told me he just knew from the sound of their voices. So, he marches past them and goes upstairs and sees that our parents' bed is now in a mess. Then he goes to the kitchen and beats up Sean."

"He beat up a grown man? Wait, how old was he?"

"He was fifteen, but tall. He wasn't known for his fighting, but I knew he could, especially if he was mad. Frank told me he hit Sean several times, bloodied his face good, but then figured out that Sean wasn't going to fight him back. That's when he quit."

"Wow. I can't picture my dad fighting."

"My mom was still crying in the kitchen when I came home. Frank must've been upstairs in his room. I tried to clean up the blood from the floor, but ended up making a bigger mess, so Mom sent me away and she cleaned it."

"When was this?"

"A couple of months before the murders."

"Oh, damn."

"Yeah. Once the cops heard about that, they questioned Frank over and over. But he stood tough through all of it. I confess I was proud of my big brother. Sean's nose never did heal right...always had a bump right in the middle."

"But my dad was gone on the day of the murders."

"Uh-huh. The cops questioned him, but he wouldn't say where he was, not even to clear himself. All these years...he never budged."

"What did he tell you?"

"He said he promised to keep something secret. And people did talk, but the cops had nothing to link him to the murders."

"Did they arrest my dad?"

"Nah. They knew they caught the killer when they arrested Walt. I don't really know, but thinking back, they wouldn't have known there was an accomplice right away...and of course there had to be someone to take the bodies away in the van. That driver would have had plenty of time to get clear before the fire trucks came. The house was a huge mess, all charred black and wet. I stayed that whole afternoon. They worked a long time before they could clear the rubble. The house didn't all burn, but it collapsed into a mess."

"And it would take awhile to know for sure that there weren't any bodies. They would need to check the shelter, too."

He nodded.

"Wait, you said the van had plenty of time to get away before the fire department came. How do you know the van was there when the fire started?"

Bill looked at his knees. He knew something.

"When you were playing in those tunnels, did you stay underground that whole time?"

He closed his eyes, his face contorted with agony.

"I-I never liked staying in those small passages too long…always had to come up and get some air." He stopped.

"And you looked out and saw something."

He nodded. "I didn't think much of it at the time, but I saw a blue van parked in the Quinn yard…but I never saw anybody."

"What time was this?"

"I don't know, but must've been in that same hour. I went back to playing then Clay, he was the one with the watch, said he and Andy were late for lunch. When we came out, we saw the house was on fire but no van or truck was around."

"Did you tell this to the police?"

"No, we all just said we were playing in those tunnels. They asked if we saw anyone and we all said no. I was a chicken-shit twelve year old. I didn't say anything…never even told my brother. I didn't understand the significance of the van for years. Just a dumb, dumb kid."

"Did you never see Walt's truck at the house that day?"

"No."

"Did you see it there on other occasions?"

"Probably…but maybe just for parties, like the one the night before. Oh, and, Mary and Julie shared a banana-yellow Ford Galaxy. That was there at the time of the fire, but it was parked over by the barn. They used the barn as a garage in the winter for the car."

He scratched the late-day whiskers on his chin. "Been carrying that information on the van all these years. I'd appreciate if you kept it quiet."

"I'll try, but I can't promise that. I need to walk," I said rising from his sofa.

"You can't go alone."

"Then come with me. No, I don't want to talk. I just want to clear my head."

He grabbed a pair of tennies, which were huge like all his shoes and boots. As a kid, I teased him by saying I could float down the Platte River in them. But right now I didn't feel like joking. My grandma committed adultery with Sean Quinn. How could she do that to Grandpa? I needed fresh air.

Soon, we were wandering through the Seven Dwarfs. I didn't talk, as promised. After a few minutes of silence and a good blast of wind, his shoulders dropped as he relaxed.

He stopped by one of the rocky mounds and asked, "Which one is this?"

"Oh, that's Sleepy. See how it slopes on the north side? Derek, Vonny, and I could lie down out of the sun. We'd make up stories."

"Who was the storyteller?"

I smiled. "Usually me. I'd get some idea from a movie or the *Little House on the Prairie* books and go with it. What did you guys play up in those tunnels?"

"Oh, pirates or gangsters. Once your dad decided to be a leper from *Ben-Hur* and chased us. Or we'd just try to recreate whatever movie—"

He froze as he looked westward. We saw two black plumes rising in the distance.

"Damn! That would be Thornton land. You got your phone?"

After I called emergency, Bill took me by the shoulders. "You can't help with this. You need to go home and stay there and keep Brian with you. Will you do that for me?"

As soon as I agreed, he ran back to his house. I did go home, yet questions nagged at me as I trudged through the buffalo grass. Where was my dad that day? Did people suspect him? If they did, would they admit it to me? I didn't like that a cloud of suspicion hung over him. I needed to clear his name and the only way to do that was to solve the mystery.

Chapter 17

An hour later, Uncle Bill called, stating two Thornton barns had been set on fire within minutes of each other. The fire departments involved gained control of the fires, and the livestock were rescued, but the buildings collapsed. Were these fires somehow related to the investigation? Just when I thought I had an inkling of something, it became more muddled. Maybe that was the killer's intent. Did I even know he was still around?

Even though it was after nine o'clock, I went to the War Room and called Officer Merritt. He'd heard of the burning barns, but hadn't been called in to aid the night crew. I told him of Chief Joe J's background and his klutzy harassment of several people regarding the Quinn murders for which he had no jurisdiction.

"I think it's time to charge Chief Joe with hacking into my computers, as well as harassment and trespassing," I said. "Hacking is the only significant charge, but it's probably enough to get him out of here and back to his other employer, the FBI."

"I'm glad that you're not planning to make another citizen's arrest," he said.

"Nah, I'd only do that with unarmed insurance executives."

"How do you know those computers were hacked?"

"They were. Your expert computer nerds will verify it. You'll see."

"What was he looking for?"

"He wanted to know if we knew Linda Sharpe was his mother. Actually, we hadn't gotten that far, but I'd appreciate it if you didn't let him in on what we know."

"He probably doesn't know who his father is."

"And if there was a rape. There wasn't, at least according to my client, Hank Eldritch, the father. Now you should treat that as confidential. I don't want Joe going after him."

"Is Hank Eldritch in the area? Where is he?"

"I prefer not to divulge my client's whereabouts...though I confess I don't always know. I'll ask that you don't go looking for him...that will tip off Joe J. Tell me if you need him. I'll find him then advise him to cooperate. Oh, and I'm dropping all charges related to the killing of my horse."

"Uh-huh. Gotcha."

"Oh, and Clay and maybe Andy Bolger is back in the area. All three of those brothers should be watched. I just have a feeling one or all of them are at the heart of this."

After I finished talking to Merritt, I wondered about the arson. Bill sounded confident the fires were intentionally set. Why would someone burn down two barns? And who did it? Why would the Thorntons be targeted? Did the death of Mary Quinn, a Thornton, intend to punish or wound the Thornton family? Was Linda connected to the Thornton family? Buck and Adam would have been close in age to Linda. I strongly sensed Beulah knew all about the relationships between the people of the ranches. Her obstinate silence infuriated me.

I worked late the next day, arriving home at nearly seven. The burning of the barns was the talk all over town. I was eager to find out what my uncle knew. I came in through the door from the garage that opened into the rear of the kitchen. My mom was setting out the plates on the kitchen table. She looked at me and smiled.

"Hi, Mom. Have you—"

I froze, aware that a figure in a doorway was neither Brian nor Patty, who both stood by the table. Beulah tentatively emerged from the threshold of the dining room. If she hadn't been hiding from me for weeks, my reaction would probably have been different. Instead, I flushed warm with anger.

"Well, hell. Can't even have privacy in my own home."

I walked past Brian and headed up the back stairs. Patty said that I would soon return. The hell I would. I dumped my purse on the bed and then changed into jeans and a top. I went back down the stairs and out the back door. Brian ran out after me and tried to stop me on the patio. I just kept going. Brian explained that Patty drove Beth and Beulah to Sidney this afternoon, which was why Beulah's Chrysler was down the block at Bill's house.

"Come on, she's your friend," he said.

"Yeah, well, when was the last time she acted like it?"

He followed me as I skirted Rufus and headed onto the rocky soil. I walked right next to a prairie dog hole. Brian caught his toe on it and fell forward into the dirt and buffalo grass with a thud. I looked back at him but kept going. It was rotten of me not to warn him, but I was feeling mean, and if he didn't know to be careful out in my wild land by now, he was a pathetic fool. He didn't say anything; he stopped then turned toward the house.

Our family's biggest secret has just been revealed to the county gossip. Shit.

Heading due north, my anger didn't abate even after I climbed the three hundred-foot bluff we called the Beast. Just to be sure nobody could spot me by climbing Big Leo and using my binoculars, I scaled the bluff from the north side.

I sat and stewed and then I stewed some more. For twenty-three years I'd lived in a lie. Then I discovered my mother wasn't dead and my strange yearning was for my twin. And right now, all of it stabbed me deeply, like a dull knife twisting around in my guts until it found the spot to wound me the most. Perhaps I was being hormonal, or maybe it stung so badly because my whole being, the very core of me, was preparing for motherhood. I hated that I decided to continue the lie by pretending my mother was my aunt. But I didn't want her or my dad to face the scorn of the community. Yet I knew, as did she and Bill, that the lie would become exposed one day. I even prepared for it by creating a one-day town newspaper revealing the story. Well-protected in my new laptop, all it needed for printing was a date. I knew the date now. Still, I dreaded the questions and the gossip.

I looked to the west where the sun was setting into an orange glow. Two vehicles pulled off the highway onto the old Hexam Road to the north, kicking up dust the south wind swirled then dispatched northward. The first auto was my uncle's silver Ford pickup; the second was a maroon Chrysler. She had come for me, led by my uncle. They wouldn't know where I was—they meant to wait for me to come to them. I didn't even consider escape; it was time to face her. By now, my mom and Bill would've told her the whole story.

I descended the bluff, reaching the bottom a dusty mess. I walked the quarter mile to the north and climbed into her car. Bill started his truck and drove away. For the first time, I looked at her. She looked on the verge of tears as she handed me a soapy washcloth for my hands. Then she handed me a cooler the size of an old-fashioned school lunchbox. Inside was a bottle of water, napkins, and plastic bag with a turkey sandwich. I drank from the water bottle.

"You know my secret, what's yours?"

She took a deep breath then knotted her bony fingers together. "I'm the one who told the police that Hank may have raped Linda Sharpe."

"Why would you say that? It wasn't true."

"I need to go back. I know you would have been investigating all of this, so you know about the Fourth of July party. Hank and I came together. You see, he was my beau. But that Linda was a friend of Julie's and she started comin' around that spring and she was at the party. The first time he clapped eyes on her, I knew we were finished, but I tried to hold on to him. I knew him growin' up, but we'd only been courtin' a year or so. But that Linda was a beautiful girl of, oh, eighteen, I think. Then at the party I saw them walk off together. I knew that was it. To be honest, I think I was a bit relieved."

"Now how old were you then?"

"Hank and I were both twenty-nine. Damnedest thing to be datin' when I was that old. Me and everybody thought I'd always be a spinster...and that was right for me. Never could tolerate some man thinkin' he possessed or controlled me. Too ornery, I guess."

"Yeah, that's you."

I didn't like feeling controlled either. My father tried to control everyone around him, but I always fought against him. I don't think he respected those who allowed his bullying. I wasn't a bully, but I needed to hold the reins of my life. Last winter I realized my extreme desire to protect those close to me. I finished my sandwich.

"So, tell me more—why was Hank arrested?"

"Well, me and Julie were supposed to be watchin' the boys in the Quinn house, but Julie left for a while. I don't know where she went, but she was gone for a time. When she came back, she acted shook up. Then Linda came inside and went up to Julie's room. Julie took me aside and told me Linda was upset...but she wasn't sure why. Julie said she thought Hank raped Linda."

"Did you ever talk to Linda?"

"No. But the next day the policeman...guess he would've been State Patrol...insisted I tell him everythin' Julie said or did at the party. So I did. But that got Hank arrested. I never told him what I told the police. He would think I was being spiteful."

"He got released. He says he didn't rape Linda. In fact, they're living together now."

Her eyebrows rose, then she nodded.

"Did you ever see Linda after that day?"

"Nope, never have. Hank tried to take up with me again, but I wasn't for it. Then some people started saying Hank was involved in the murders. That probably came from Ellie Bolger, that old witch. He ran away. I did too, after a while…had to get away from all the pain."

"And Sean ran away, too."

"Yeah. I felt so bad for him. He wasn't a good man…bit of a snake."

"As in adultery."

"Yeah."

"Including my grandmother."

She gasped. "How could you know that?"

I shook my head. "Who else did he mess with?"

"I kept my distance, I could see what he was…always was. Mary had to know. I always wondered if he messed with one of the McCracken sisters…that would've been way back. But if he did, it didn't last."

"What was Julie like?"

"Oh, nice to me, but she could be kind of uppity. Didn't like living on a ranch. Thought cowboys were scum. If your pa had been older, she would have liked him…or the idea of him…someone smart who wasn't going to be a cowboy. Me and ever'body thought he'd be a banker like his pa."

"Did Julie ever date anyone around here?"

"There might have been someone in Potter for a while, but I'm not sure. We weren't close…me being ten years older. Bert useta be around the Quinns a lot. Julie treated him like dirt. But he kept comin' and helpin' with things. I saw him fix a screen door once that was hangin' funny. Bert was good with that stuff."

"Do you think he wanted to date Julie?"

"Not sure. Always wondered. Mary was mean to him, too. Bert just took it."

"That's strange if he was being nice. Bert's a mean old bastard nowadays. So, how did Sean treat him?"

"He just ignored him."

The sky had darkened around us.

"Hon, I'm gonna need your help now. I don't general-ly drive in the dark…'specially out in nowhere."

"Hey, now. This is somewhere—it's my backyard. I'll drive you home."

We switched places and then I circled around and headed back toward the highway.

"The Docket family secret wasn't going to stay quiet," I said, avoiding eye contact. "I was planning to revive our town newspaper for a day. I'll be doing that sooner than I thought."

As we headed down Benson Street, the headlights be-hind us stayed close behind. I drove past Beulah's house.

"You past it," she said.

"So did the car that's following us."

My phone vibrated right when I pulled it out of my back pocket. It was Brian.

"It's me behind you," he said.

"Why'd you wait so long to tell me? I thought you were a stalker."

He chuckled. "Sorry."

"Oh, you think it's funny? Do you think this is a game?"

"No."

Great, someone else to piss me off. I circled around the block and returned to Beulah's house. She pushed the gar-age door opener and I drove into her single car garage. I turned off the ignition then pressed the button to close the door just as Brian pulled into the driveway.

In the dim light of the garage, I turned to her, "Who do you think killed Mary and Julie?"

"God be my witness, I don't know. Walt doin' it never made sense."

"Someone else was involved…someone took those bodies away."

"All these years I been hopin' those bodies would be found…get a proper burial…give them some peace. I suppose that's what I think about most. But yeah, there was someone else."

"By the way, Hank wants to see you," I said.

"Really? You won't tell him what I said to the police."

"I see no reason for that. It may be awhile before he can see you. But don't talk about him. Oh, and here's a heads up. Chief Joe J is in trouble and will get arrested if he hasn't already."

She gasped. "What did he do?"

"It's better if I don't tell you. Just say he did something fishy…you like that phrase."

"Yeah, said it many a time. Okay, that's what I'll say."

She worked at moving her old silver Timex around her wrist. Her hand looked shaky as she did it. Finally, she said, "You're not still mad at me are you? You've been that way for weeks…tonight was the worst."

"Mm-mmm. Tonight was my fault," I said. "But you've been hiding when you should've been helping."

"I know."

Certain her flimsy watch would break, I pressed my hand over hers. Her beady blue eyes penetrated my skull.

"We'll be good friends again." I leaned over and kissed her veiny, winkled forehead. "It's time you went to bed, young lady."

She cackled. "Yep, yep. Need my beauty sleep."

Her warm hand clasped mine, holding it tightly.

Chapter 18

The next morning, I rode with Brian to his Sidney office. He dropped me at the jeweler's while he attended his morning appointment. At lunch, I waited till Beulah walked back into the kitchen then followed her. I handed her a small box.

"Heh! What's this?"

She unwrapped and opened the silver box. Inside was a note that read: "Best Friends," with a silver Seiko watch.

"Oh, hon! It's gorgeous. Seeko."

I didn't usually correct her, but it seemed appropriate in this case. Then I held up my watch, which was identical to hers.

"Oh, pshaw!" She wasn't a hugger, but she grabbed my shoulders and gave them a shake. I winked at Blaine, her nephew, who stopped to watch the scene.

"Oh, and you were right," she said. "It's the big news. The State Patrol arrested Joe J this morning."

"Yeah, what did he do?" asked Blaine.

"Something fishy," I said.

As expected, Joe J arrived at the firm that afternoon. More than likely, the FBI bailed him out. I quickly set up my desk for his appearance. When he came to the door, Zane, who had been tailing him, entered the firm when Gus opened the door to Joe. Zane frisked an uncooperative Joe as Brian and I looked on. When Gus removed a handgun from Joe's rear waistband, Joe growled then stomped into my office.

As I sat down at my desk, Joe stared at my Glock, which I had placed at the center of my massive desk. He didn't notice that I slid my hand under the front cover of an open bankruptcy manual then pulled it out again. Instead, he slammed shut my laptop. He must have thought I planned to film and record him. I mustered a poker face to stifle my smile.

"You know I'll get off, the FBI will make sure of it," he said.

I shrugged. "That's possible, but you've been charged with a felony. And you knew better than to come to my office with a weapon. That should get you back in jail. You aren't making wise decisions. The question is—why do you think I'm the enemy? Yes, I've been looking into the Quinn murders. And I also know your mother was never raped. That was faulty information caused by the clumsy work of the State Patrol. They charged a man, Hank Eldritch, without ever having anything more than the speculation of a dead girl. But it ruined his life here and aroused the anger of the bastard son—you."

"You are my enemy because my mother, my birth, has nothing to do with you," he said.

"Sure it does, because it involves my client, Hank Eldritch."

"You represent that son of a bitch? Now you listen to me. I know about you, more than other people do around here."

"Excuse me for a moment," I said as I picked up the office phone and pressed the button for Melanie's phone. "Go ahead," was all I needed to say. "Okay, now what were you saying that you know about me?"

"That your Aunt Beth is really your mother, Elizabeth, and your parents divorced then lied about it. Now listen, you've been keeping those secrets, but that's blown unless you drop all the charges against me."

"Are you blackmailing me?"

"Whatever."

"You just keep making one bad choice after another. My guess is that you stayed on here because you wanted to find out who your father was. It's Hank Eldritch. He's a nice man who loves your mother." I handed him an envelope. "That's a writ ordering you to stay five hundred feet away from Hank Eldritch. And you've just been served."

I closed the book then picked up the mini tape recorder. As I held it up for Joe to see, I picked up the phone, pressed a button and hung up.

"You bitch! I'll get you for this!"

I clicked off the recorder. "We'll see."

My office door burst open. Joe was quickly surrounded by Brian, Gus, and Zane as Officer Merritt put handcuffs on him.

"You'll want this," I said as I handed the tape recorder to Merritt. "By the way, Joe, your scheme to blackmail me won't work." I held up a copy of the *Dexter Gazette*. "I revived our newspaper for a day. While we were talking, my family's story was being distributed around town. I'm sure it will make its way throughout the county in no time."

I followed them out the door and into the lobby, gloating with every step I took. Zane walked toward the front door without looking over at Melanie. She was watching the events, but I didn't see her look at him. They had been dating—did I miss something?

After I returned to my office, I closed the door and called Judge Dean Shelton. Maybe I could convince the judge that my enemy needed to stay behind bars for a while.

I left work soon after Joe was arrested. A pile of work higher than Mount Doom needed my attention, but I needed some mental health time. When I got home, I told my mom this was the day. I'd discussed revealing our family secret over a week ago, so she was ready. I called Uncle Bill so he'd know, then Mom and I went out to Rufus with a jug of iced tea.

"I confess, I feel relieved," I said. "Now, nobody has anything they can hold over me."

"Beulah says everybody knows Bill and I are dating," she said. "It was nice of you not to mention Bill and me...you know, before the divorce."

"I didn't see the point. I don't think people will think badly of you—"

"You mean for letting you go."

"My father is the one who comes out of this looking bad. That's how people will see it."

The south wind brought us the sound of the back door slamming shut. We both turned to see Patty escorting Beulah across the patio. My mom and I hastened down to her.

"Now what about those Seven Dwarfs I always heard about?" asked Beulah, in a voice I could barely hear in the wind.

"You want to see them? We'll take you." I said.

"Don't wanna see Grumpy."

I laughed. With me on one side and Patty on the other, we steadied her as we skirted Rufus to get to the small buttes. After we'd led her through the first couple, she laughed.

"There's only five."

"That's because Vonny named them before she could count," I said. Pointing eastward, I said, "That's Big Leo."

"Oh, I've heard about him." She looked out over the wild land. "I got somethin' I need to tell you, Megan."

"Okay, should we go back to the house?"

She nodded, so we led her back to the house. We sat together on our sofa as she caught her breath. Patty brought us glasses of ice water.

"Got any bourbon?" Beulah asked then cackled. "Better give me some ice."

"You won't be driving home, get that in your head, young lady," I said.

She smiled and nodded as my mom brought out some Fritos and ranch dip. Patty set the bourbon on a coaster.

"Oh, I love this…could eat it all day." Then she showed off the watch I bought her to Mom and Patty.

As soon as Mom and Patty left, her demeanor changed.

"Got to tell ya somethin' else." She took two sips of the bourbon. "Remember I said I was watchin' the younger boys inside when it got late?"

"The boys watched *Star Trek*."

"Right. But there was some comin' and goin'. Bert was never with us. Frank left for a while then came back…gone um, fifteen minutes maybe. Julie left for a long time. Then she came back and said Linda was all upset. I wonder about that. Anyway, Mrs. Quinn and Mrs. Bolger were also there. They sat in the kitchen…soon got to arguin'."

"Did you hear what they said?"

"Well, you know me. I got up and sat in a chair closer to the kitchen, but where they couldn't see me. Mary was tellin' Ellie to keep her son at home and that he was not wanted. I assumed she meant Bert. Mary said Sean 'hates' him. I recall her sayin' that exact word. Ellie gets to sputterin' when she's mad so I couldn't tell what she said. I saw somebody, had to be Frank or Bert because it was a skinny guy, go by the window. It was dark out and all the fireworks were done. The men were off drinkin'. Frank came back in the kitchen, so that stopped the women from talkin'. I betcha I was the only one who noticed the dirt on his knees."

"On my dad's knees?"

"Yeah. He was in shorts. Like I said, never saw Bert, not after the fireworks. Little while later, Julie comes back in. She runs upstairs…couldn't see her face from where I was sittin.' I wanted to go to her, but I didn't want to leave those mischievous boys alone. Ellie came stompin' in and got Clay and Andy then they left. Then Julie came down a while later in a different top and shorts. That's when she said Linda was upset. Then she leaves again. Soon, your grandpa came by and took Bill and Frank home. Buck and Adam were the only ones left and they were asleep. When I left the house a little while later, I couldn't find Hank. Never did see Linda." Beulah took a big swig of whiskey. "I've speculated over the years what happened and if anything happened. But I don't think we'll ever know."

I wanted to sit and think, but Brian came home. Then Bill came over. Soon, the house began to fill. James and Zane came, then Hank and Lew. I assumed they came to show their support for us. It was kind, but I wanted to think. Then Hank found Beulah and me sitting in the family room. He lifted Beulah off the sofa and gave her a big hug.

"How ya doin', Blue?" he asked.

"Blue?" I said.

"Yep, that's what I called her." He smiled at her. "You look healthy."

After a stunned pause, she said, "Nah, that's just the orneriness you're seein'." She turned to me. "Salt had trouble saying my name when he was little, but he knew the color, so that's what he called me."

Later Zane helped me set up the picnic table in the back yard for supper. When no one was around, I asked about him Melanie.

He shook his head. "Nah. We're finished. Just as well. You were a lot easier to date. I mean, you never expected chocolates and flowers and a fancy dinner on your birthday. She's kinda petty, when it comes down to it. And she didn't think too much of me living with my mom. But hell, I haven't even started working yet. The opening in survival gear doesn't start till July first. She didn't understand that either. She just didn't understand me at all. So, ah, we just fizzled out."

"I would've thought she'd be more compassionate," I said.

"By the way, that was pretty nervy what you did today—not nailing Joe J, he was putty in your hands—but about your folks."

"Yeah, thanks. Should've done it before."

"It's all people were talking about. I saw people just standing on the sidewalk reading your newspaper."

"Well, I'm not planning any more editions," I said as Brian joined us. "They'll get the scoop on Joe J tomorrow."

"Oh, yeah. Art Meyer came by the office, but you'd already left," said Brian. "He said the town council fired Joe J. And then he said Officer Merritt brought his badge to the station. And get his—Judge Shelton put off his hearing till morning, so even the FBI couldn't spring him. He'll be stewing in jail all night."

"Planning his revenge on me." I said.

"Well, you probably went too far in punishing him," said Brian.

"Ah, hell no," said Zane. "That hot-head got what he deserved."

Brian looked peeved the rest of the night, but I couldn't help that. The impromptu party lasted longer than I wanted. Brian wasn't interested in making love, still annoyed at my bravado in subduing Joe and perhaps in Zane's support. I was disappointed when he didn't budge from the edge of the bed, but it gave me the chance to think about Beulah's narrative. Sleep took me before I could grasp anything concrete.

If Brian was irritated with me, he got over it once we went to my obstetric appointment the next morning. When we returned to the office, he sought out Gus and Glenda and anybody who would listen to him say, "We heard the heartbeat today!"

I was excited, but I got a particular kick out of his joy. Well into my fifth month, I was starting to swap my normal dress slacks for ones with elastic waistbands. As I was watching Brian, Glenda pressed a note into my hand. It was a call I expected.

I shut the door then dialed the number to Robert Foxworthy of the Denver FBI.

"I warned you, but you didn't listen," I said, preparing to play my ace.

He insisted I drop the charges against Joe, but I refused.

"What do you want?" he asked.

"I want him gone or incarcerated—somewhere he can't get me. And he will try. By the way, he now has two restraining orders against him. If he comes within five hundred feet of me or my client, Hank Eldritch, he'll be back in jail."

"Dammit, Megan."

"Oh, you know he brought this on himself. But listen, there is one deal I will make—I'll drop all the charges against Joe if you commit the necessary resources for finding the bodies of Mary and Julie Quinn. You know they pulled the van out of the lake and that this is a case the FBI never solved."

Long pause.

"You think about it. Oh, and do you have an undercover cowboy out here named Tony?"

"How'd you know? Did he give himself away?"

"I've never seen him...I just know how you operate. This time you knew better than to tell my uncle."

Chapter 19

I spent the next day, Saturday, catching up on work at the office. Sunday afternoon, I sat in the War Room, trying to grasp what happened at the last Quinn party. Beulah didn't see or hear what happened, but she thought something did or she wouldn't have made a point of telling me about that evening. So, maybe Julie was the one who was upset. Did she have sex or was she raped? If so, by whom? Bert and drunken men were in the area, as was my dad--he had dirt on his knees, he beat up Sean Quinn, he was a young male, fifteen, and just starting to get really horny. Did I know that boy? And then there was Bert, who was a truant and a bully, but was kind to Mary and Julie Quinn despite their aversion toward him. None of it helped me to understand the characters in this horror story, except that Julie may have been deceitful, maybe even cruel.

I studied each of the poster boards. By now, my mom or Patty had found photos for every person—short, tall, fat, skinny, and those in between. The one sentiment everyone agreed on was that Walt Bolger wasn't the kind of guy that would murder two women. Yet he'd been in jail or prison for forty-five years as of this July. He argued with his wife, it had been a rocky marriage, yet Ellie never divorced him, even after his conviction.

Beulah's narrative did succeed in shifting my focus to the younger generation. Patty, here on a day off, stopped in the doorway.

"Somethin' new?" she asked.

"Nah," I said, not even looking back at her. "Just thinking."

Her footsteps retreated down the hallway. Maybe it wasn't possible to understand more than the War Room crew and the original police investigators knew. Still, Walt didn't drive the van, those weren't his clothes, and the van was at the house just before Walt would have arrived. Walt had protected someone all these years—sons were likely candidates, but they had alibis. I needed to clear my head and get out of this creepy room.

I saddled Strider as Rohan protested his neglect. Then I remembered my promise not to ride without protection, so I called Bill and let him know I was riding. Strange thing, I hadn't even thought about asking Brian to ride with me. This was a time to think and then to clear the mind—he didn't understand. He thought we needed to chat all the time. He always *needed*. Sometimes I found it necessary to be alone. Maybe that's why I'd kicked him out of my bathroom and gave him his own dressing room, closet, and bathroom. And right now, I wanted to be alone, in the intimacy of my family's desolate land.

Out in the wind, we galloped in the smooth pasture land. We didn't go onto the rough land, for that took too much concentration. I went over Beulah's narrative once again. Then a gust of wind hit me so hard I grabbed onto the saddle horn and ducked low. When the wind abated, I straightened myself in the saddle. As if the gust had taken it all away, I needed to let go of the details, a hard thing for an attorney to do. But it was clear—go back to motive—it was the key to everything. And I still didn't know it.

The next afternoon, the movers brought the Meyer files. Melanie herded the burly, sweaty men like cattle, insistent that the files be set up in alphabetical order, as I instructed her. As soon as the cabinet with the Bolger files was unloaded, I started perusing the file at the big Meyer desk. Nearly all of it was business in nature, purchases, sales, and leases of sections of land; contracts for the purchase of cattle, machinery, trucks. Soon, I was yawning despite the continuing bustle of the movers. Glenda brought down coffee and a cinnamon roll, for I didn't want to leave the file unattended.

The caffeine and sugar did help as I worked my way to 1968. I located the bill of purchase for the Ford pickup Bert bought on July 5, 1968. The copy indicated the sale was finalized at 2:20 p.m. Either he had been indecisive or he lied about when he arrived at the car lot. Then I found the record of a sale by Ellen Bolger of a 1961 Chevrolet station wagon at 1:45 p.m. She needed to sell her car so Bert could buy the truck. It also put them at the car lot around the time they claimed, maybe a few minutes later. It was a twenty-minute drive to Sidney. I felt disappointed. Bert was an evil man—I'd felt certain he was involved.

After that, the file changed to one of disaster. Art Meyer didn't represent Walt on the criminal charges because he didn't handle criminal law cases. The original attorney disappeared after the family filed for bankruptcy in 1969. Most of the land was sold, except for the rough area to their north, an area of rocky ridges and gullies much like my backyard. No one probably bid on that land. Ellie and the three boys were left with the house, a barn, the Ford pickup Bert bought with his mother as co-signor, and a Ford station wagon. She'd replaced the one she sold, though I didn't see any purchase record for that vehicle. After the bankruptcy, a new defense lawyer was listed, probably a public defender. Yet the file contained notes taken by Art, so he was working with the family to help them stay afloat. The family finances then stabilized, probably when Bert started working for Smokey in the repair shop. The family no longer needed or wanted Art's aid, so the file ended in 1972 with a record of another pickup purchase, this time from Smokey, with Clay Bolger as the buyer and Ellen as the co-signer.

I looked up to discover that the movers and Melanie were gone. I walked into the room and noted the well-organized double row of file cabinets. I located the Quinn file and returned to the desk. After several minutes, Brian cleared his throat.

"I think it's time you quit," he said. "These will be here tomorrow. It's almost five and I'm ready to go home."

"No, I'll stay and call somebody for a ride home."

"You're obsessed. It's time to quit."

"I disagree. Goodbye."

I looked back down at the file. So what if it's nearly five o'clock? We usually worked past then. He said something else, but I was busy sorting through the records of deeds. Brian huffed then started walking back and forth in front of the desk. At some point he left, but I didn't notice because I'd found the will of Sean Daniel Quinn. I skipped to the last page which indicated it was signed, witnessed, and notarized on March 16, 1965. I went back to the first page which bequeathed all his assets and land to his wife, Mary, if she survived him; if she didn't survive him then the estate would pass to Julie A. Quinn and Bert R. Bolger, equally.

Holy cow! Motive!

I read it again. My blood pressure rocketed to the outer stratosphere. I raced through the file until I found the will for July 5, 1968. But this will omitted Bert. The property upon Sean's death would go to Mary, if alive, otherwise to Julie and only Julie. Why the change and on that day? The appointment wasn't booked until eight in the morning of that day. And the will was never signed, witnessed, or notarized, even though Art writes a note to "RUSH" the will. The secretary was to hurry up and type out the will, probably for that day. Wait—Sean never returned to the law office because his wife and daughter had been murdered and his home set on fire. Art hadn't remembered the 1965 will, nor had he reviewed the files before he sent them to me. The next will was properly attested and dated July 10, 1968, giving all his property to two cousins.

I skimmed through the file to make sure nothing else of importance existed. Then I locked the files in the cabinets and then I secured the room. Upstairs, I called Zane for a ride and an invitation to supper. Then I called Mom and asked her to invite the crew along with Beulah, Hank, and Lew for supper and a War Room meeting. I extended my own invitation to Trooper Warren Merritt.

I was too anxious to eat—my gut feeling was now vindicated. I paced the hallway in front of the War Room while the others ate. At one point, my mom, yeah, I could now call her Mom in front of anyone, put a napkin and a ham sandwich in my hand. Patty gave me a glass of water on my next pass. I ate and drank, the slab of ham was warm—we must be having ham for supper—and my mom swept up my crumbs. Brian looked at me and scowled. Go to hell. My mom understood, why couldn't he? Zane had driven me home and let me think in silence. Brian would have scolded me about something. He thought I was too intense. Playing Husker football must've been intense, but that was over ten years ago for him. What would he ask next—that I should shutter the law firm and become a stay-at-home mom? With Mom and Patty here, the child would be far from neglected. I planned to come home for lunch to nurse then go back to work. He or she would wake up every afternoon with Beulah's beady blue eyes peering into the crib.

Babies. Oh, I dearly wanted one. Bert was once a baby. He'd been Ellie and Sean's baby, yet Sean neglected, probably even denied him, apart from the 1965 will. Did Walt know? Had it been a quickie fling? Ellie was only a teen, preyed on by an older man, well five or six years older, I needed to check the board, no, five was right. Then Ellie quickly married Walt, probably only a month or so later. My brain and my bones told me I was right.

As Officer Merritt hadn't arrived and supper was eaten quickly, Bill and Zane made a dash to Shavers for more root beer and vanilla ice cream. Meanwhile, I escorted Beulah, Hank, and Lew into the War Room. They walked around, studying the boards. Beulah stopped at the Quinn board where she reached out and touched one of Julie's photographs. Three quick sobs shook her then she lifted her head as Hank put his arm around her. The doorbell rang. James and Brian brought in additional chairs for the extended group. Merritt came in, stopped by each board then sat down as Bill and Zane took their seats.

"The one thing that's been missing all along has been the motive for the killings," I began. "Today, I believe I found it."

I discussed the three wills, which made some nod in understanding, but made others scrunch their brows or scratch their heads. Meanwhile, Mom took notes.

"So, we have young Ellie McCracken, age sixteen, impregnated by Sean Quinn, who people often described as a womanizer. But he spurns her, so she is forced to go after Walt Bolger so her child would be legitimate. That was a rough marriage with plenty of bickering. Bert was born then another son four years later. But Sean neglects Bert, maybe even denies that he's his son. Sean marries Mary Thornton and Julie is later born. Bert tries to be nice to Mary and Julie by doing work for them, but Sean ignores him."

Both Hank and Beulah nod.

"Bert probably never knew Sean put him in the first will. Meanwhile, Ellie is angry and resentful of the Quinn prosperity. But time passes, Bert becomes a young man, one whose father rejects him, and it begins to eat away at him. He becomes an angry man. Then the Fourth of July party approaches. Bert steals a blue Chevy van from Kimball—"

"Wait," said Brian, "how does he get there?"

"Mommie Dearest. They've become an ultra-sinister version of Uriah and Mrs. Heep. Bert hides the van overnight, maybe in one of the bigger gullies of their wasteland north of their house, which is like the area north of this house. Something happens at the party, probably to Julie by or with Bert…she was upset…use your imagination. It angers Sean so much he makes an appointment first thing the next day, July fifth, with Art Meyer to make a new will omitting Bert as a beneficiary."

"But Bert has an alibi," said Brian.

"A partial one. Ellie tells the police that she gave Walt and Bert lunch at twelve-fifteen. That's either a lie or lunch was never served. Clay and Andy were playing in the tunnels on the Quinn land. Bert gets the van, drives over to the Quinn house where the blue van is seen by a witness over the lunch hour and shortly before the fire."

"I don't have that information," said Merritt.

"It's new. That witness would like to avoid being named if possible. So the van is there. The murders are committed. Meanwhile, Ellie tells Walt what Bert plans to do. Walt rushes over to the Quinns, but he's too late. All he can think to do is burn down the house to destroy the evidence against his son. As Bert puts the bodies in the van and drives away, Walt starts the house on fire, but is caught quickly. Bert hides the van and Ellie picks up Bert and they drive to Sidney. Ellie is forced to sell her car so Bert can buy a pickup. The sale and purchase transactions place them in Sidney at the time the fire is still being investigated. It's all quite possible if you realize Ellie is a part of the scheme and lies about the time of lunch. She sends Walt out after Bert, knowing Walt will probably get caught. Ellie and Bert avenge the wrong Sean did them by killing the two people Sean loved the most. His spirit is beaten, so he sells his land and leaves."

"What about the bodies?" asks Beulah.

"Bert hid them then he ditched the van in Lake McConaughy even before the police knew to look for the van in connection to the murders. Bert chucks the murder weapon in the big lake. He figures the van will never be found, so he takes his bloody clothes and leaves them in a plastic trash bag that he sinks with the van. The trouble is the plastic bag preserves the clothes, to some extent—and they aren't Walt's size. Bert moves the bodies probably more than once to evade the searches in the area. So Walt confesses to the fire that he set, but denies the murders he didn't commit. He refuses to give up his son."

"Do you think Walt knew Bert wasn't his natural son?" asked Bill.

"He probably figured it out. If Walt wanted to protect his son completely, he would have confessed to stealing the van and killing the women earlier in the day and hiding the bodies. Maybe he was giving Bert the option of confessing to the murders, but Bert never did."

"Walt and Bert never looked alike," said Bill.

"No, it's rather obvious that Clay and Andy look like Walt with the stocky build and hairy arms. Bert is lean and pale like Sean, though all three sons have noses like Ellie."

"Bert was always a mean kid, but nowadays he helps out over at the Breeley and Zimmer ranches for several hours each week and never takes a dime," said Bill.

The group becomes quiet as they contemplate the information.

"Why has Joe J been on your case?" asked Beulah.

"Because he knows someone around here is his father, but he didn't know whom. Then he hears about the rape rumors, but those never involved him or his mother. If someone was raped, it was probably Julie, but perhaps not. We'll never know unless someone confesses. But Joe just thought I knew it all or would find out before him. It also made him angry that the reason he stayed on here as police chief became so obvious, but that was his own clumsiness."

Officer Merritt stood up. "You've made some interesting points. Evidence is an issue. I will add that Walt was caught because he had two flat tires, which had been punctured, probably by a knife."

"So, Ellie or Bert wanted him caught. And I agree that evidence is a problem," I said. "But maybe there's enough to help Walt earn parole in August."

"I'll be going," he said.

Patty left to walk him to the door. When she returned the room was still silent. Beulah gave me a slow, sad nod.

"But now you've fingered Bert as the murderer...he's bound to hear about it," said Brian.

"So, how about some root beer floats?" I said.

"I got to get out of this room," said Beulah.

The group slowly rose and drifted out into the hall. Zane stayed in his seat grinning at me. Brian was looking out the window. If he scowled long enough would his face stay that way? I followed Mom out of the room. She took my hand as we stood in the hallway.

"I'm worried for you," she said.

"I am, too. I called Jackson, the elder on the Pine Ridge Reservation. He said they would hide me if I needed help."

People ate their floats and drank bourbon as they milled about the main level. An hour after he left, Officer Merritt called. Patty gave the phone to me. I listened, thanked him, and then went to the family room to announce that Bert Bolger had been arrested.

That night, I lay awake in bed for hours. Brian was a still mass beside me, but I could tell from his breathing that he didn't go to sleep for quite a while. The floorboards creaked in the hall outside our bedroom—my mom wasn't sleeping either. Maybe I'd done this wrong, but I thought the crew and other interested parties deserved to hear my theory. But even if I'd told only Merritt, Bert would still get arrested and he'd somehow blame me. In the morning, I'd call Ernie and Art and tell them. James offered to call Derek and Vonny, who he'd kept informed of the investigation. The new SUV wouldn't arrive till later in the week, but the Shark was parked in the garage, its repairs now completed, so at least I had transportation if I needed it. Should I leave now for the rez? I could sneak away to avoid putting anyone else in danger. I trusted Jackson to hide me, but it rubbed against my grain to run.

Father Almighty, please keep that bastard in jail. Oh, sorry about the language, but I was frightened. Yet I lacked that intense, queasy sense of foreboding when danger was close—so maybe I still had some time.

Later Mary and Julie's screams jolted me awake, convincing me that I'd done what was necessary to preserve my sanity and find peace. How could I be a good mother if shrieking women haunted me?

Chapter 20

I awoke in a sweat at five, my heart hammering the walls of my chest. I stumbled to my bathroom to choke down some cold water. Fear throbbed in my veins and made me dizzy. I spent the next hour sitting in a chair, envying Brian's blissful, ignorant sleep. At six, I called Zane from my bathroom to warn him. I struggled to eat a piece of toast as my mom looked on.

Before Brian and I left for work, I took my mom by the shoulders and said, "Stay close, stay alert."

At work, I did my best not to alarm anyone. I'd done that before, alarming my staff and destroying office productivity for the day. So I kept my nose in a book or stared at the blurry words on the computer screen. Suddenly, my pulse quickened. I started making calls—first to Bill, and then to James. I was concerned Bert might go after Mom, so cowhands were dispatched to keep watch. Within a few minutes, James parked his truck across the street. At noon, Brian and I went across the street to James.

"Why aren't we driving? You look out of sorts," said Brian. "Why is James here?"

I nodded to James and we walked onward. Getting in a car would trap me, maybe that didn't make sense, but I didn't want to get gunned down stuck between two men—I needed to be able to run. And if Bert was watching, he'd be looking for Brian's Jeep. We walked two blocks in silence, though Brian kept looking at me. As we neared Custer's, dread hit me so hard I bent over and gasped for air.

"Are you okay?" Brian asked.

"He's out," I said, straightening, mindful that I needed to stay alert.

My phone rang, I handed it to Brian as I switched my purse to my right shoulder. I slipped my hand into my purse and grasped the handle of my gun. The strange bulge of a gun handle at the back of Brian's blazer reassured me that he was ready.

"That was Trooper Waters. He says Clay Bolger posted bail, so Bert was released a half hour ago. Merritt is on his way."

James was following in his truck, I didn't want to ride, though a big part of me wanted to run, but I was wearing two inch heels. Now, if I could summon the courage to calm my pounding heart enough, maybe we could make it across the street to Custer's and form an army. Just before I reached the corner, I knew I would never make it that far.

"He's here," I said.

I sensed the need to turn left as I came to the corner of the brick building.

He was right in front of me, so close I could smell his jail breath and the stench of his pants. My heart pounded. I needed reinforcements. Talk, I told myself, though pleasantries seemed ridiculous as I stood facing a man who probably wanted to kill me.

"Hey, Bert, you smell like urine…get a scare spending the night in jail?" I said.

"You're a real smartass. I was just comin' to get that steak you promised me."

The traffic on the street stopped and people began to gather around us. A block behind Bert, Zane sprinted down the sidewalk. Something was running down his face.

"Is that so? Good idea. They won't serve you steak in prison."

Bert scowled. Stall, I must stall. Brian was standing beside me, but I needed Zane.

"You killed Mary and Julie. Why, Bert?"

"Because I hated them. Too bad I never found Sean…I'd have done him, too."

"How could you let Walt rot in prison all these years? Were you punishing him because he wasn't really your father?"

"Bitch!"

Bert's left hand reached back then came forward as the switchblade flicked open. I caught his wrist with my left hand.

"You're a bit slow, old man."

Brian raised his gun and barked, "Back off!"

Bert looked from Brian's gun to his face then sneered. I yanked my gun from my purse. Bert reached forward and grabbed my neck with his right hand. I could feel his big, greasy thumb press down, just as his left hand came forward. I wasn't strong enough to stop his knife, so I fired.

Tearing. Falling. The sign for the dry cleaners above me. Blurring. Empty hand. Gunshots, many. Searing.

Blackness.

Lights. Tubes. Numbers flashing. A form beside me.

"Where am I?"

"Boulder, Colorado."

"Do I have a room with a view?"

"Not in ICU."

"Am I murdered?"

Blackness. Panic so deep, as deep as I go, down to the core.

"Stat!"

Whiteness. Jolting. Blackness.

The swirling water rose over my head. Violently tossed about in the darkness, I reached my hand above me, but nobody took it. As I foundered, I reached out my hand into the blackness below, but no little hand reached back. I struggled back to the surface, back to the light, out of the maelstrom. I knew.

A room with wires and tubes hanging down. Red lights. A squiggly green line on a box. A stent taped to the back of my hand. Tube at my nose. In a hospital. Forms approached. I closed my eyes to think.

I lived. She didn't.

I could feel the tears run down my jaw and drip onto my neck.

"Megan."

I opened my eyes and said, "She's gone."

"Yes."

I turned to the voice. It was my mom, but she wasn't quite in focus. She squeezed my arm. Bill and Brian stood on the other side of the bed. Bill's warm hand was in mine.

"My head is floating," I said.

Uncle Bill said, "Just rest."

"Where am I? This isn't Sidney."

"Colorado," said Brian. "And sorry, no view from this room."

I looked at him. "What? Make sense. I'm tired. Where in Colorado? Never mind, I don't care. Brian, our girl is gone."

The tears started again. Beeping. Two forms in aqua came in. They were in a hurry. Why? They pushed Brian and Bill away. I stared at the ceiling.

No big brown eyes. No dimples. No smiles. Nothing. Gone forever.

"You must rest," said a voice.

"You had surgery, hon," said my mom.

"Oh," I said. "Gonna sleep." And I did.

Later pain woke me. I coughed and that hurt. I looked around for water, though I didn't feel like moving. Mom came to my side.

"What do you need?" she asked.

"Water."

She poured me water in a beige plastic cup and I drank several swallows.

"Do I eat?"

"Just through a tube."

"Don't feel hungry. Who's here?"

"Just me in the room. They let me spend the night in that recliner."

"Oh, is it night?"

"It's about midnight. Brian will be here at six."

"Mom, my baby is dead."

"Yes, she is."

I thought about the knife and the hand on my throat. "Bert stabbed her?"

"Yes."

"Did I kill him?"

"Yes."

"Heard lots of gunshots."

"Brian says Zane came and just kept shooting Bert till the bullets were gone. He's here. He brought Beulah and Patty."

I knew the answer to my next question: "I almost died, didn't I?"

"Yes, hon."

Tears formed in her eyes.

"How'd I get here?"

"By helicopter from Sidney."

"Really? So, what day is this?"

"Thursday."

"Oh. And what day did…?"

"That was Tuesday."

"And I killed Bert and Bert killed my baby. We didn't even have a name…we didn't know…but I know…she was a girl…a girl with no name."

The tears came and so did an aqua form.

"Just call her Sweetie."

The tears kept coming, but I smiled at her. My mom lifted the oxygen tube and wiped my nose for me. I would never hear her voice, not even in the wind.

"Hon, I'm so sorry." She kissed me on the cheek. "It's time for you to go back to sleep."

"I hurt."

"This will help," said the short aqua.

It did. Just as I began to float away, I saw my dad's face. No one would doubt him now.

The next day, visitors were allowed in my room, though Mom and Brian were always around. Brian didn't say much, just a few comforting words. Just after lunch, Bill and Patty came in then Beulah and James. Then Zane, Derek, and Vonny were permitted in after my lunch of red Jell-O. Zane had a bandage on his forehead.

"What happened to you?" I asked.

"I had a run-in with Bert. My Pathfinder smashed into a tree on Elm Street."

"I'm glad he's dead," I said.

"Lots of people are," he said. Then he looked down at his feet and back up. "I'm so sorry I didn't get there in time. I'm just sick about it."

I just nodded. What could I say? My brain was whirling with drugs and heartache, so articulate thought became impossible.

Later the doctor came in. He had black and gray hair, silver glasses, and an enormous head. "We'll be backing you off some of your meds. We'll move you to a private room after breakfast tomorrow."

"Was I stabbed just once?"

"Yes," he said.

Bill and Patty came and stood next to me.

"What killed the baby?"

"The knife."

"But she would've been so little."

He nodded. "You suffered tremendous blood loss. You have quite a few internal and external stitches. You also received a blood transfusion."

My brain worked hard to absorb the information. "Is she...ah...out?"

"Yes, along with the placenta. That was all taken care of during surgery."

"Do I still have my uterus?"

"Yes, you do. You'll make a complete recovery and your uterus will heal and become functional."

Great, I'll be functional. I closed my eyes; I wanted everyone to go away. My baby took a knife for me. My Sweetie saved my life. That's not how it's supposed to be. I'm supposed to die for my child, that's what a parent should do. It was beyond understanding. I nearly died—I comprehended that more because I still felt it deep inside where I was weak and afraid. My near death left a wound. Sweetie's death left an abyss.

Chapter 21

I was glad to get out of ICU and get unhooked from the IV and other machines. My new room did have a view of the mountains. It also allowed unlimited visitors. When I needed to be alone, I simply shut my eyes, then most people would leave and those remaining became quiet. I was suddenly delicate—how I hated that and the tragedy that kept me weak. I vowed to overcome my frailty; though, I wondered if I'd ever recover from the loss of my girl.

I opened my eyes. James stood against the wall, looking particularly sad. So I asked him to recite Psalms Twenty-Three. He recited it two years ago in our basement as a tornado raged overhead.

"Of course, anything," he said. "The Lord is my shepherd; I shall not want; he makes me lie down in green pastures. He leads me beside the still waters. He restores my soul; he leads me in paths of righteousness for his name's sake. Even though I walk through the valley of the shadow of death, I fear—"

"I died," I announced, as much to myself as to others. "I know I did."

James dropped his jaw into his lap.

"What?" asked Brian with clear annoyance in his voice.

"It's true," said Mom. "I was hoping you didn't know. It was right when we got to Colorado. I was with you in the ER before surgery. Brian, you left to check her in." She paused, her face strained. "All of a sudden there were all these machines beeping and more staff rushed into the room. They put those paddles on you twice before you came back. Then they asked me your blood type."

"How long was I gone?"

"It seemed like forever…not even a minute…not nearly enough for brain damage they said later, ah, after the operation."

"Since Miggy has a way of getting into these situations, maybe you should tell all of us her blood type," said Derek with a smirk.

Mom smiled. "A positive. Size six shoe. Size small gloves."

Bill and James chuckled.

"Size of head—jumbo," said Brian.

If that was supposed to be funny, it failed, landing with a thud.

Vonny gave Brian a cutting look then turned back to me. "So do you remember being dead? What was it like?"

James and Beulah stepped forward; Brian leaned back against the wall.

"It went white. It had been black. The knife tore into me and I pulled the trigger and then blackness…I remember now. No idea about time. Then it was white. Then it went to blackness again. White…that's all I saw…didn't see anything…but I saw it clear…I didn't feel anything…I didn't feel pain like when I woke up here…here I feel my body. I'm sorry none of that makes sense."

No, it didn't make sense—I was Dorothy trying to explain Oz.

"Heh! Makes sense to me," said Beulah. "Yeah, white, no pain, no pain. That doesn't sound bad to me."

James came to my bedside, "Don't you worry. We didn't let that killer get buried in our cemetery. Everybody was stirred up about it. You can still go there like you do sometimes and know only friends and loved ones."

I nodded.

Beulah wrapped her hand over my shoulder. "You remember—your girl, your Sweetie—no pain, no pain."

"I need some air." Brian yanked open the door and left.

I kept looking at Beulah; my tears came, but I smiled.

"I'm sorry, would you continue, James?" I asked.

"I fear no evil; for thou art with me; for thy rod and thy staff they comfort me. Thou preparest a table before me in the presence of my enemies; thou anointest my head with oil, my cup overflows. Surely goodness and mercy shall follow me all the days of my life; and I will dwell in the house of the Lord forever."

I nodded. "Now I think I need a nap."

"I'm gonna go check on Brian," said Derek.

I closed my eyes. Yeah, my friend, you check on my husband. I didn't understand his behavior, nor did it keep me awake.

For supper, they gave me green Jell-O, joy of joys, and some chicken broth. I wasn't going to miss that damn stent driven into the back of my hand. Yeah, there's lots of veins to stick, but there's also bones and nerves. Two of those aqua nurses came in then shooed everyone out except my mom. It was the first time I'd been awake to see them change my bandage. My belly looked shrunken and wrinkled, now with a four-inch gash in the middle, a bit to the right. I guess they had to enlarge the knife wound to get to my girl and to stitch up my other parts. Oh, yeah, that knife was a long sucker—the thought of it made me shudder.

I looked up at Mom and said, "I guess my bikini days are over."

Her faced flushed with emotion as she attempted a smile.

Aqua instructed my mom on wound care; I didn't really listen as the medication the nurse gave me was kicking in. I fought sleep, certain that'd I see Brian's face above mine any second, but he didn't come and I drifted away.

When I awoke, everyone was back. They had to be bored, so I suggested we try and find a baseball game.

My mom came to my bedside. "Hon, I want to tell you that they're keeping Sweetie for you—if you and Brian want a funeral."

I looked over to Brian and he nodded.

"Yes, but back home," I said.

"James and I can help with that," said my uncle. "We'll make the arrangements."

"Okay," I said then I nodded to James.

He picked up the remote and found a Rockies game. After a few minutes, Brian left and Derek followed. Zane scowled until he noticed I was looking at him then he smiled at me.

Then an aqua walked in, I was starting to notice them, this one was short, middle-aged, and Asian Indian.

"The reporters are still here," she said. "Do you want to talk to them?"

"No, never." I turned to my mom. "Maybe we need to reissue another entry of the *Dexter Gazette*."

"Charge a buck a piece and you'll fund our food bank," said Patty.

I nodded. Patty walked over to Mom and they started talking quietly.

"I'll take care of them," said Zane. He left with the nurse.

Just then a chime sounded in the hall.

"What's that?" I asked.

"End of visiting hours," said my mom. "We all need to leave, but Patty and I can help you to the restroom first."

Everyone said their goodnights and left. Mom and Patty helped me untangle myself from the bed sheets and slide down to the floor. It was pathetic that I needed help, but I still felt "puny" as Beulah called it. The doctor told me I could go home when I could walk on my own, so that was my goal.

The next morning, Vonny came into my room alone, a few minutes before visiting hours.

"There's something I need to tell you," she said. "Brian keeps leaving because he wants to go drink."

"I don't blame him. I'm sure when I get off these drugs I'll want a big Jim Beam Black on the rocks."

"Oh, that's not strange…we all hung out at the hotel bar last night. But it's what Derek says that bothers me. He says Brian is very upset, but all he talks about is the baby. He's even mad that you knew the gender and he had to ask the doctor if you were right."

"Well, he's just not worried about me. I'm okay…or I will be. I bet I feel a lot better once I get home."

"I'm sure you're right," she said.

"I know you're trying to warn me. I appreciate it."

She squeezed my hand as an orderly walked into the room and set a vase of various flowers on the window sill, next to a long row of fragrant color in clear or white vases, then left.

"I haven't been on Facebook in ages," I said. "How would this post read? How about—'Hi from sunny Colorado. I'm on drugs cuz I almost died and my baby did. Sad face. And I killed another man. Third year in a row. But I'll be home soon. Happy face.' Do you think I'll get any Likes?"

"How much morphine do they have you on?"

"Not enough, maybe. Hey, will you help me off this bed…it's a hell of a drop."

Vonny kept me from sliding off the side of the bed too fast. I steadied myself then took small steps toward the restroom with her help.

"This robe hangs on you like a muumuu."

"Thanks. Hey, will you help me wash my hair? Otherwise, all I get are sponge baths."

The shampooing was successful yet exhausting. I was asleep with my head still in a towel when Robert Foxworthy arrived. I awoke to a broad-shouldered African American man in his fifties and my Dexter support team. Brian walked in during our discussion.

"We think the State will move up Walt's parole hearing," said Robert. "He'll likely be paroled since you managed to get a confession out of Bert. It's hard to say if there will be a new trial. It may depend on whether Walt pushes for one."

"Brian, the FBI has agreed to a deal I made," I said. "I'll drop charges against Joe if the FBI agrees to provide resources to help find the bodies of Mary and Julie."

"Well, hell," he said. "I thought you were done with this. I mean, it's great for Walt, but c'mon. Where's Sean? Let him find the bodies."

"I wasn't asking your permission."

"That would be a shock."

I felt as if we'd unleashed our first arrows at each other. What would it be like when we were alone? The machine for my blood pressure beeped and revved up, the numbers rising with each moment. I flicked the Off button on the side of the blue metal box. I hated that my distress was being broadcast to the whole room.

"You missed the doctor, again. They'll probably release me tomorrow morning. Maybe you should go back early and make sure everything's in order at home and at the firm. I'm sure you have plenty of work to catch up on."

"Yeah, maybe," he said as he rose.

"You can drink at home."

He stared at me for a moment then walked out the door.

I tried to divert the conversation as quick as possible to save face, so I asked Robert, "Will you be setting up an office in Dexter?"

He answered in the affirmative, but my mind shifted to Brian and the sound of those wailing women. What a jerk.

Yet Brian did leave after lunch. The room felt different after he left—we were more relaxed, no longer concerned whether something would set him off. I wished he was here supporting me, but I had a room full of people ready to do that. Beulah began telling stories about her siblings that made us all laugh. However, I discovered laughing made my guts hurt, so I restrained myself as well as I could. Nobody said it, but we all knew we were better without him. How long would that take to change?

I awoke from one of my many naps to discover the gang had left for supper. They all joked about the lousy hospital cafeteria food, so they left for town. I guess it's all about perspective, for I thought my food tasted good; then again, I'd been fed through a tube for three days—was it three? I couldn't worry about that for I needed to head to the restroom. Someone tapped at the door. Zane's head poked around the door.

"Oh, you're awake," he said.

"Yeah, come in." I was wishing it was Mom or Patty or Vonny, but I didn't hear them coming. Dang. "Um—"

In a flash he was at the side of my bed, looking eager to get me something.

"I need to make a pit stop and it's a long drop down," I said.

"Oh, sure."

I gingerly swung my legs to the side of the bed.

"I'm afraid to touch you. What should I do?"

"Here, lean forward and I'll put my hands on your shoulders and lower myself down."

"Okay, I'm ready."

My feet landed on the cold linoleum, but I kept my hands on his shoulders to steady myself. Last year Zane kissed me when his brother convinced me to go rouse him from his PTSD funk. The strange impulse to kiss him right then hit me, so I dropped my head. I felt his gaze on my face.

"I'm okay now."

Even as I shuffled toward the restroom, I could still feel his shoulders in my hands and my face flushed warm. Surely, I was longing for Brian. He had strong shoulders like that, too. When I emerged, Bill and Mom were standing together against the wall. Getting down from the high bed was tricky, getting back in was even worse. But after four days, Uncle Bill knew what to do—he scooped me up and gently deposited me on the bed. Mom helped me get back under the covers.

My gang stayed till visiting hours ended. I was more than ready for sleep. After they left, I plunged into a deep sleep. But it didn't last—with the decrease in the potency of my drugs came heightened awareness of my dreams. I panicked at the sensation that I was going under, but there was no stopping my plunge into the black. At first, I saw only the taillights of Brian's Jeep. Then that disappeared and I was falling. Blood left a trail behind me—I was bleeding for her. Looking down, I thought I saw her, but it was only a flash of pink. Five months. She had been more than a flash; she was part of me, a part that died; now I was only a fragment of a person. Was I dying? I could no longer breathe. I reached for Brian's hand in the light, but it wasn't there. Panic, choking. He's gone. She's gone. I'm drowning in the deep with blood pouring out of me. It swirled around me and covered me and washed down my throat. Let go. Let go. She's gone. Then I don't need to face it, face anything or anyone. Just let go—but I can't. I fight back, kicking and clawing my way through the blood. I would save myself—I breathed.

Did I just relive my death?

A dimmed fluorescent light hummed behind me. I was dry and clean and alive. Anger rose up into my chest, into my throat. Why did I live when she died? I would have died for you, Sweetie. Tears drenched my neck. That cursed blood pressure machine beeped, I rolled over to try and shut it off, but the effort sent stabs of pain deep into my gut. Damn nurses—they'd moved it out of my reach. I fumbled for the controls then pressed for the call button. At least they could give me more drugs.

I spent the long night falling. The sight of the sun on the mountains revived me. After breakfast, Zane drove Patty and Beulah home in his mother's SUV. After lunch, a freckled aqua gave Mom and me a lecture and a list of instructions. I was loaded into an ambulance for the trip home with Mom holding my hand. Her left hand was still in an air cast she'd told me she was eager to ditch. Bill and James followed us home in Bill's pickup.

I slept through the first part of the drive. When I awoke, Mom was gazing at me.

"I'm glad you're here," I said.

She smiled as she squeezed my hand. My next comment made her cringe.

"He blames me for her death." She started to say something, but I continued. "I do, too."

"You're both wrong. How could you have known talking to people and making poster boards about two deaths forty-five years ago would lead to your baby's death?"

"But if I hadn't done all that, she'd still be alive," I said.

"You're a lawyer and you've forgotten something very important—foreseeability. Yeah, I know that term. You couldn't have known Bert Bolger would stab you with a switchblade. No more than anyone could have known RT and Chief Dobbs would kill poor Davey. You bear no guilt. None at all."

I quietly pondered her words as the miles rolled by. After a few minutes, Mom cleared her throat.

"Um, there's something I need to tell you," she said. "Bill and I are engaged."

"That's great!"

"He even bought me a ring, but I can't get it on my hand till I get this blasted cast off. We planned to announce it, but things got kind of crazy."

"Crazy, yeah." I held her in my smile. "I'm so pleased for you."

"I wondered for years if I'd ever get the nerve to try marriage again. But Bill is just right for me. I love him. I have for a long time…but I was chicken. I think when you announced our family history it seemed to make us feel free and finally truthful."

"At least something good has come out of this summer. When were you planning to have the ceremony?"

"We'll wait for you, of course. Will you be my matron of honor?"

"I'd love to."

I arrived home with my mother's joy still in my heart. I was incredibly glad to be home. Uncle Bill accepted my congratulations then carried me up the stairs. Once there, I burrowed under my own pillows and plunged into sleep.

Chapter 22

I awoke later that afternoon when my favorite teenager peeked under the pillow at my face. When I smiled, Kayla pulled the pillow off my head. I could tell my motherless friend wanted to hug me, but was uncertain to. So she scooted next to me on the bed and dropped her head on my shoulder.

"I'm so sorry," she said then wept.

The sudden outpouring of emotion sent Patty from the room and made my mom bite her lips. I handed Kayla a couple of tissues.

After Kayla wiped her eyes and nose, she said, "We didn't know if you were gonna make it. But James and Zane kept calling us with updates. Lots of people packed into Custer's and the bar or just stood on the sidewalks waiting for news. Beulah tried to call once, but she got so choked up Patty had to take the phone from her."

"Wanna know something weird?" I asked.

Her eye brows nearly hit her hairline. "What?"

"I did die...just for a minute or so."

"Ohhh! Did you see God?"

"No, it must take longer."

"So, can you walk and stuff?"

"Yeah, I can walk...but I'm probably not ready for stairs. Mostly, I just go to the biffy and back."

"Ha! 'Biffy'—that's what Beulah calls it."

Patty brought a tray into the room. "Okay, Kayla, that's enough for today. Megan needs her meds and some supper."

"Gotta go. I'm glad you're back."

Her exit wasn't as gentle—stabbing pain seared my guts when she bounced off the bed, but I stifled a gasp and gave her a smile.

In the evening, I sat up in my chair for an hour or so. After breakfast in my room and a sitting shower with the aid of a footstool, Brian carried me downstairs where I took up residency on the family room sofa. Kayla read get well and sympathy cards with me. Brian stayed in the background, polite, but quiet. The house was filled with flowers, baked goods, and casseroles. Patty let in a few visitors to see me, but mostly she took the pie or lasagna, thanked them, and then told them I was sleeping. She did allow Jim, Brian's dad from Sidney, to sit next to me on a dining room chair. He said comforting words and asked how I felt. Otherwise, he sat quietly holding my hand. After a half hour, he left for work.

A bit later, I found an opportunity to talk with Zane in private. He sat on the edge of the recliner looking tense.

"Somebody told me you emptied my gun into Bert after I shot him," I said. "What was the deal with that?"

"Just anger...but it felt good. You remember what I told you about that boy when I was stationed in a dinky town north of Kabul, don't you?"

"Yeah, you were chasing down some sniper when one of your shots went through a window and hit that boy."

"It killed him, but not before he could look into my eyes. That sent me over the edge...but I still had missions after that...four of them before we were sent home. I was worthless, couldn't shoot worth crap. It was a jittery mess. So firing into Bert, one shot after the other, right into the enemy's chest...you already blew away his face...it was a bizarre sort of therapy."

"Got your mojo back?"

"Still sick I didn't get there in time to help you."

"Stop worrying about that. I've thought of a hundred things I should have done differently, but it's over."

He leaned toward me and said quietly, "Did you realize Brian has been standing in the hall listening to us? I
could see his shadow, but he's gone now."

"That's strange, I wonder why he didn't come in?"

Zane shrugged.

Before bed, I walked down to the study. All the
boards, stacks of notes, and any piece of evidence of our
investigation were gone. The low western sun cast a golden
hue into the room. It pleased me that the room was once
again our study. I walked over to Brian's desk where the
edge of a yellow sticky note was visible under the office
phone. I slid it out and read: "Jessica Fenton" with a phone
number for Sidney written in Brian's tidy handwriting. I
stuck the note in my jeans pocket, too tired to worry about
it for now.

My nights were better, though I still awoke at least
two or three times with a terrifying notion of drowning or
being covered in blood while I reached my hand out to that
ever elusive flash of pink. Meanwhile, Brian slept in the
dressing room, claiming that he was afraid he'd bump me
during the night.

On Tuesday night, Mom, Bill, Brian, and I drove out
to the cemetery where we met James and Pastor Ryder, the
minister of our dinky Presbyterian church. We stood, well I
sat, around the Docket headstone and the individual marker
for my father's grave. Pastor Ryder said a few words and
read scripture, none of which I heard, for I was too busy
staring at the hole in the ground and trying to keep my head
above the water. When the pastor nodded to James, our
friend handed a sealed silver box to Brian, who knelt down
and placed the box into a small grave, dug three feet down
in a rectangle James made sure was perfect. James then
placed a blue velvet cloth over the top of the silver box.
And it was done.

God in heaven, how could you permit this? I sobbed a
few times then wiped the tears from my face and neck and
dabbed my nose. I rose, stubbornly refusing to shed any

more tears in public. I turned to Brian, expecting him to take my arm and lead me back to his Jeep. Instead, he stared straight ahead then abruptly turned around and strode toward his vehicle. Surprised, I just watched him walk away. The hell with you, buddy. Mom and Bill looked equally stunned. The Jeep charged down the black top at a disrespectful speed.

As Brian had been our driver, we were now stranded, at least till the pastor offered to drive us home. As we left, James began gently scooping dirt into the burial pit with his hands. I stepped over to my dad's grave. Sweetie would be with him in heaven, not me. How bizarre.

At home, Patty and Beulah awaited us in the kitchen.

"Where's Brian?" asked Patty.

"Who knows," Bill said. "He abandoned Megan at Sweetie's graveside."

"Lordy, Lordy," said Beulah, scowling. "If that don't beat all."

Exhausted by the drama of the day, I eased into a kitchen chair. Later Bill carried me upstairs then Mom helped me get ready for bed. I fell asleep before my head hit the pillow.

A few hours later, I awoke to noise. It took my head a few minutes to clear. Then a crashing sound and the spewing of profanities got me out of bed. I put on a robe and went to my door, but didn't open it; instead, I listened. I recognized the voice—it was Big Joe McCready.

"I don't know how many he put away. Johnny Two Rivers called me at home. So Carlos and I brought him here. Bo came, but he let us take him 'cause we promised to make sure he stayed home."

"He was trying to start a fight with Lew and then with anybody he could," said Carlos Hernandez. "Some of Bill's cowhands tried to contain him. But we all feel so bad for him. He gave Bud a hard gut punch. He still wasn't standin' when we left."

"Thank you for bringing him home," said my mom. "Take him to the room on the left. I don't want him disturbing Megan."

"I can walk!" growled Brian. "Let go of me."

I opened the door. Brian yanked his arm from Big Joe's, so he could turn to me.

"It's your fault she's dead!"

There, he finally said it.

Mom stepped between us and said to Brian, "Go to bed. Now."

Carlos and Big Joe both nodded to me then Carlos shoved Brian into the dressing room.

"Mom, don't let him sleep in his contacts."

"Go back to bed, hon."

I nodded and closed the door then I crawled back into bed. Was he right? Yeah, he was. I cried myself back to sleep. Soon, I was plunging back into the watery darkness and searching for a tourniquet for my bleeding.

In the morning, I struggled through a shower then applied a new bandage to my abdomen. In the face of terrible tragedy, two people who loved each other should grieve together; but in his pain, Brian chose to hurt me rather than help me. Was this a chasm we could ever close?

I dressed then stood at my window gazing out over Rufus and Big Leo. I would love to go sit in my Fort atop the bluff, but I wouldn't make it much past the edge of our lawn before I crumpled to the ground. I'd been known to bolt out into the hills in times of distress, now it angered me that I was too weak to even attempt it. I wanted to hear Beverly's voice—she would soothe me.

Sweet Jesus! Had I lost them both? Please God, don't let it be.

At my request, Patty served me breakfast out on the patio. Brian's door had been open when I came down, so I assumed he went to work. Patty and Mom sat out on the patio in silence, waiting for me to talk. We drank iced tea as it was too hot for coffee; soon, it would be too hot for me to stay outside. I was so damn weak. Yet, I recalled so well the fear, the sensation of coming so close to death that exertion scared me. The natural part of me that wanted to force my way back toward strength was subdued.

I thought of Brian. He probably felt like crap this morning. It would have taken a handful of aspirin to quell his hangover so he could work. I'd always thought of us as a team—we did different things well. His strengths were brains and brawn, yet he could show flashes of immaturity, even though he was five years older than me. Would he want to continue punishing me? Reconciliation seemed far away, he barely spoke to me, except now to accuse me.

When we first met, he probably saw me as my father's puppet, the new attorney struggling in a new job. He fell in love with that woman, not the strong, willful one that emerged after my dad's death. Last summer he'd committed adultery. I punished him by kicking him out of my house and life, and by changing my name back to Docket. Months later, I decided I wanted him back, and he came back, penitent and full of love for me. But I knew him well enough to know he'd never reach his hand out to me; he'd continue to punish me—he'd pull me down into the blackness, where the pink flash no longer existed. Then what? Would he ever pull me back to the surface? Maybe he'd just leave me to wallow in the blood.

Later in the week, Gus and Melanie came over in the afternoon to discuss some of my more pressing files. I thanked them for working extra hours to cover for me. As they were gathering the files to leave, Gus cleared his throat then spoke.

"There's something you should know, Megan. People are still stirred up about, well you know, lots of things. But Brian is taking some of the backlash. And Beulah's been telling everyone how he abandoned you at the gravesite, and how he's been leaving you alone to go get drunk every night."

"People have been cancelling appointments with him," said Melanie. "And nobody will sit with him at lunch. Beulah even kicked him out of your booth."

"Well, that's actually true about the drinking, but I wish they wouldn't punish him. It's none of their business."

"Well, everyone thinks the Quinn murder case is their concern, and I can understand that." said Gus. "So, by extension, the deaths of Bert and your baby are their business, too. Brian's behavior is none of their business, you're right, but folks see it as a natural next step. And you know folks around here. They think Megan Docket is their business."

"People are very concerned about you," said Melanie. "I went out to the cemetery last night and well…you need to go see it."

Soon after they left, I convinced Mom and Patty to take me out to the cemetery. The sight stopped us in the middle of the road. From the Docket headstone, twenty feet in every direction, was a sea of bouquets. James had moved the flowers off the new sod so he could water it in. Once I waded into the heap of flowers, I realized flora and note cards weren't the only offerings of sympathy. Dolls, all brown-haired, were nestled in among the bundles of wild flowers and tidy florist shop arrangements. Babies. Little girls. Barbies. I dropped to my knees, scooping up a plastic baby in a pink blanket. My hands shook as I drew her to my chest. I knelt there for fifty thousand hours, my mom's warm hand resting on my shoulder. When I looked up, the family standing off to the side quickly set down their gifts and backed away. Overwhelmed, I wanted to bolt, but realized I'd gone to lead.

"Can you help me up?" I asked, as I placed the doll back in her nest of pink carnations.

Mom placed her hand under my arm, but that didn't budge me, so Patty put her hands under my armpits and yanked. Once on my feet, she placed her hands on the outside of my shoulders, turned me, and then pushed me toward her car.

"I need to buy you some waterproof mascara," said Patty, handing me a tissue.

"I need to collect all these note cards," I said.

"We will, I promise," said my mom, who seemed overcome with emotion.

That night, Brian came in the front door, drunk again. I was still in the family room.

He looked in at me and said, "All those damn dolls have brown hair. Brown! Who do they think the father is?"

I shrugged, I could do that now without it hurting, and said, "Everyone knows dark genes are dominant. Just go to bed."

He growled and stumbled up the back stairs. It was a relief to know he wouldn't be in my bed—I could have my nightmares in peace.

As soon as my head hit the pillow, I went under. Around me floated pink carnations, babies in pink and yellow blankets, dolls in polka dot dresses, Barbies in sequins, even a blond Ken doll and a G.I. Joe. They all sunk with me into the black, until I remembered to breathe. When my head broke the surface, I awoke. No blood—there hadn't been any blood in the water—that heartened me. Brian's persistent absence disheartened me. Wait, had he been there?

The next night, we invited Hank and Lew to supper; Patty told me they'd been asking about me. The men seemed nervous though they both managed to express their condolences.

"We seen the grave," ventured Lew, though he wasn't able to say anything else.

"Bunch of young gals gatherin' cards," said Hank. "I brought a few more." He pulled a handful of cards from his back pocket and set them on the end table. "There's still people comin' out. I saw Dawes County license plates."

"Thank you." What else could I say? As an attorney, I should have been able to say something, if not profound, at least appropriate, but my tongue went to lead.

CRIES IN THE WIND

"I'm glad Bert's dead," said Hank. "I know it ain't respectful to talk bad about the dead, but that's the way I feel. But…um…there's somethin else. Ah, would you be willing to meet Linda? She's mighty grateful that you cleared my name."

Stunned, I nodded. I hadn't been thinking of her, I'd been wrapped up in my own calamitous life.

"And Jackson Draper would like to come see you," said Patty.

I was curious to meet Linda. I thought back to the poster board entry for her. She wouldn't be the eighteen-year-old I'd always pictured; she'd be in her early sixties.

As I was pondering Linda, Brian pushed back his chair and left the dining room. A few minutes later, the door to the garage opened and shut. I avoided Hank and Lew's glances, so nothing was said.

Chapter 23

On Friday morning, Patty brought Laura Meyer into the kitchen as I was finishing breakfast.

"I've tried calling Ellie, but she won't answer," said Laura, "Art and I went out there on Tuesday, but she wouldn't let us in. She has no income at all. The committee tried to deliver food to her on Wednesday, but she chased away first graders—she threw paperback books at them. None of the other poor families have been mean to the little kids." She shook her head and took a sip of tea.

A big part of me wished she would broil in hell, but that wasn't Christian of me, even if I thought she was probably the brains behind Bert's alibi and Walt's capture. With Bert's death and no concrete evidence against her, the State Patrol would let Mrs. Bates live without Norman and rot in her chair.

"So how do we make sure she eats?" I asked.

"Well, yesterday, kids delivered another box—I told them when she takes her nap. I drove by this morning and the box is still there. She can be so stubborn. Maybe she doesn't know it's there."

"Who could take another box of food out there that she'd respect?" I asked.

"Well, she's always a big supporter of the military. She always wanted one of her boys to join the Air Force."

"Zane, of course. I'll give him a call right now."

I called Zane and he agreed; he even said he'd put on his Army dress uniform.

After Laura left, I ventured from the house for the first time. I admired my new Acura in the garage, parked next to the repaired Shark. I had offered the Shark to Patty and she accepted it as an early birthday present. Once I was off drugs, I would start driving my new SUV. But for today, Patty drove Mom and me into town. After we stopped at the clinic to get my stitches removed, we stopped at Art Meyer's old law office, recently converted to headquarters for the digging.

Officer Waters greeted us and brought us into the room. Two women and two men sat at rented banquet tables, typing or studying their laptop screens. One of the women was Trooper Rachel McNeill, a former friend and the mistress of the DEA agent I killed. She looked up at me as I paused. She nodded at me then looked down at her screen. What was there to say? I walked on. At a table with several old county maps were men in their seventies and eighties. One man in a wheelchair looked to be even older.

I gave Officer Waters an inquiring look.

"You'll never see the State Patrol and the FBI working so well together. All these men worked on the Quinn case. You succeeded when they failed."

I wondered if they might be resentful of me, so I started to back away.

"Hey-ooo!" yelled one of the men. He rose to his feet and shuffled over to me, grabbing my hand and giving it a vigorous shake. "I know your face. It's in all the papers. You shoulda been a cop. You even got the battle scar." He pulled on my hand, leading me to the table where all the veteran cops wanted to shake my hand. "I'm Ben Anderson. I was State Patrol back in the sixties and seventies. These are the contour maps of this area."

I introduced my mom and Patty as they walked up to the table. Meanwhile, Ben hung onto my hand. He nodded his head, which featured as many age spots as his hands. I took his gesture as his means of expressing his sympathy. I nodded back to him as he released my hand.

He held up a copy of the Dexter Gazette, volume two, the one my mom put out from Colorado based on my solution of the murders. "Brilliant, this was. Everybody here thinks so."

As I looked over the maps, Officer Waters said, "We're digging out at the old distillery tunnels and the Quinn house shelter. We figured those were good places to start. Officer McNeill will supervise the digging on the Thornton ranch. It makes sense 'cause she grew up there."

I nodded, for it did make sense, though I still thought she was a bitch and a sap. I worked my way around the table to the map of the Docket land. In the center were aerial photos of the various plots of land. I picked up the one of my former playground.

I held up the map to Ben and said, "That's Big Leo. My uncle built a hut for me up there for a Christmas present."

"How old were you when he built that?"

"Twenty-eight."

Ben chuckled.

"I still go out there. It's my backyard."

"Where is that on this map?" asked another elderly volunteer.

I ran my finger from the house to the bluff, Big Leo. "Right here."

To my surprise, he marked it with a black marker. Soon, the man, Lloyd, wrote in the Beast, Pooper's Canyon, Rufus, the Seven Dwarfs, Miss Gulch, the Joker, Strider and Rohan's barn, the old Eldritch barn, and the location of the former Eldritch house, demolished last spring.

"See, this helps us," said Ben. "We need people who really know these areas. Officer McNeill marked her land, too, but her family wasn't nearly as creative as you and your friends."

"Just remember, there's only five buttes in the Seven Dwarfs and I refuse to answer any questions regarding the naming of Pooper's Canyon."

I heard chuckles from around the table.

I wasn't ready for Custer's, physically or emotionally, so we made one more stop before we went home. Patty parked in a lot close to Bill's house. We slowly made our way over the crunchy soil to the barn. Bud was supervising Strider and Rohan's lunch. He took off his hat to us. Then he stepped toward me as we approached the doorway.

"Glad to see you out and about, ma'am, I mean, Megan. Strider's been lonesome without you. Ain't eating as much."

I walked into the barn. Strider and Rohan looked up from their troughs. Strider whinnied and bobbed his head. When I reached my hand out to him, he became still. He dropped his head down and sniffed at me. Rohan snorted. Then Strider gently rested his head against my shoulder.

"They know you're injured," Bud said. "They sense it, they smell it."

I stroked Strider's neck. "Someday, I'll come for you."

When we arrived back at home, Zane was sitting in his mom's SUV in our driveway. He looked shaken. Mom led him into the house. Patty gave him a glass of brandy. He took a swig.

"I went to the Bolger house with one of those food boxes. She didn't answer the door, so I peeked through some gauzy curtains she has in a side window. I could see her sitting in a chair in the front room, so I called the cops. Me and the deputy busted down a side door. The shotgun was still on her lap. She'd put it in her mouth and fired."

Ding dong...the Wicked Witch is dead.

"Oh, Lord!" said Patty. "Maybe we shouldn't be surprised. She could never show her face in town again. She'd have to rely on charity to live."

"I just came from the Meyer house," he said.

"I'm so sorry you had to see that," I said, worried that it would stir up memories of the deaths he saw in battle. "Drink up. Have you had lunch? We were just going to have ours."

He shook his head. I looked to Patty and she started making sandwiches.

"Why don't you stay and watch the Cubs game with us?"

He nodded.

Later that afternoon, Mom came back from a visit to the Meyers' house. I followed her into the hallway.

"The county sheriff has ruled it a suicide. Laura says they'll bury Ellie with Bert. There's a cemetery out in Banner County that took Bert, with a generous contribution from Art. They said they'll accept Ellie."

"With another generous contribution," I said.

"But the location is supposed to be kept in confidence."

"The secret is safe with me," I said.

Mom was quiet for a few minutes. I leaned against the wall, for I wasn't used to standing for long periods.

Finally, she said, "It seems like bad timing, but I think we'll get married pretty soon."

"That's great."

"You're on your feet, but you haven't plunged back into work. I suggested we wait on a honeymoon."

"Why?"

"Well, you still need looking after and it's really best to wait until the herd is sold. He'll have more free time then."

"The last part makes sense." I said, as I slid down to the hallway floor. "I'm fine. So, what are your specific plans?"

"We're thinking very small…small as in a minister and you." She sat down next to me.

"What about Kyle? Bill's son should be invited."

"We've talked about it. Bill says Kyle won't come, but he agrees we should send him an invitation."

"He should know that his father has gotten remarried."

Just then the door from the garage opened. Brian walked out into the hall. Heaviness descended upon the house. Zane came from the family room. He had taken off his blazer and tie. I wished he had taken off more. No, I didn't just think that.

Brian looked at him and asked, "What are you celebrating?"

"I guess the news hasn't gotten out," I said, as I struggled to stand.

Strong hands took mine and pulled me off the floor. Zane quickly stepped over and also assisted my mom, who didn't need help, but knew to let him. Zane knew better than to look over at Brian, whose face flushed red as his cock shrunk.

"Mom and Zane will tell you," I said. "I need my drugs."

I didn't really need any, in fact, I was trying to shift to Advil and ditch the opium. But I walked down the hall so they could talk without me present. I seemed to aggravate Brian with anything I did and said. So I crawled onto my bed and thought about the F word. Mom said Sweetie's death wasn't foreseeable. Was it? Legally speaking, no case law, no court, no jury could find my actions in investigating the Quinn murders as a foreseeable act that caused my baby's death. Then why did Brian's blame haunt me so?

A month ago, it would have been Brian waking me from a nap for supper; and he would have come up in time for some loving. Yet a month ago I would've still been at the office.

"Time for supper," said Patty. "Bill's here—we already told him about Ellie—and we convinced Zane to stay."

She headed back downstairs and I followed, but a thought slowed my steps—was it Brian's blame that bothered me or was it just Brian? I pondered the question during dinner. As soon as he ate, Brian left. Zane stayed.

"He's off to go get drunk at the Cowpoke," I said to Zane. "He does it every night. I called and asked Johnny Two Rivers not to kick him out, though Brian's always trying to start fights. I figure if he's really plastered, he can still find his way home, better than if he was driving from Kimball or Sidney. Bo often follows him home—it keeps the State Patrol from arresting him for drunk driving."

Zane nodded. "That place is too loud for me."

We spent the evening watching a hockey playoff game. Patty left soon after supper. Once again, I'd forgotten to ask her about the note I found from Jessica Fenton. Patty would probably tell me it was a phone call for Brian made by a young woman. Would adultery be his next method for punishing me? Maybe I deserved it. After Zane left, I was alone with Mom.

"I said that we'd get married soon because you're back on your feet," she said. "But you aren't, not really. You've lost your fight…something you always had, even as a toddler. Maybe it's your wound or the drugs or the grief or all of them, I don't know."

"And you've never felt beaten down?"

"Oh, sure. But I never thought I'd see you like this…not for this long."

"I'm tired." I rose and left the room.

That night I lay in bed feeling alone and desperate. God, help me, I begged. Yet, I was doing it again—pleading for God's help when I was guilty of so many sins—pride, ingratitude, neglecting God, lusting after Zane when I was married to a man who repulsed me—just to name a few. I did pray and I usually went to church and I read the Bible on the weekends, but I wasn't the Christian I should be. Still, once again I was in trouble. I hurt so badly. I lost my Sweetie. Maybe I had lost my willpower. And I didn't know what lay ahead with Brian, but it would get worse. He'd lash out at me, and I felt so weak in my heart that he'd beat me down. But, I'll ask again anyway—God, help me, comfort me, lead me to green pastures and still waters, and restore my soul. Even if I plunge back into the blackness of the deep, please bring me out of the water.

Chapter 24

The next morning, I dumped my meds in the trash. I ate breakfast alone then went out to my car. I backed the dark red Acura out of the garage and messed with the features for a few minutes. Then I took it out onto Highway 51 and then Interstate 80. Man, that 300 horsepower engine blasted down the road in a quiet hum. I drove west to Kimball then sped back toward home. Oh, yeah, this was a fine machine. It ate up the pavement with a voracious appetite. We already had the Shark, no, this was the Barracuda.

After lunch, I spent a few hours in the office. The overflow of work took up most of a card table set up next to my desk. Glenda typed out a list of new clients seeking appointments—the first of which was made the day after the "Showdown" as it was being called. How could they know I'd live? Breathe, just breathe. It doesn't all need to be completed in a day.

Late in the afternoon, I drove out to the east pasture. I stood just inside the gate and waited. I knew he would see me. Soon enough, Strider came charging toward me. This caught Rohan's attention and he followed. Strider slowed to a stop when he was twenty feet away then he walked to me, sniffing as he came. He was soon gently nuzzling me. Rohan tapped his head on my hip. I walked forward into the green short grass of our prairie pasture with a horse on each side of me, close yet never touching me. Bud was right, they sensed my injury. They were kind, certainly more than Brian, yet they were tentative, like the people around me; well, except for Mom, who accused me of weakness. She thought it would do me good, and she was right. And as a person who had lost a child, she was the only one who possessed the nerve and the right to chastise me.

Once again, Brian left after supper; once again, the mood improved in the house with his absence. A few minutes after he left, Zane arrived. I poured us both bourbon on the rocks. I turned to find Patty, Bill, Mom, and James behind me.

"You can't drink that!" said Patty. "You can't mix Vicodin and liquor. That kills people."

"No, but I can mix bourbon and Advil," I said. "I dumped those pills. They kept me in a fog…they're damn effective, I'll say that. But I need to get those out of my life. So go get your own and let's watch some hockey."

I winked at Zane. He smiled at me in a way that made my anti-perspirant stop working.

Bill came in with his Jim Beam and sat in the recliner, which we reserved for him.

"So, Zane, Megan says you start work at Cabela's soon," said Bill as the others returned to the room.

"Monday, in fact," said Zane. "I'll start management training in about three months. Until then, I'll be in survival gear, hiking, that stuff."

"I would have thought they'd put you in guns," said Bill.

"They tried, but I refused. I'm not going to sell people AK-47s. Nobody outside of a war zone needs those."

"Makes sense, young man," said James, nodding.

"Hey, Uncle Bill, you ought to go down to the bank building and look at the excavation maps. You'd remember if there were old barns and shelters on our land."

"I'm way ahead of you. I took Officer Waters out to two old barns and one old shelter we used when I was a young man. People think you're right about the bodies being moved more than once. Waters got all excited about one old shelter where the ground looked to be recently disturbed."

"Really? Where's that?" Patty asked.

"On one of the far eastern pastures, just north of Smokey's. They've cordoned off the area. On Monday, they'll have a complete State Patrol and FBI team ready to dig."

"They'll need to bring out the heavy equipment—some of those shelters go pretty deep in Tornado Alley," said James.

"I bet they go at it with spades," I said. "They're looking for decomposed bodies, so they'll need to be careful. They'll have everybody except the oldsters digging."

"I saw something like that on TV," said Patty. "If they find even a toe, forensics will start digging with spoons." She looked me. "Your butt is buzzing."

"Yeah, thanks," I said with a smirk as I pulled my phone from my back pocket.

"Yes, hi, Hank...Wednesday? That would be fine. Right, Jackson on Wednesday also? Hang on." I looked over to James, who sat in his favorite chair near the bookshelf. "James, would you mind hosting Jackson for a couple of days starting Wednesday? I'm sorry, this isn't much notice. And Bill could you handle Hank and Linda?"

They agreed and I relayed their acceptance to Hank.

"I'll try, but no promises. Okay, bye."

"So we finally get to meet the mysterious Linda," said Mom.

I nodded. "Do you realize they'll be visiting on the forty-fifth anniversary of the Quinn murders? Patty, is this some Lakota tradition?"

"Lordy, I hope not—it's so creepy."

We collectively took large swigs of our bourbons and shifted our attention to the hockey game. After the game, we switched over to a late west coast baseball game while Mom, Patty, Zane, and I played Monopoly. By ten-thirty, my vision began to blur with fatigue. Suddenly, the front door burst open, banging against the door stop.

"Oh, Lord, he's in a nasty mood tonight," whispered Patty.

"Maybe you shouldn't have given me his spot in the garage," said Mom.

"Oh, he's bothered by other things...mainly me," I said.

Soon, he was standing in the doorway to the family room.

"Damn! It's a houseful. No privacy, never."

He turned away. His feet pounded the wooden steps of the back staircase, echoing against the walls of the stairwell. His heavy footsteps were audible even in the carpeted upstairs hallway. We all waited and listened. Drunkenness was new to this family, dating back to my great-grandparents who built this house.

At the sound of smashing glass we all jumped to our feet. Normally, nobody could have beat me up the stairs, but now everyone passed me except James, who kept saying, "You take care, Megan. You take care."

The crashing of furniture continued even after I made it to the top of the stairs. I ran down the hall to the nursery, where Mom and Patty were standing. I squeezed past them into the room. Brian stood panting next to the window with the colored vases and glasses that he had demolished with the wooden bassinet Lew made. The wind whipped the curtains into the air. Bill and Zane stood in the room. Bill was attempting to calm Brian.

"You embarrass me," I said.

"Everything is yours!" Brian ranted. "This house, the firm, these people, they're yours. It's your frickin' world and I'm just a guest."

He picked up the bassinet and heaved it through the window to the yard below.

"Know what you also don't have?" I asked. "Strength, as in strength of character. You are shit in a crisis. Now before—"

He stepped toward me, but in a flash, he was on his knees, his neck in Zane's chokehold. Brian fought against Zane, but even a strong drunk couldn't break Zane's technique. Brian's face reddened and the veins in his neck began to bulge. Brian stopped trying to hit Zane or knock him over. Soon, Brian began to sink to the floor as Zane held on. Then Zane let go and Brian dropped face forward onto the floor, choking and sputtering.

"Watch out for the glass," said Zane, shaking his head.

Brian lay panting on the floor.

I bent down and said sharply, "Go to bed."

He rose to his hands and knees then crawled to the door frame as Patty and Mom backed out of the way. He pulled himself up and staggered down the hall without looking back. Making sure he went into the correct room, I followed him down the hall. As he started to close his door, he looked back at me.

"You push and you push and you don't know when to stop."

"Go to bed," I said, unwilling to argue with a drunk.

Brian came down for breakfast just as we were leaving for church: otherwise, he kept his own company that day. After another walk with Strider and Rohan, I found Brian in his room, sitting on the chair in the corner with his elbows on his knees and his head down. I told him about the impending visits of Linda and Jackson. It stirred his interest.

"You know, there were times when you were very interested in the Quinn murders," I said. "You did plenty of investigating."

"I thought of it as a hobby, a puzzle," he said. "I never thought we'd actually figure out what the FBI couldn't. But you did and look what happened."

"I did try hard to figure it out. There's a man in prison who shouldn't be there. I think that's unjust. My dad's good name was muddied till I cleared it. And Hank has been an exile from his home. How terrible would that feel? Mary and Julie have haunted me ever since I first heard them wailing. Every night I hear their screams. This was never just a game to me."

"You took it too far."

"You said that last night. Yeah, I finish things, and yeah, there can be consequences, good and horrible. But with you, there's always going to be something you can't handle. It happens over and over—you sulk, you commit adultery, you turn into a lush. I wait for you to get stronger, but you don't. We should be bearing this together, that's what couples do. Instead, you abandon me for booze."

"Anything else? Are you going to tell me I need to grow up?"

"Brian, you're a great guy as long as there's no crisis. But if one comes along, your character is just not equipped to handle it."

"Yeah, I remember the 'you're shit in a crisis' and 'you embarrass me' lines. I wasn't that drunk. And you had to say them in front of everybody. That was cruel."

"You were drunk or stupid enough to tear apart the nursery. That's when I was embarrassed for you."

He got up from the chair and walked to the window.

"Did you clean up your face? You have a few scratches from the glass."

He nodded.

"Who's Jessica Fenton?"

"Huh? Oh, just a client."

"As in Fenton Trucking?"

"Ah, yeah, I think so."

"Are you having an affair with her or anyone else?"

"No. Are you cheating on me with Zane?"

"No. I'm married. I wouldn't do that to you."

He continued to stare out the window. That would be something he'd do to get back at me, though he'd enjoy thinking I didn't know.

"Let me ask you this," I said. "Do you think it was foreseeable to the Shusters that Davey would be murdered when they trained him to work at Custer's?"

"Foreseeable? No. They couldn't have known it would happen."

"But you think it was foreseeable that when we started looking into a murder committed forty-five years ago our baby would be killed."

"That's the goddamn argument of an attorney."

"Actually, it's Mom's argument."

He rubbed his chin. "So what do you think?"

"I can't seem to separate guilt from grief. Maybe I can see it more clearly at some point, now that I'm off that drug."

He was quiet. If he was an attorney, he'd know to look at it from another direction and point out that the Quinn investigation put me in danger and, therefore, our baby. Yes, I had been reckless, I was guilty. But he was an accountant, he saw things in columns. He applied the tax code, he didn't argue against it. He couldn't even find a valid argument for my guilt—he simply chose to drown his uncertainty and his disgust for me in booze. I left him staring out the window.

I downed Advil and worked four hours on Monday and six on Tuesday then collapsed on my bed till supper each day. On Wednesday, I worked six hours, even though it was a holiday, collapsed again, but roused myself to prepare for our guests, which involved downing a handful of Advil then changing out of an old Husker t-shirt and cotton shorts into a nice top and khakis.

Jackson looked the same; in fact, he'd probably looked exactly this way for decades, with his short, wiry stature, deep wrinkles, and thin, silvery hair. While we still milled about the foyer, Jackson announced they'd held a Sun Dance for our baby on the rez. Brian and I thanked him as we nodded solemnly. Then Jackson whipped out his cell phone and showed us photos. It became bizarre—Sun Dances probably originated hundreds of years ago and we were viewing the gathering of the Lakota tribe on a cell phone.

We waited in anticipation for the mystery woman. A few minutes later, Hank, Lew, and Linda arrived. Linda was a beauty at sixty-three, with high cheekbones, long, black hair that she probably colored, and a quiet, long-suffering manner. As we greeted, I thought how she would have been better off if she'd possessed Patty's take-no-shit personality, but she was probably too firmly settled for change.

Then we heard the tapping at the door. James and Zane escorted Beulah inside.

"Heh! Hank, you old rascal. I wondered if you'd come back...and Linda, dear, so good to see you again," said Beulah.

After supper, Brian stayed, not because he experienced any sense of reform or softening toward me, but because he was curious.

Linda approached me and asked for a few minutes alone. As Bill and Brian were setting out chairs in the family room to accommodate the large group, Linda and I retreated to the study. I started to draw two chairs together, but she stopped me, insisting she move them. We then sat down together with our root beers.

"I thank you for clearing Hank's name," she said. "He's waiting till you think he should go out in public."

"I think it's okay," I said. "I know Smokey would like to see him—that would be a good place to start. And if Beulah gives him her approval, nobody will bother him at Custer's. I can tell Lew likes having him around."

She nodded then slipped into her own thoughts.

I gave her a minute then said, "I can help you get a divorce. We need to track down your husband, if we can."

"Yes. I want that."

"Now what about Joe? Are you ready to meet him?"

"I'm scared to. What if he hates me?"

"He's been on a search for his father and probably for you, but he could have found you easily enough. He's probably scared, too. Do you know about my family's history?"

"Yes, Lew sent us a copy of your one-day newspaper."

"The breach can be mended. It takes time, that's for sure."

She nodded. Her gaze wandered as she pondered the situation.

"Did you read the second edition of the Dexter Gazette that gives my version of the Quinn murders?"

"Yes, and I think you're right."

"Did Bert rape Julie at the Fourth of July party?"

"I think so, but I'm not sure. She was distressed…that was clear. The next morning, she said she was too upset to drive me back to the rez and that I'd have to wait. But I needed to get out of there—I had my own things to deal with. So I asked your dad to drive me. He was only fifteen, but he'd been driving awhile on one of those early permits the ranch kids get."

"Did he know why he needed to drive you?"

"Yes. I told him I thought I was pregnant and I needed to go home."

"He kept that secret to his grave."

"Your dad was a good man, but Bert was wicked right down to his bones. And Julie taunted him…used to walk in front of the window in just her bra when she knew he was around. She was kind to me, but she could be mean. I heard about the digging. I hope to God they find them. They'll never be at peace till then."

"I was just thinking, Joe may demand a paternity test. I could help you set—"

"No!"

She rushed over to the door and listened then returned to her chair.

"You know I was in the assimilation program at the school by Potter. Well, I did begin to change after I was there for a while. It was always hard going back to the rez in the summers. I didn't seem to fit anywhere—not Indian, not white, just confused, and sometimes mocked, even bullied. But I figured out I had to marry a white man, and make that my place in the world. I didn't want to date boys, they're stupid. Well, except for your dad, he was nice to me."

"I'm glad."

"Now you can't tell this to anyone, but I started dating Walt Bolger."

I nearly dropped my root beer.

"He said he hated Ellie, and he wanted to divorce her. Well, after a couple of months, I knew he wouldn't leave...I think he feared problems with his sons more than anything. So I ended it. I had met Hank and knew I liked him and he was single. But then I decided I was pregnant. You know that feeling when you think you're either pregnant or you have the stomach flu?"

"Oh, yeah." I recalled it as a strange mixture of misery and joy.

"So, you see, Walt is Joe's father, not Hank—but I wish Hank was. I don't want Joe thinking he's the half-brother of a murderer and the son of an arsonist. And after that party, and making love to Hank, well, I just ran away."

"Why didn't you come back after the murders and talk to the police?"

"I was ashamed to be pregnant. And I didn't think I could help, because I didn't know who the killer was, but I didn't think it was Walt. So, I was afraid to come back, not knowing who to fear. The killer might have thought I knew something and then I'd be next."

"I promise to keep all of this in confidence. Does Hank truly think he's Joe's father?"

"Yes, he's thrilled that his son went to college and became an FBI agent. But it made him angry that Joe was bothering you when you were protecting him."

Secrets—they make such a mess out of life.

Chapter 25

When Linda and I joined the others, Beulah was in full-story mode. Patty offered us bourbon, which we both accepted.

"I got tired of workin' in my cousin's business. Rentin' out canoes and sellin' packaged food, that was his business, not mine. But he was nice about it...helped me build my shack out on that island once I got the right root beer mixture. Had me a good business. Never sold liquor, people could get rowdy as was. I had me a bow and arrow with a suction cup on the end. When guys got unruly, I shot that arrow at 'em. Didn't hurt, but it embarrassed 'em. If they kept on, I'd let my Lab, Buddy, chase 'em away. He'd—"

Beulah went on with her story, but my butt began to buzz. I looked at the caller ID and hurried out of the room.

"Hello, hang on." I stepped out on the back porch. "Yes, Joe. You're where? In James' driveway? Did you follow them here?" Pause. "Yeah, I'll meet you. I'm on the back porch, I'll be right over."

I walked over to the Wilson driveway. Joe was standing next to his white pickup.

"Okay, so let me say two things, Megan, before you say anything."

I nodded.

"First thing—I'm sorry I gave you such a hard time. It was wrong of me...but I thank you for dropping the charges. And second, I am so sorry about your baby. Truly, I am. Did you get my flowers?"

"Yes, I did. They were lovely. Did you get my thank you note?"

"Yeah."

"It took me awhile to get those out...didn't trust myself when I was so drugged...thought I might send one to Dr. Suess. So?"

"Yeah, I followed them here. I'm suspended from the FBI until January."

"Does that mean you want to meet your parents?"

"Lord, above, I'm feeling chicken shit right now."

"So is Linda. She says Hank is thrilled that you're his son."

"Really? Huh. So, how do we do this?"

"Well, let's see. Okay, hold out your arms." I frisked him. "There, now. Some people think you're dangerous, so I can tell them you're unarmed."

"Damn, I've never been frisked by a hot chick before. But you're moving around all right so you must be better."

"Yeah, yeah."

"Hey, you've been followed."

I backed up then turned around, expecting to see Brian. It was Zane. I waved him over.

"I wondered where you went. Hey, Joe. Oh, I get it...next up...family drama. Good luck with that."

"Yeah, and you can help," I said.

The plan was set and executed—Zane led Joe through the front door to the study, while I asked Linda, Hank, and Lew to follow me down the hall. I sent them into the room then Zane and I exited the room and shut the door.

A couple of hours later, the house was finally quiet. I sat in the kitchen with Mom dunking graham crackers in milk. Zane and Brian sat in the family room drinking bourbon and watching baseball.

"Mom, will I ever get over losing Sweetie?"

"No."

"I was hoping for a little optimism."

"Well, it's only been two years since Scottie died, so maybe I'm not the right one to ask. But you look around for good things, replacements, diversions."

"Oh, I'm diverted all right and we've replaced the nursery window. But I don't see anything good ahead besides your wedding." Footsteps sounded in the hall from the family room. "Speaking of diversions." I dipped another graham. But it was Zane.

"Right," said Mom with a grin.

"I know you can't resist these," I said.

"Oh, yeah," said Zane.

I shoved the box over to a seat at the table.

"It won't go well with this." He left his half glass of bourbon on the counter then took a mug out of the cupboard and poured some milk.

"I taught him to eat Mush," I said, referring to the odd Docket tradition of crushing up grahams in a bowl, adding milk, and eating it like cereal.

"Your uncle still eats that," Mom said as she dipped. A chunk broke off and fell into the milk. "Oh, no! I'll need to make a rescue."

We laughed as she used a dry piece to pull the milk-soaked piece out of her cup. It felt good to laugh.

Then Brian lumbered in and set his empty glass on the counter. I told them of Linda's disclosures, including my dad's whereabouts, yet omitting the paternity issue.

"Nobody ever thought your dad was guilty of anything," said Brian. "You just got worked up over nothing."

He walked out of the room without another word, his lingering presence dampening our spirits, well, at least for Mom and me. Zane kept on dunking. After a few minutes, Mom loaded her cup and a few other glasses on the counter into the dishwasher, kissed me on the forehead, and said goodnight.

"I should go," said Zane. "Walk me out to my car…I'm afraid of the dark."

Once outside, I saw that he'd replaced his bashed up Pathfinder with a junker pickup.

I started to make a smart remark when he said, "It's temporary till I earn a few paychecks."

"Yeah, it's—"

His lips found mine and locked on.

I dropped my head into his chest. "Ah, Zane. Don't tease me. Your timing is really bad, you know."

"Oh, I think it's perfect. Brian won't get better. You two are going to finally explode and you'll get rid of him."

"What if you're wrong, what if—"

His lips were on mine again. My legs went rubbery. He squeezed me tight, then relaxed his hold and placed his hand right on my wound. I could feel the heat through my top.

"You okay? I didn't hold you too tight, did I?"

He sent a charge through me when he kissed me again. I needed to stop kissing back.

He stepped away from me and said, "You'll see I'm right." He climbed into his truck and drove away.

In bed, again alone, I thought about the day. I was so pleased at Joe's reunion with his mother. They still had issues to deal with, but I predicted an eventual happy resolution. I didn't feel the same about my resolution—mostly I felt Zane's lips. Was Zane right? Or could I turn around my current life with a man who accused, embarrassed, and annoyed me? No, it was more than annoy, it was detest. I didn't like worrying about the trouble he might be creating when he went to the Cowpoke, but I dreaded his presence and preferred his absence. The notion of love for him was like a speck shrinking in the distance.

Like usual, Brian left after supper on Friday, but Bo delivered him to our door a little after nine. Bo informed us that Johnny kicked Brian out of the Cowpoke permanently. Brian left Bo at the door and went to the kitchen. I thanked Bo then closed the door behind him. I took a deep breath then went to the kitchen where Brian was pouring a large glass of bourbon.

As he walked by me, I said, "Well, you've done it now. Bo is probably sick of you. You're lucky you didn't get arrested."

"Get out of my way. And who are you to criticize me? You know this is all your fault."

He went up the stairs; I stewed for a few moments then followed him. I pushed open his door and flipped on the lights. He was sitting in a chair with the bourbon glass on an end table beside him. When he saw me, he took a big gulp.

"You're so ready to blame me...well, I have a question for you. Why didn't you do something? He's got a knife inches from me and he's preparing to choke me, and you just stand there. Why the hell didn't you shoot him? Huh? Give me an answer."

He sat so still, he looked fossilized.

"I'll tell you why—you don't have it in you. You weren't man enough to do what you needed to do. Pull the trigger and you save both of us. You'd be a hero—a real one, not a college football player. But you're not a hero. You don't have the guts, the strength for it. Instead, you blame me and try to drink away the truth of your cowardice."

There, I said it.

Before I entered my room, he shouted, "You're the reason she's dead!"

In the hall, I turned to look back at him and said, "Know what else I did wrong? I didn't divorce you last summer when I realized what a pathetic piece of shit you are."

I closed my door, stood in front of the window, and gazed out into the night. That's where we're at, complete darkness. My God, can two people get any lower, any more vicious? He knew I spoke the truth—I'd cast the blame for her death on him. He wouldn't take it, especially since I insulted his manhood. In truth, he simply froze, as some people do in a crisis, and gender had nothing to do with it. I'd also implied that he was weak in the midst of my strength. And I argued with a drunk, which was unwise. But was he really getting drunk all these nights? He didn't really seem wasted tonight.

I gasped. Something changed and it scared me. God help me! Fear welled in my chest and rammed into my throat. It was here. My bedroom door slammed against the wall.

"Not man enough?" he yelled from the threshold.

He strode toward me, clenching his fists. Oh, sweet Jesus! He's going to kill me! Luckily, he'd drunk just enough to slow him and I was able to duck as he swung. But his hand grazed the top of my head, spinning me around and knocking me into the end table next to my chair. The lamp, table, and I crashed to the carpet. I cowered for a few moments, trembling. After a few breaths, I stood up. A trickle of blood rolled down my neck. He unclenched his white-knuckled fists and dropped his head onto his chest.

"I'm sorry."

Mom and Bill rushed into the room. They saw the blood and the overturned furniture. My mom whirled around to look at Brian. He stepped back.

"Get out, you monster!"

Brian strode out of the room and closed his door. I sat down in the chair.

"Did he hit you?" asked Bill, his face red with anger.

"He tried, just barely got me. I ducked and I hit my head on the table."

Mom dabbed at the blood on my neck then found the broken skin above my temple. She pressed the tissues to my head.

"It doesn't look like more than a nick," she said. "You won't need stitches."

"I've had enough of those."

Bill picked up the table and lamp. He left with Mom's instructions. She helped me clean up in the bathroom until Bill arrived with an ice bag. The cold made my head hurt, but that isn't why I started to cry. Bill left and returned with a snifter of brandy.

"A restorative," he said.

I nodded and drank. In time, I stopped crying; in time, I went to bed, weeping anew. He hit me. He wanted to hurt me, first with words then with violence. If I hadn't ducked, his fist would have smashed in my face. He wanted to hurt me. As I wiped my eyes, I slid out of bed and locked the door, then scampered back under the covers as if they could somehow protect me. I'd been lucky this time. Would he hit me again? Sweet Jesus, how could I live with this fear?

Brian left the house in the morning and stayed away all day. Bill, Patty, Mom, and I spent the day boxing Brian's things and putting his suits in plastic bags. Around noon, James came home then wandered over to inquire about the commotion. Once he was told, he sat down on the front porch steps and put his head in his hands. Kayla wandered over in the afternoon. I took her inside and told her Brian was leaving. She sobbed into my shoulder. By supper, Sherman Locksmiths changed the outside door locks then we set a new security code.

Brian arrived in the early evening. He loaded his possessions from the unlocked garage and drove away. I called Derek and Vonny to tell them my plans. According to my instructions, Patty turned Zane away that evening, but told him he could return the next evening for supper.

Later I went out to sit on Rufus in the early dusk. Brian wanted to control me, but he didn't possess the strength to alter my course of action. Only one person could have done that—but my father was dead. Even so, I doubted that he could have stopped me completely. It was ironic that the man who could have influenced me was also part of my motivation to solve the mystery. In the end, I endangered not only myself and Sweetie, but also Brian and Mom in my zeal for truth. As I sat there, guilt lashed against me, whipping hard at my body, slicing into my soul, forcing me back to the red-brick refuge of the house and the shallow recourse of the bourbon I intended to consume.

Monday morning, I filed for divorce. When I returned from the courthouse, I told Gus and the rest of my staff. At lunch, I cornered Beulah in the kitchen and gave her the scoop, but I asked her to keep it in confidence for now, word would soon be out and she could confirm the news if she heard it. I stressed that I filed for the divorce—I guess that was my ego talking.

Yet when I thought about it, Brian would hopefully face less censure if I was the one to take action. Then again, that's how the book of our marriage read—I was the one to take action. During a bout of Brian's sulking, I faced Salt Eldritch, and fought him to the death. While Brian slept late, I confronted RT and Chief Dobbs, and fought them to the death. With Brian unable to act and Bert ready to kill me, I fought him to the death. I suppose it was more than any guy could expect from a marriage. Maybe it was all too much trouble—maybe I was too much trouble. He was now free of me.

Brian said I pushed and pushed. He was right—I insisted on doing things thoroughly, to completion, even if it meant extreme effort. What would have happened if I backed off? Once Bert decided I was the enemy, he may have persisted in getting at me. He was a sadistic killer, who probably never reformed, living with his scheming witch-mother. But retreat would have meant weakness—recoiling from a challenge, losing my self-respect, giving in to fear. This was me. I paid a heavy price, and learned the lesson of caution, maybe even some wisdom; but I knew I wouldn't change, not substantially.

I came home early, considering all the work I needed to do. Zane arrived a few minutes after I did. I grabbed a couple of beers and we went to sit on the patio, despite the heat.

"So you filed…is it to shape him up or are you dead set on ending it?" he asked.

"Dead set," I replied. Then I told him Brian tried to hit me.

"My God. I confess that really surprises me."

"He'd been drinking, but I think it accurately reflected his mind state. All along he'd been blaming me for my baby's death, so I accused him of being too weak to act."

"That last part is sure true. Brian should have blown Bert away the second he saw that knife. And he knows it. That's why he's been leaving you every night to get drunk—he can't face himself."

"That moment, facing Bert, then facing the consequences…maybe it's more than we could ever overcome. Forgiveness—that's possible, but it's more than that. His behavior in so many ways, especially when he hit me, showed me something terrible about his character. Maybe he'd try to hit me again or do something else…like cheating on me like he did last summer. I'm not going to put up with any of that. I need to move on and away from him."

I felt his eyes boring a hole in me, stirring something inside I wasn't sure I wanted to deal with. In that moment, I realized I'd been measuring Brian against Zane ever since Bert put that knife in me.

"Do you know why it didn't work with Melanie or anyone? They weren't you."

"Oh, Zane, don't do this."

"But none of them could have hurt me the way you did."

"I'm sorry…I know I hurt you."

"Why did you break up with me? I know it was seven years ago, but I never let you explain anything."

"You pushed too hard. I needed to breathe, I needed space."

He nodded.

"Good grief, why did we come out here? I'm frying."

He followed me into the house.

"I guess supper won't be for a while. Maybe there's a baseball game."

When I turned toward him, his lips were on mine. First, I kissed back then I pushed back when the feeling of suffocation hit.

"Look, Zane, I need air and space."

"And time to grieve," he said. "For the time being, I'll be working late on Tuesdays and Thursdays. And I'm off on Sunday and Monday. I'll only come over when you want me to."

"Sounds fair," I said with a grin.

"But you can visit me—I moved into that empty duplex."

"Which side?"

"The good one. Joe lived in one side and Paul and Kayla lived on the clean side."

I nodded. "I need time...lots of it."

"Yeah, I get it."

"But there are some things you need to know about me."

"Things I didn't know in college?"

I nodded. "So can you come over when you get off work on Wednesday?"

"I'll be here."

I didn't doubt that, but I doubted myself. Was I ready for this? No, not even close. I had no desire to date someone right now—so close to Sweetie's death and the very week I filed for divorce—that would be skanky.

On Wednesday just before lunch, I stopped by the excavation office. Both Ernie Sedlacek and Art Meyer had joined the search. They were standing along a wall discussing the set of maps hanging from the walls. Ernie apprised me of the latest activities then showed me a large map of the area with blue markings for projected digging sites and red for completed excavations. The map was covered with red marks, but only a few blue marks remained. I studied the markings on our land. I'd been told the site Bill showed them on our land indicated recent shoveling and tire tracks, but they'd found no bodies after an extensive excavation. The dig was failing.

Chapter 26

By five o'clock, Zane and I were wandering through my backyard. He knew about Rufus, and the Seven Dwarfs from playing here as a kid, but we'd never taken him farther. This was special land to Vonny, Derek, and me; naturally, we kept its secrets from other kids. In the late afternoon heat, Zane and I meandered northwest to Pooper's Canyon and the cottonwoods along Raccoon Creek. Then I took him along the path of my escape and entrapment of Salt Eldritch. Zane learned about the boy trapped in a well and the wailing woman, who turned out to be my twin brother and my mother.

"I've read about connections between twins," he said, trying to encourage me.

"And I felt the heart attack he had."

He nodded thoughtfully.

"When I'm alone and I'm not angry, I can hear Beverly."

"Who? Oh, Mrs. Wilson. Right…you were always close to her, anybody could tell that. So, um, do these voices say anything?"

"They're just sounds. But it's nothing I'd ever tell a shrink or really very many people."

"So, who knows you hear voices?"

"Just the Harney Street gang. Even Brian believed me in time—and he was with me when I knew my dad had that heart attack and when I knew where to find Davey."

"Does anybody else hear voices?"

"Yes, but I'll keep that in confidence."

"So, something about this place and some people, ones who yearn, I bet. I think I could guess a couple, but I won't."

"You might guess right, but I still wouldn't tell."

"Do you ever hear voices of people who aren't close to you?"

"Just once," I said as I came to a halt at the chilling memory of it. "I went out to where the old Quinn house stood. It's all covered in dirt now, but I heard the tortured cries of Mary and Julie Quinn."

"My God."

"I can't even begin to describe how horrible that was. I haven't gone there since...don't need to. I hear them most nights."

A cloud rolled under the sun and gave us a few minutes out of the late afternoon rays.

"I suppose you think I'm crazy—feeling things, hearing things."

"Nope. You have a special sense...two, I guess...other people don't have. It's impressive, awesome really."

"And no, I don't see dead people, but it can be creepy. On the Pine Ridge Reservation, they call me The Woman Who Feels."

"Yeah, I get that."

We walked along the gulch to the spot where Salt Eldritch fell in. Suddenly, I saw something that made me gasp. I ran ten yards down the gulch, my guts churning.

"We don't have any animal around here that would dig like that," I said. "Look how the ground has been disturbed then patted down."

"Should I jump down there?"

"No, if Bert was here, we don't want to disturb anything. But we do need to get to the other side to see if there are tire tracks. I'm not sure I'm up to the task."

"I'll go. Just tell me where."

I walked north a few yards. "There! See the rocky edges on this side and then down a ways are footholds for you to climb up the other side."

"Gotcha."

Zane descended into the gulch and climbed up the other side. He turned and walked near, but not too close to where the digging took place. Then he began to scan the area away from the ditch. Then he froze and slowly knelt. He rose and bent over as he examined the ground. He turned and jogged away from the ditch, always looking at a specific distance away from him. He backed away then ran back to the ditch.

"Tire tracks!"

He climbed down into Miss Gulch then out again. I pulled out my cell phone and reported the discovery to the State Patrol.

"Zane, I gotta confess, I'm done in, walking this far in the heat. I'd like to stay, but I need to head back."

"Okay, we'll mark it."

He took off his shoe then yanked off his white crew sock. He set it under a rock at the edge of the gully. As we started back, he took off his shirt and draped it over my head.

"Sorry it's so stinky, but we need to get the sun off you."

We started on a direct path to our house, but then I abruptly veered toward Big Leo, without understanding why it drew me in. Zane followed.

"I really hope we found it back there," I said. "This is Big Leo up ahead. See that little hut up there? That's the Fort, my Christmas present. I'll take you up there once I'm strong enough to climb it."

"Yeah, I'd like to see it. I could carry you up."

I felt excited yet queasy from our discovery; still, I kept walking toward the bluff. A sinister force smacked me in the face as the wind shifted from the south to the east and intensified. I spotted two dark spots on the side of the bluff, right below two scrub trees. I worked my way against the wind, now feeling exhausted, but compelled. As I trudged over to the bluff, terror shot adrenaline through my body. At the base of the slope, I returned the wail that hit me, knocking me to my knees.

"It's them! Oh, God, in heaven, it's them!"

Two forms were tied to squat conifers on the north side of the bluff by ropes; nooses were wrapped around two dusty sheets. God above. Bert hanged them. In the presence of such evil, I crumpled to the ground.

"It's time to get you out of here."

Zane scooped me up and carried me, running back to the house. I pulled out my phone and called the State Patrol again. By the time we made it back to my yard, two State Patrol cars awaited us in the street. As Merritt and Waters came around the house, Zane put me down. I gave Zane his shirt back.

"I found them," I said.

The weight of those words made me drop to my knees.

"Zane, show them."

"I'll be right back," he said to the officers.

Once again, he lifted me from the ground. Patty held the back door for us. He deposited me on the sofa.

"Are you okay?" he asked.

"Zane, go! I'll be fine."

He dashed out of the room. Patty rushed to my side. I must've looked exhausted, for she switched the ceiling fan to its highest setting then brought me a large glass of water. Within a few minutes, Mom, Bill, and James were hovering over me. I told them of the discoveries then I collapsed onto the sofa pillows an enervated heap.

A half hour later, Officer Merritt came to talk to us. He stood for a few moments then said, "Looks like it's them. Megan, I'm sorry you were the one to see it." He shook his head. "It'll be a crime scene for a day or two."

"Then it will be a tourist attraction," said Patty.

"The hell it will," I said. "Bill, I'll need to borrow a few of your hands. Anybody who trespasses will be caught and prosecuted."

"You'll want to use Barnaby and Traddles," said James.

He was right; a couple of dogs would be good look-outs, especially at night.

"Officer, I think it's time to find Sean," I said. "And we'll need to organize a funeral service."

"Why don't you leave that to me and Patty," said Mom.

I nodded and rose. "I need to make a phone call."

In the study, I called Brian and let him in on the news.

"Whoa, shit, that is so sick," he said.

"Where are you?" I asked.

"In my Sidney office. I'll be looking for an apartment this evening. So, you filed. Bo brought the papers just before his shift."

"Ah, right. Well, I hope this will go smoothly. We should be able to settle our finances okay, just know that you won't be getting any of my father's life insurance money. But I don't plan on kicking you out of the firm's office."

"You don't?"

"No, you're valuable to this town and to Gus. But you need to rebuild some goodwill you erased by boozing at the Cowpoke every night. People will give a man a right to grieve."

"But what about Friday night?"

"Only my close group knows. And it will stay that way, if you cooperate. I did file a police report with Bo, but he won't make that accessible information to the public."

"You've got me by the balls."

"You tried to smash my face in. You really wanted to. And it's a good thing I ducked and you didn't connect—it would be impossible to hide. Then you'd have no career anywhere around here. Use your imagination...picture the headlines. So, like I said, we will make an amicable break. And you'll cooperate. Oh, and I do think you're cheating on me. That's more ammo."

It was time to ease my grip on his man-parts.

"So, meet me at Custer's for lunch tomorrow. We'll show Dexter that we plan to handle this like adults."

"All right. See ya."

"Brian, you're gonna be fine. You just need to marry someone normal, someone who isn't haunted by voices and stuff like that. By the way, do you want Rohan? If you don't, I'll buy him from you. Think about it."

"Are you going to date Zane?"

"Eventually. He still has PTSD, but he's better. Okay, see you tomorrow."

When I returned to the family room, supper was almost ready. Zane sat with his elbows on his knees at the edge of the chair.

"I gotta say, I've seen some gruesome things, but that was pure evil," said Zane. "Bert must have known he'd get caught."

"I think he knew he was going to die," I said. "What a bastard. Derek and Vonny will be pissed that he buried them in Miss Gulch. Then he hung them on Big Leo, my favorite bluff, so that I'd be the one to find them—if I lived. That S-O-B defiled our land."

"Sean was guilty of wronging him, denying him," said Bill.

"That must have eaten at him," I said. "But people get screwed in life all the time. Bert must have been fertile ground for evil to take hold. And Ellie...she gouged him till his wound festered and burst with heinous pus. I'm sorry Laura lost her sister, but the world is a better place without them."

After dental records confirmed their identities, the funeral was held the following week. Melvin Poots, who had known the family well, led the service. Chairs were set up in a swath of grass along the cemetery, as the churches couldn't provide seating for the throng of people who attended the interment. After the service, nobody moved—it was as if everyone wanted to see those caskets placed in the ground and covered. Even then, people milled about in the Saturday morning sun.

A wizened old man who had been sitting near the front during the service, came to my chair. I knew who he must be. I suggested we walk away from the crowd.

"I think you know who I am," Sean said. "And I've seen your picture in the paper."

"Yes, I was certain the FBI could find you," I said, noting the bump on his nose my dad gave him.

"I've spent the last couple of days learning about all that has happened. And I am thankful to you and to all that helped in...resolving this. And I'm really sorry about your baby."

"At least you were man enough to show up. Walt sent me a note giving me his thanks, but he says he never intends to return to this area."

"Walt is a good man," Sean said.

"But you are not," I said. "You once thought you were hot stuff—screwing your neighbors, including my grandmother. I don't know if my dad ever forgave her for that. But you never thought about the consequences, did you? Just the conquests. The torture you inflicted on your wife and daughter was horrible. How many were there? Huh? Could you even keep count?"

"Don't you think I've been tortured?"

"Oh, you deserved punishment, just not as much as you got. And now you know it was the bastard monster you created that killed your own flesh and blood, so your torture is multiplied. Bert told me, before he killed my daughter, that he would have killed you if you had been there."

"It would have been better if he had killed me then."

"Your wife and daughter have finally been put to rest, and I'm glad. Still, you need to go away and never come back to haunt us."

As he walked away, it occurred to me that Sean was western Nebraska's version of Dr. Frankenstein, an egomaniac who had created a monster out of his reckless, demented zeal. That creature turned on him, killing his family and inflicting misery on him for decades.

On a Sunday afternoon, Bill and I drove out to the old Quinn land. As we passed by the Joker, I thought of all that had happened in the last month—my baby died, I ended my marriage, the mystery of two homicides was solved, a neighbor killed herself, and I shot another man.

Bill, who had been quiet, cleared his throat then said, "Strange, if you think about it—when we bought this land last year, we mostly wanted to seed it with wild grasses so the topsoil wouldn't blow over us in a cloud of dust."

"We couldn't have foreseen all that would happen," I said. "The land was cheap, but the price I've paid is high. I lost someone special and my marriage ended sooner rather than later... in time it would have collapsed. I told Brian to find someone normal."

Bill chuckled. "I'm not always sure what normal means, but you're not it."

"And neither is your upcoming marriage...but that's okay. Some good things happened, too. I've been trying to remind myself of that. Linda and Hank have been reunited with their son and Lew has a family again."

"And the creepy mystery that has hung over us for all these years has been resolved. You've not been real social lately, but folks are grateful to you."

"Don't forget my firm has a tornado shelter," I said with a smirk.

"Hey, that's right. And you now have all those files. I bet there's a ton of secrets in them. Beth says there's rows of cabinets."

"Secrets that will be kept."

We approached the oak trees Brian and I visited in June. The scorching July heat prompted Bill to park in the shade of the aged bur oak.

"Megan, are you sure about this?" Bill asked.

"Yeah," I said. But I wasn't.

Still, curiosity had been eating at me, even waking me at night. We walked forward, pausing as we approached the site. A mound of dirt showed the marks from the spades where the State Patrol diggers smashed down the earth they dug out of the shelter to search for the bodies. I knelt down to find the edge of the concrete frame of the Quinn house. Once I located it, I ran my hand along the edge for a few feet.

"That's the house, isn't it?"

I nodded as I stood. I trembled in memory of what I might hear. But I finished things and I would finish this. I sucked in a deep breath then stepped onto the dirt-covered floor. In the house of terror and death, I heard only peace.

About the Author

JUDY Bruce is a resident of Omaha, Nebraska, USA, where she lives with her husband and two children. She has a law degree from Creighton University. Judy is the author of *Voices In the Wind, Alone In the Wind,* and future stories in the series, as well as *Death Steppe: A World War II Novel.* She maintains a website at judybruce.com and a blog at heyjoood.com.